UNDERCOVER IN BANDIPORE

Ashok Kaul

Vitasta
LET KNOWLEDGE SPREAD

Published by
Renu Kaul Verma
Vitasta Publishing Pvt Ltd
2/15, Ansari Road, Daryaganj
New Delhi - 110 002
info@vitastapublishing.com

ISBN: 978-93-86473-97-4

First Edition 2020
MRP ₹ 395

This novel is entirely a work of fiction. Names, characters, events and incidents are entirely imaginary. Reference to real places, actual regions, institutions or community practices has been made in a fictitious manner. Any resemblance to actual persons, living or dead or actual events is purely coincidental.

Typeset & Cover Design by Somesh Kumar Mishra
Edited by Manjula Lal
Printed by Vikas Computer and Printers, New Delhi

Dedicated to
Kamlawati Kaul and Jaikishori Mattoo,
for their blessings and affection for me

Acknowledgements

My wife Anita and my daughter Aparna are always a source of strength and inspiration for my creative ventures. I am thankful to my former colleague Dr Neha Kala and doctoral student Susmita Shukla who were generous enough to read the first draft and give some valuable suggestions. Finally, I am grateful to Vitasta's Renu Kaul Verma and her editor Manjula Lal for this publication.

Preface

The inspiration for this book is to hold up a mirror to the turmoil in Kashmir that was a conflict zone for at least four decades. It unfolds several dimensions of militancy and its different trajectories in Kashmir, one of which was the imposition of political religiosity that has made structural changes over the years to the social core of the Valley. It has provided an escape route for youth to affluence, influence and identity in secessionist upsurges.

In an unusual web of narratives, it brings into sharp focus how a rank outsider, in his search for education and a larger cause, gets entwined in a fight in which he has no personal stakes and a mission which he slowly realises can never be accomplished.

The kindly, wise persons who mould his life normally remain unsung in the public domain, and this book pays tribute to the *Babb*s who were once universally revered in Kashmir. The blended cultural-spiritual capital has buckled under the weight of imposed religiosity, depriving the younger generation of a vast heritage of language and literature.

And finally, it is a story of ordinary people who want to seek respite from this forced political turmoil, once they understand the cure of the collective ailment is not *azadi* but in the organic, ever-evolving cultural traditions of Kashmir. Power play and distant referents only complicate their lives without bringing any kind of salvation. My purpose was to weave a powerful and absorbing mesh of narratives that has, so far, remained untold in stories about Kashmir.

Eight long years have passed since Parash's father took his last breath and left this world at the age of ninety-nine. *Babb* could have lived for 120 years, he would say, but then fate took a cruel turn and his desire for living slowly faded away. He witnessed a drastic change of fate that forced him to relocate from his native place, Bandipore. He could never reconcile with his sudden uprootedness. He spent the rest of life with his sons but their homes were just houses and quarters for him—his home and heart were in Kashmir.

He was a proud father and they, in turn, served him well. He often shared his poetry and discussed literature with his sons. Iqbal and Ghalib were his favourite poets and Kalidas and Shakespeare were his choice dramatists. *Babb*'s reading habit and enthusiasm for life would have inspired anyone. His recitation of classic manuscripts in Sanskrit, Persian and Arabic was so lucid and mesmerising that it surpassed great orators of the world.

His youngest son Parash often felt that his own international exposure, doctorate and University position were like shadows hiding in the summer noon in comparison with his father's intellect. Had *Babb* managed to acquire some political power or influence, his literary talent would have been easily recognised and his work would have become prized literature.

Babb was a product of the freedom movement. Irrespective of faith and position, everyone in Bandipore held him in high esteem. He was respected even by Mama Sahib, the Imam High of Bandipore. He was spiritually inclined, devoutly religious and strengthened the public good with his personal conduct. There was no contradiction in the two realms. He had grace with assertion, wisdom with compassion and unfailing optimism with pragmatism. He was not a romantic realist but an institution in himself, a catalyst for transformation.

After that fateful day in October 1990 until his death in 2010, he spent his post-displacement years proportionately with his three sons, who were in three different cities. Everywhere, his daily routine was unchanged: two hours meditation (morning and evening), reading literary and philosophical books and teaching the needy.

Barkat had come to him in Varanasi through his son Parash. Barkat was a taxi driver who drove his son from a conference in Allahabad to Varanasi. Coincidently, five days later, Parash had to travel again to Lucknow and the company sent the same driver. During the return journey, Parash engaged in conversation with Barkat out of boredom. Gradually, Barkat opened up and told Parash about his life's aspirations and dreams, one of which was to qualify for some degree. Parash's interest grew when Barkat told him that he was an orphan raised by a Baba at Mughalsarai, who in all probability would have liked him to take up a salaried job when he grew up.

Knowing his father's passion for teaching, Parash introduced Barkat to *Babb* when they reached Varanasi. As expected, his father wholeheartedly welcomed Barkat and promised all help in his studies. Since Barkat had no family, Parash's father took him under his wing and treated him like his own son. He first brought out his *Nichpatre* (religious calendar) to find an auspicious day, date and time to start the teaching. Under his tutelage, Barkat passed his tenth, eleventh and twelfth class examinations through correspondence and joined computer classes after that.

During those years, Barkat invariably stayed for hours at a stretch with his 'Teacher *Babb*', who desired to see him settled well in life. *Babb* would invest time, energy and money in preparing him for the competitive job market

One day, Parash and his parents had to leave for Jammu to attend a marriage of a close relative. When they came back after a month, Barkat did not come to visit them. In between, Parash's mother passed away, creating a big void, especially in the life of his father.

Despite his bereavement—or perhaps because of it—*Babb* had difficulty accepting Barkat's disappearance. He kept waiting for Barkat to turn up. When he could wait no more, he asked Parash to find the teenager. On his insistence, Parash went innumerable times to Mughalsarai where Barkat grew up but failed to find him.

Parash's father was annoyed with Parash because he felt that his son had not done enough to find Barkat. His protégé would pop up daily in his conversation after his morning meditation. He had wanted Barkat to graduate in English Honours. His endeavour to transform Barkat's life remained an unfulfilled desire in the twilight of his life. He was restless, saddened by the void left by the unaccomplished mission—even though *Babb* had lived a contented life with abundant achievements.

Parash's father desired to return to his eldest son who lived in Jammu. There he was hospitalised with high blood pressure. During one of the visits to the hospital, Parash held his hand while he was sleeping and whispered to him in a broken voice, 'We will miss you, *Babb*'. *Babb* was awake. He quickly responded, 'Do not miss me, find me'. He died in 2010 months before his hundredth birthday.

Eight years have gone by. Not a day passes when Parash does not remember his father. He feels his presence and he feels *Babb* is urging him to find him Barkat. The question is: How to find him? He tries to find him in his father's poetry, which is published as an anthology. He hears his words ringing in his ears as if he is still asking him to find Barkat. Parash keeps looking for Barkat as an attempt to find his father.

With advancing age, Parash's desperation to find Barkat intensifies. On many long visits to Assi Ghat, Parash thinks about this metaphysical chase, like Keats' 'Grecian Urn', a pursuit that would never end. His father becomes both attachment and engagement; real as well as notional for him. Attachment of roots, continuity of tradition, nourishing of universal values, intense engagement with his profession and reconciliation with the pain of uprootedness are inherited traits.

The sad demise of his father makes Parash look more to the grace of the Ganga and divinity of the place that had nurtured and privileged him for the last forty years. The Ganga becomes his companion in the lonely hours.

The weather in Varanasi is very different from that in Kashmir. December is cold and the chill continues till mid-February. Then comes the hot and dry summer followed by the sultry, humid monsoon. Showers after the scorching heat are a great relief and create a longing and an intense desire for reunion with departed ones.

Parash murmurs to himself, 'The months have gradually glided into years and my life circle has entered its last phase, perhaps its winter, leaving behind the traces and shades of a legible memory. Has everything come full circle? I don't dream now, nor do I have any qualms. My passion has lost its wings and it remains shuttered. Yes, some strange memories still scare me and make me shiver. But I feel I have lived life to the fullest.'

With eyes closed, he remembers the deities of the Himalayas and pays his respects to them. This brings a sense of tranquility.

On one of his routine visits to the Ganga, without any explanation, he hurries to Assi Ghat, as if he wants to be in conversation with himself. Mirrored in the Ganga, Shankar and Husna, Barkat, Hasan and Rashid appear before his eyes in different avatars, bright and dull, in full reel, painting a tapestry of messed-up lives in a faulty world order. He becomes restless to complete the narrative. Perhaps the years of militancy have locked up the music of humanity in his heart and he wants to play it. It needs to be told: the story of Kashmir and its estrangement.

Parash can still remember the spring breeze and autumn winds which stir his conscience, urging him to open the knots of his epochal heritage—knots which are tight but not impossible to unravel. His heart is still in Bandipore. He was raised and groomed by those gushing rivulets, green-yellowish paddy fields, crimson spring flowers, autumn golden apron, wintry white snow carpets. He was moulded layer after layer by Pirs, saints, pilgrimages and distant tales with divine connects. All the colours woven in that divine Shaivite mould have given him the identity of a Kashmiri Pandit.

At an early age, he moved out of Bandipore for higher studies but religiously came back for summer and Durga Puja vacations. In 1989, the whole family had to flee from Kashmir for safety and survival. They lost their home, their ancestral abode.

It has been more than thirty years now and each year they find themselves further away from home with imagined cultural nearness and social distance. Yet, the beautiful memories of the last summer in Bandipore when Parash loafed around the banks of Madhumati river with his friends Hasan and Rashid are etched in his mind. These memories take him back to a time when everything was normal in the Valley. Life was different before that fateful year of 1989. Relationships were concrete and youths were engaged in playing, farming, learning and chatting.

There was an air of romance then, unlike the terror that prevails in Kashmir now. The army was in the barracks, police sleepy in their stations with not much work to do; schools and colleges, fields and playgrounds, shops and vendors, mosques and temples, men and women, girls and boys were all bound by a predictable routine. The equilibrium was functional and changes seemed to be holistic.

There was a gradual evolution in the linearity of transformation. The Pakistani green fervour was tacitly concealed in mosques from early 1960s, but it permeated through different layers of those institutional structures which had uniformity as well as distinctness.

As time passes, everything changes but it is difficult for Parash to forget the memories of his childhood. Due to the physical distance and the time lag, the warmth he once shared with his friends has dwindled. Still, he is concerned about them and their families and hopes that they too fondly remember him. Parash often wonders how the displacement of Kashmiri Pandits might have left them desolate. One disadvantage of being a *Batta* (Kashmiri Pandit) is to understand the plight of not only one's own community but also friends from the community left behind. Kashmiri Pandits might be rootless and homeless but Kashmiri Muslims, although rooted and living in newly-built houses, are also not at peace.

It is over a month now that Kashmir has been on the boil again. Parash has not heard from his friend Hasan. He is eager to know how Hasan is doing, for the television talk shows, news and narratives in *Rising Kashmir* or *Greater Kashmir* make him paranoid. Recently, Rashid had also sent a dispatch from Srinagar in which he had lamented the miserable condition of his homeland. He had not been in touch with Parash for a very long time and his letter seemed like a desperate attempt to experience a normalcy which was now elusive.

Parash wonders how his friends in the Valley live with such uncertainties and presumed there must be some outlets which allow them to take their life forward. Fortunately, this Sunday morning, Parash is able to talk to Hasan. The moment his call connects, Parash asks anxiously, 'Hasan, How are you? How is your family?'

'Everything is the same'.

Parash senses the hopelessness in his voice. They talk for a few minutes about their kids and then Parash asks, 'Hasan, what is happening? Is there any end to it?'

Hasan replies, 'No, there is no respite. Summer is over. They say it will go on till the Darbar move.[1] I wonder if it was all planned or was it sudden, sparked by the killing of Burhan Wani, whom they have presented as the mystic local hero. It has plunged the entire Valley in the darkness of uncertainty. Guns are back,

---

1 Until 2020, in a practice started by the British in all hill stations, the state administration would move from Srinagar to Jammu as it was impossible to function during the harsh winter.

people are suffering, the sudden and surprise attacks on police checkposts and army convoys are frequent. A new normal with manufactured uncertainties has feigned consensus to keep this happening. Hurriyat and Pakistan's establishments are preparing weekly 'Calendars' to keep discontent on the boil. They make announcements of shutdowns and protests to close down offices and institutions, orchestrate *taranas* (songs) in nearby mosques, and engage children in stone pelting from noon till evening. In return, the state uses teargas. The next day, the vernacular press exhibits affected boys and children in the news.

Sane voices are rejected or are quickly vanishing. The Education Minister requests the Hurriyat chief, known as Senior Pir, to spare education from the shutdown Calendars. In return, he is threatened with his life. He tries to clarify with an open letter to Senior Pir and is rebuked like a schoolboy. The vernacular press has been fueling the fire, creating war-like conditions despite believing that war is no solution.'

'I feel horrified when I think about the life you are living now', Parash tells Hasan.

Hasan says, '*Yaar*, we are going through a difficult time. Medical shops are closed, schools are burnt and public transport has vanished from the roads. We have nowhere to go. The rich can go anywhere in their private vehicles. Their children have shifted to schools in Jammu and Delhi. Some are doing online courses. The poor and the general public in villages and towns have to face the consequences. All our plans for the future have failed. We are the unfortunate ones. *Achcha, Khudais havale* (Okay, go under God's protection).

Hasan ends the conversation abruptly. Perhaps, the continued conflict without any visible resolution has made him weary. This vicious cycle of shutdowns and violence become a sickness from which there is no respite. Everybody is avoiding everybody else. It has become a conundrum for all.

Bandipore, like any other place in Kashmir, has undergone a change in its social composition after the 1990s. Those who are rich and able to afford city life have moved. Hasan is not one of them. Throughout his life, he remains burdened with the family responsibilities that he chose at the cost of his future. He stays in Bandipore with his wife and two sons—Niyaz and Mumtaz—and two daughters: Sadia and Shaman. Shaman is yet to be married. He is depressed at times that his close friends are not around when he needs them most. They have either moved away from Bandipore or left Kashmir. The morning fog and chill further cloud his mind.

Hasan often broods over how to engage his children so that the irritation caused by the stagnation would decrease. Confinement within the four walls of the house and then the staleness and uncertainty since militancy started have made them weary. Life remains out of gear in broad daylight and the hustle-bustle of the night only adds to the murkiness.

Many teenagers who are working as sales boys have lost their jobs. But most of them are back with a new mission: 'Now or never'. They wait eagerly for the Calendars covering the next two weeks prepared by the Hurriyat, the umbrella body of anti-India outfits. These schedules for stone pelting, lockouts and strikes are usually announced in the evening and within hours, reach all the districts of the Valley. News outlets update them. Police officer or CRPF personnel, businessman or salaried person, each is eager to know where to go and where not to go and hence wait in suspense for these Calendars.

October has now come to an end and the November sunshine is tinged with chill from the far-off mountains. It has not rained for many months but the peaks have turned white. The dry weather, shrunken streams, encroached spaces in the midst of the ruins of old *batta makaan* (Hindu houses) cast a deep shadow over an ashen autumn. Nothing seems to be in its rightful place. Three decades ago, the same place was blooming and flourishing in the golden crescent of departing autumn, but it is now filled with dullness and deep melancholy in its countenance.

Kashmiris do not see any promise in the spring breeze and are disheartened to see an entire generation turning into stone pelters and militants. Schools remain closed for indefinite periods and the energy of youth is channeled through slogan shouting. Children leave home after the morning tea, assemble in the street and led by face-covered gun-toting leaders, engage in violent stoning of the police and the army. Stone pelting has become fun for them but it invariably causes suffering to their parents, who understand the agenda of the masters across the borders. The young are induced to it. These stone pelters are mainly from villages and small towns who are led astray due to unemployment, rural-urban disparities and the ruthless competitive system. Stone pelting has become a means for them to escape their failures.

There is also a notion of 'holy cause' as professed by Hurriyat, which is one of the major causes of increasing participation of youth in stone pelting and militancy, leading them to untimely deaths. Their mothers do not even get the time to dry their tears and the Hurriyat issues a fresh Calendar. The doctrine of Hurriyat is a concoction of appalling principles—*azadi* from schools, *azadi* from moral policing and *azadi* from social institutions. They want the situation on our side of Kashmir to deteriorate just like they did in the part of Kashmir which is occupied by Pakistan, known as Azad Kashmir. The motive of

Hurriyat is to use boys for the 'greater' cause of *jihad.* It has brought misery to women and the older generation. Stone-pelting and slogan-raising on the streets occur throughout the day while the whole night, it is business as usual and deals are struck for plying of private transport and execution of emergency tasks. The state-run schools, hospitals and other institutions remain shut but salaries are credited into employees' accounts without fail.

Also, a huge cash inflow has brought asymmetrical affluence to Kashmir. Although money is in circulation, there is no legitimate economic development. Months pass but there is no end to these disruptions—only a strange pandemonium is prevalent everywhere.

Rashid spent the happiest time of his life at Bandipore, where he was born and schooled. He moved to Srinagar with his uncle for graduation in engineering and then went to Michigan for a doctorate in international politics. He spent seven years teaching at Klagenfurt University, Austria. Decades of teaching experience and exposure to the world shaped him differently from other Kashmiri Muslims. Although he cannot relate to the Azad Kashmir movement, he is saddened by the degradation of his land and people—the people for whose welfare he wanted to work when he came back from Germany.

His idea was to return to Bandipore but his wife was from Srinagar and least interested in moving to a remote region. So they ended up living in the state capital.

After many years, he decides to visit his cousin Muza in Bandipore. Dropping his bags at Muza's house, he heads directly to Hasan's house. Hasan opens the door and is surprised to see Rashid after so many years. They hug each other and with hands on each other's shoulders, enter the sitting room. After the initial catching up on each other's lives, Rashid asks him about his mother.

There is instant seriousness, deepened by the dim light in the room. Hasan sadly says, '*Mauj* has left us.

'Was she sick?' asks Rashid.

'She was not seriously ill but was perturbed and disheartened with this new turn of events and had no will to live any longer', replies Hasan.

'Our *amal'* (deeds), intones Rashid.

'What could we do? I am also worried about my children.' He adds, 'Niyaz is a graduate while Mumtaz never went to college after completing his higher secondary education. They are both unemployed.'

'What about your daughters?' Rashid asks.

'Shadia is well-settled. Her husband has an electronic goods shop here. We are relieved for her. This winter, we wish to marry off Shaman too. Let us see what His will is....' Hasan's voice trails off. Clearly perturbed by the uncertainties in Bandipore, he says regretfully, 'I should have moved to Srinagar back then.'

He asks Rashid about his kids and wife. 'Both my sons are studying in a technical institution in Noida and Itika has opened a beauty parlour,' replies Rashid.

'God has been kind but peace is elusive and uncertainties are looming everywhere in Kashmir. We all worry about our families. Our boys form clusters and hardly ever befriend boys from other communities. People now have covert agendas which are controlled by unknown forces, unknown persons. We were lucky that we had a sense of geography and cultural familiarity. The rapid pace of change is strange. In our time, we would be happy to interact with tourists, take them home and befriend them with a sense of pride. Nowadays, no one extends such hospitality. There is a valid reason. Interactions with people are shallow and fake. The boundaries are blurred and the conversations are guarded. The human soul is dead. Through digital glamorisation, the modern generation is deceiving itself. They reveal everything about themselves and expose the details of their personal life. They display their illusionary self through social media, as if they are celebrities; in reality, their life is not the perfect picture it seems on Instagram. They need to realise that they can fall prey to organisations sitting in remote locations, hunting for vulnerable youths who can potentially be easily trapped to serve their agenda. Religious institutions also have become centres to catch these teenagers and brainwash them...Digital technology is being used as the main instrument to lure youths into *jihadi* engagements. We are exposed in such a way that anyone can misuse our willful displays of emotions to control us and channel our energies for their agenda without being accountable', Hasan says sadly.

'Burhan Wani became a popular star among Kashmiri

youths for his videos encouraging them to join militancy through social media platforms like Facebook. People said that Wani would never be caught by the armed forces and suddenly, we hear about his elimination without any resistance. Everyone is baffled by this idolisation, then mystification and finally elimination. This new trend of youths ready to perish for the cause of *jihad* is disheartening', Rashid states.

He adds, 'What is annoying and terribly depressing is this new phenomenon where families are forced to eulogise the death of their dear ones the moment the dead bodies are brought home. Their wailing and agony are turned into revelry by the presence of *mujahideen* (freedom fighters) who celebrate the snuffing out of lives. The funeral processions from their homes would resound with songs celebrating martyrdom: *'Kusund gubar...ghar drav, imis mauja marhaba...Pakistan ka mutlab kiya'* and '*Saladin say rishta kiya...laillahiallahla*'.

'Something similar happened at the funeral of Faizan, a schoolboy turned militant from Tral who was killed in a military encounter. Songs praising his mother and eulogising the boy's heroism were sung, as if the elite commanders across the border get vicarious pleasure from the blood-scented songs of these young boys. Faizan was the only son of his parents and his death left his mother distraught. After the funeral, she sat alone in a corner of her house, wailing and cursing the entire Valley, Pakistan, Hurriyat and the police in one breath', continues Hasan.

He pours out his anguish, unable to stop. 'The radical Islamists have their international agenda of mystifying the *hoor* and *kasoor*.[2] This is how they have brought primordial passions into youthful lives. It is meant to increase the number of armed youth through inducement and glamorisation.

The youth feel that these activities would bring instant fame and money. They will get relief from deprivation without being in a government job. Alas, it is a self-defeating and willful choice in favour of destruction and premature death. Their dreams are far removed from reality. Mass participation has become the new mantra in which public, local militants and non-local commanders with a Hurriyat shield go for the final assault. This system of terror works through a non-state organisation, Difai Pakistan, through which our neighbour has been indirectly experimenting and interfering with Kashmir to bleed India and internationalise the issue. China is accepted as its big brother to weaken India', Rashid states.[3]

---

2 These are the privileges to be enjoyed in heaven: *hoor* is beauty and *kasoor* is drink.

3 Difai Pakistan is an anti-India group of retired Pakistan Army officers and clerics who work for the Kashmir 'cause'.

'Let us see how it works. It has taken a toll on our youth, as if they are meant to perish on a daily basis. We are caught in a rut; Pakistan identifies and India terminates them. Unemployed youth, especially of remote rural towns, are progeny of a new rich class groomed over the years on unaccounted funds. They have no role models except for the *mujahideen*', replies Hasan.

Rashid comments, 'Funds without accountability and concealed sources of wealth have played havoc with our families. Inter-generational relations are no longer cordial and the traditional middle class has not grown much. We remain where we were. But people from far-off villages, who were uneducated and very poor during the 1960s and 1970s, have now taken all the cultivable land of our towns, built big bungalows, hotels and schools. It is rumoured that Rahem Sahib, a separatist, has accounts in overseas banks.

'Everyone knows that his sons had acquired these riches through ill-gotten funds. The eldest son was killed at the border, and the other two sons, who were school dropouts, got associated with the Hizbul Mujahideen. The youngest son, after persuasion from his parents, joined Kashmir Police in 2007. The family has become rich beyond imagination. Rahim's second son runs a Jaamat (school run by the Jamaat-e-Islami) and is still tacitly associated with Hizb. All those who could not study beyond school level due to lack of money or capabilities in 1960s-70s have now become influential people, solving feuds between villagers and deciding about closure of schools and shops. Their children are studying and enjoying life in different cities and they do not care about the future of our children. It is a money-centric world. The material game is played under different covers with new ethics and has become the new normal.'

Both Hasan and Rashid are lamenting the Valley's predicament when Imitiyaz, a neighbour's son, enters Hasan's room to inform them that stone-pelting has started on the main road near the shopping centre. Rashid had met Imtiyaz's father while coming to Hasan's place. He had sent a warning that making his way home, he should take a back lane, crossing a rickety bridge, to go home, where his cousin Muza lives.

'Hasan, I must go now. Muza will be worrying and waiting for me. Give me leave. I shall ask Imitiyaz to guide me home', says Rashid. Hasan does not insist on lunch but makes his friend promise to visit again before leaving for Srinagar. '*Chalo*, go with God's protection.'

With Imitiyaz's guidance through a route clear of stone-pelters, Rashid safely reaches home.

Muza, his wife Zoya and their daughter Razia have already eaten, as it is 3 pm. The four engage in a light conversation while Rashid has his lunch. Muza has three kids: his elder son Bilal, who has completed his studies and is unemployed; his younger son Uzma, who is in college while his daughter Razia has studied till Class 10.

Since Bilal and Uzma are nowhere to be seen, Rashid asks Muza their whereabouts. In a despondent tone, Muza says, 'I have no idea about Bilal's life these days. He does not eat at home and often stays out for days on end without informing anyone. In case anyone in the family tries to question his suspicious behaviour, he gets agitated and hurls insults to avoid giving any explanation. The whole family is scared of his growing entanglement with the wrong crowd. He is turning out to be a bad example for his younger brother Uzma, who is still studying. It seems that he will join the *tanzeem* and bring shame to our family.[4]

'Now I avoid asking him anything. It is becoming more and more difficult to tolerate his outbursts. Lately, Bilal has started keeping a long beard and wearing trousers up to his shin. Also, he is often seen with an Urdu booklet in his hand. Uzma says that he has become religious. However, the people around him look like they are from across the border, similar to the Taliban. Bilal occasionally brings them home. These days he is hardly seen around clean-shaven people. This type of Islamic cult is being seen in our family for the first time.'

---

4 *Tanzeem* literally means organisation, a term commonly used in Pakistan.

The news about changes in Bilal's life shock Rashid. His mind registers the gravity of the situation in Kashmir for the first time. He assures Muza that he would talk to Bilal and Uzma and try to dissuade Bilal from walking down the path of destruction which leads to untimely death.

Trying to shake off his pessimism, Rashid wonders where Uzma has gone. Suddenly, stone-pelting and police firing starts outside. At that moment, Uzma enters the house and heads straight to his room after a hasty '*Assalam Aleykum*' to Rashid. The simple 'Salam' has gone out of fashion and this traditional way of greeting maulanas, a West Asian mannerism, has become the fashion.

Uzma's attitude agitates Rashid and he asks Uzma to join him for a walk in the courtyard.

The autumn evening does not allow them to shake off their gloomy mood. There is an eerie dryness emanating from the pallid trees standing dispossessed of their golden crown by the mountain winds from the north that had spread an ominous shadow across the courtyard. The whole landscape looks half-naked and exposed.

Rashid notices how different this part of the Valley is from Jammu and the plains. In the plains, these were the cherished months, full of hustle-bustle. Here, the pre-winter season is oppressive and cloudy, bringing despondency as it multiplies despair with its dark cloak. Expressing his sadness, Uzma says, 'Our beloved Kashmir is in the Dark Ages. The entire south is crammed with soldiers. There is a huge concentration of army; the *mujahideen* attack the army and then there is counter attack; these operations have caged us in our own native land. There is no respite for us. Right now, we have no idea what we can do to make the situation improve. The real danger is the continuation of the status quo for too long—it will make us myopic, enclosed in shells with insecurity and primitiveness which will bring misery to the common people who are living like aliens in their own homeland.'

Uzma becomes emotional and further opens up about the difficulties in the Valley, especially after the death of Burhan Wani. He says, 'Bilal has become a major concern for the family. I regularly come home from hostel to keep Bilal stable and sane. How long could I hold him? He is unemployed and at any time could join the *tanzeem* as his friends have already introduced him to it. It is difficult to go against the current tide of youngsters hating Indian rule. With the new accord between BJP and PDP, everything that was Indian about this place has changed. Maybe it is running its final course. Either India will kill all the boys or Pakistan, along with China, will help them to force India to decide about Kashmir's *azadi* (freedom). With Narendra Modi as Prime Minister, India is becoming a depressing mirror image of Pakistan.'

Rashid understands the sense of panic. His thirty years of service as an executive in the Power and Works Department in Jammu and Kashmir and deep association with the political elite of Srinagar have kept him aware of the disappointments of this *azadi* agenda. Even the Hurriyat leaders who run the anti-India campaigns are confused about it. 'I think that there is no turning back for Hurriyat. Back in 1980-90, they survived in the post-Cold War era, when such movements were treated as ethno-national uprisings. However, changing political developments, both nationally and internationally, have polarised the whole world. The world order is fluid and national governments are no longer held accountable for the perpetual violence. Armed violent movements are no longer considered as ethnic movements but are connected with new agenda of changing the world order on the basis of religion. There is a tacit understanding between the superpowers not to interfere in bilateral disputes.'

Pondering over these concerns, Rashid speaks, 'Kashmiri Muslims are not like the Muslims of Middle East or even tribal Pakistan. We are not conservative. We practise monogamy and do not have many children, unlike our fellow Muslims across the world. In such a social setup, the current trend of youth perishing in the name of *jihad* has brought unimaginable despair to the parents who lose their children. Their suffering is unparalleled.'

He asks Uzma to convince Bilal to come home at least during the night. His parents have become frail agonising over his whereabouts and probable future. Uzma promises to try his best.

The late afternoon brings crimson rays filtering through bare trees and dry leaves in the courtyard, a 'hum' vibration adding to the scary ambience. Zoya calls Uzma from the kitchen for dinner. Rashid smiles and they both go indoors. Razia has already set the table for the meal and they all sit down for dinner. Looking at everyone around the table, Zoya wipes her tears and says, 'I wish Bilal was here too. After ages, I have so many people eating together at the ..' After dinner, Uzma and his sister go to their room and Zoya cleans the kitchen. Muza and Rashid are left alone.

The silence which prevails most of the time in the house is unusual. It used to be abuzz with activity, as cousins, uncles and aunts lived under the same roof. There was never a boring or dull moment. There used to be a continuous flow of boisterous conversations. Everyone was content and happy. Uzma, who was passing the living area for a glass of water in the kitchen, stopped in his tracks when he saw the look of sheer joy on their faces as they recalled those times. Uzma became curious and sat with them to listen in.

'Muza, unprecedented changes have taken place

since I left Bandipore thirty years ago. I remember how affectionately our elders used to talk, discuss and engage in quality conversations amongst themselves. The daily routine was lively.' He then looked pointedly at Uzma and said, 'Although it is difficult for the younger generation to believe, Muslims and Pandits lived together peacefully. Relationships were stable and the course was straight: linearity was taken for granted. Rather than 'the new game of azadi modern youths engage in, youths of our generation used to participate in various school tournaments. The entire town used to come and watch. We loitered around the Madhumati river any time we wanted and nobody at home ever bothered about our whereabouts. We intermingled culturally without any rancour and divergence but our religious boundaries were intact. Religiosity, if visible, was disliked. Respect was mutual and there was security. These circumstances were not state-given, but were culturally evolved for interfaith accommodation. Social formation had strong roots, where common security, mutual respect, predictability of conduct were the ingredients of the cultural core. It was the strength of our culture'.

'How can it now be termed as anti-Islam or anti-Muslim, when these *Batta*s saved us from the yoke of subjugation of centuries?' Rashid laments. When he was younger, his father told countless tales which depicted the

Kashmiris, especially Musalmans, as illiterate, poor and ridden with inferiority complexes. It was only a section of Pirs and Punjabi Muslims, along with highly proficient *Battas*, who were well-to-do. The rest were despised by outsiders, especially by Panjabi Muslims and Dogra Hindu elites alike in rural as well as urban Kashmiri.

For Rashid, it is hard to ignore the memory of the *Battas* who were the transforming agency for the vast Muslim illiterate majority for decades until 1970. They were school teachers, college lecturers, engineers, postmasters, doctors, office clerks—hard-working middle class professionals spread all over the Valley. It is even more difficult to accept the truth that the participation of both Hindus and Muslims in common rituals, ceremonies and festivals—where division of labour never hindered cultural integration but brought stability and predictability to this evolving structure—has vanished too. Kashmiris have forgotten and ignored our syncretic *Reshi* (Sufi) culture. For modern youth, *Battas* have become a despised community who exploited us in the past. Youths are brought up on hate slogans and *jihad* pudding. Anti-Hindu discourses are full of the notion that the Valley must be purified by driving out the Pandits. And they believe it', exclaims Rashid.

Uzma is perturbed by their conversation and the truth of what Rashid says about his peer group in modern Kashmir. He realises that there is a conscious effort to erase the memories of peace and oral history from the minds of people, else *jihad* will not have any meaning. They are silent, lost in their own thoughts and interpretations.

Rashid mulls his decision to move to the city and feels guilt for having left Muza to suffer alone. Coming back to Bandipore has brought him face to face with ground realities. Although he never feels the warmth of those years in his new home in a posh locality of Srinagar, he played it safe for his immediate family by migrating to the city. Away from the tough times in the Valley, his kids are living and studying safely in the plains; far away from militancy and violence.

However, the situation is completely abnormal here. The generation gap and ramifications of violence and displacements are vivid in Bandipore. His nephew is on the verge of getting trapped in militancy. He realises that violence and religious extremism have played havoc here and Muza's family has suffered. The huge social-cultural capital has faded with migration to the city and with the displacement of *Batta*s from the Valley. There is a stillness in the place. For the first time, Rashid feels as if he is drowning in that unending river of misfortune which has trapped Kashmir.

The silence is broken when Razia brings *sheer chai*

(salty tea) with chapatis of rice flour. 'Rashid, have tea quickly. We must go and see Wali Mohmmad, the retired school teacher, who has been unwell for the last one month. I think he has a heart problem', says Muza.

'Yes, yes, we must visit him. I am eager to meet him after two decades. He was a good friend and neighbour too', Rashid replies.

'His eldest son Iffa completed his diploma in electrical engineering from Punjab and has gone missing. It is possible that he might have had joined the new selfie militant group', Muza informs.

'His son hasn't come back?' Rashid asks. Before Muza can reply, Uzma quickly responds, 'Who comes back once their way back home is lost? Our boys are not even wanderers, they get caged and killed.'

Rashid, Uzma and Muza go to meet ailing Wali Muhammad at his place. After the *dua salam* (greetings), they all settle down for tea and Muza enquires about Wali Sahib's health.

'My health is deteriorating just like the situation in our Valley', replies Wali Sahib in a dejected voice. He looks at Muza and Rashid and says, 'How differently our generation fought for freeing Kashmir. Unlike the present generation who believe in violent methods of stone-pelting and gun firing, our patriotism was through 'Azad Kashmir Radio' which was a mystified hope that kept us engaged until 1970. The 1971 Bangladesh war finally brought us face to face with reality, destroying our illusions. We should have listened to local legends and understood our oral history. We wanted to buy dreams which were actually nightmares. Although we hated people from across the border, we welcomed them under the illusion that they would save us. Instead, they inflicted more pain on us.'

Abruptly, he starts talking about Bilal and his son Iffa, who had gradually stopped coming home and started spending more time with militants. 'They have gone to Alusa forest with the militant group. Iffa was also spotted at Khalid's house a week ago. It is rumoured that he is having an affair with Khalid's daughter Naseema.' 'Shabir, the local SHO (Station House Officer, a police official), one of my old students, has told me that Khalid's place is under army surveillance', he adds.

Disturbed by this alarming piece of news, they say '*Khuda Hafiz*' in subdued voices and leave for namaz in the old mosque.

On their way home, Muza remarks that the attendance of teenagers and middle-aged men has conspicuously increased in the mosque. 'It is very good that the younger generation has become religious'.

Both Uzma and Rashid laugh at this naïve statement. Rashid says, 'Muza, you are very innocent. Their religiosity is a mere instrument in the international agenda and is more political than spiritual. In the modern era of lucidity, they are Muslims with covert agenda of *jihad*, making it easy for them to lose their way. Wired and caged in time and space, no place is safe for them'.

Muza and Rashid sit in the room near the kitchen to continue their conversation while Uzma retires to his room. They ask Razia to tell her mother to send tea and a few chapatis for them but not to make dinner.

'Muza, how do you know about the things you were

telling us on our way home?' Rashid asks.

'Muza replies, 'I heard about it from Pir Sahib, an old man in his late seventies who lives in a single-storey two-room cottage on the far side of Putshay mountain. There are many rumours related to his identity as no one knows where he comes from. It is said that he holds a doctorate in political science and is multilingual. He says that Kashmiris do not believe in their own narrative but pretend to be radical like the militants. Since the rule of non-natives, everything about Kashmiri culture—from language to food habits and dress sense—have been rendered inferior. I think this sense of inferiority inflicted in our worldview has made us suffer. Our leaders should have believed in the native culture just like we did during the 1939 'Quit Kashmir Movement' in order to strengthen our faith and re-establish a distinct Kashmiri society based on *Reshi* tradition. But under the influence of the non-natives, we kept rejecting our strong, rich tradition and started believing in the conundrums of fragile religious nationalism. And this process started as early as 1953, when Abdullah turned his back on Nehru.'

'Muza, you are right. We need to revive the culture of harmony in order to recreate the narratives that had given us peace in the subjugated centuries. There is a need to spread awareness about our art, great historical pilgrimages, food, music, the stunning scenic beauty and less about *azadi*. Despite subjugation over centuries, our culture survived in the past because of faith in our subdued and evolved indigenous tradition. Our traditions allowed us to laugh at our predicaments despise the non-native, through *Ladishahs* and *Band-jeshna* (types of folklore). The belief that some divine person would come and save us was perpetuated through folk tales. Our rich poetry was both godly and romantic, be it the theme and context of *gadabata* (a Pandit fish feast during snowfall*)*, or the return of *yaeosh* (prosperity) or many other celebrations during the dark months of snowy cold winter', says Rashid.

'Our elders have become silent, as if their stories are stories of *Battas*. Youth are too impatient to listen to their elders and they outright reject the narratives of the elders,' states Rashid. Muza's face falls the moment Rashid mentions the younger generation. He asks in desperation, 'What should we do? How do we get Bilal back? We do not know how much entrenched he is with the *tanzeem*. Some people say that he is a part of the band of thirty boys who recently posted videos on Facebook displaying arms and announcing their entry into militancy. They are exposed. I fear if Bilal is part of that band, he will never be able to return even if he wants', adds Muza in anguish.

He feels responsible for Bilal's growing interest in the

path of destruction. Sensing his guilt, Rashid holds his hands and assures him, 'Don't worry about Bilal. We will bring him back at any cost. Family name along with Uzma's future is at stake. He may follow in his elder brother's footsteps and turn his back towards a normal, respectable life. I will also talk to Nasir Sahi, who is DIG (Deputy Inspector General of police) as well as my friend, once I reach Srinagar. Razia and Zoya should meet Naseema and ask her to persuade Bilal and Iffa to return home by lying about Zoya's sudden illness.'

Feeling exhausted, Muza yawns and looks at the clock. It is already past midnight. Rashid stands up and tells his cousin to retire for the night. He had forgotten that unlike Jammu, people sleep early in Bandipore.

'Yes, Rashid, sleep well. I have kept an extra blanket in your room in case you feel cold. *Khuda Hafiz*', says Muza.

'*Khuda Hafiz*, Muza', Rashid replies, walking towards his childhood room on the first floor. Nostalgia grips him the moment he enters. He switches on the light and checks out the room thoroughly. Structurally, nothing has changed except for the window, which is now sealed. His eyes fall on many posters glued to the walls revealing *jihadi* messages and heroics. His mind instantly goes back to the past. Back then, the room had photographs of Sunil Gavaskar, Majid Khan, Nehru and Abdullah. He explores further and finds published booklets with the title *Ghazwa-e-Hind* (Holy War to Conquer India) on the shelf. Islamic literature in Urdu and Arabic as well as small notebooks can be seen. In a far corner are a few university books on a small iron bookshelf.

Disturbed by these discoveries, he decides to go through Bilal's belongings to understand the extent of his involvement with militancy. He switches on the laptop he finds in the almirah along with a few pen drives, military uniform, Afghan caps and Pakistani flag ribbons. He is shocked by the contents of the pen drive. There are innumerable songs of glorification of martyrdom, hate speeches against the Indian state and slogans of *jihad*. The room is no longer a typical student's den but has undergone a metamorphosis and become a militant hideout. For a while, he sits on a chair, closes his eyes and the image of the same room from the past pops up in his mind. This is where he had studied relentlessly during his boards and competitive exams. He remembers the carefree teenage days when he played a messenger's role in the love life of his friends, Hasan and Parash. In this same room, he had read letters of his friends' lovers before handing them over. Those were wonderful days of togetherness, full of adventure and fun.

Dawn glides over the darkness of the night but sleep still eludes Rashid. Bilal appears repeatedly in his thoughts. Bilal's mingling with the militants does not look abnormal any more. After all, he is a child groomed in conflict and socialised in the confessional fervour of *jihad*. His social world is built through reports and rumours of army crackdowns, encounters and relentless religious sermons from mosques. His loyalty has shifted to mushrooming militant organisations. He is driven by belief in the monolithic Muslim identity and the mystified versions of the blind discourse. The world has witnessed modernity after Islam. Domination over resources, places and people has changed. Refusal to acknowledge modernity has made God primordial. His adherents are unable to come to terms with the modern nation-state, multicultural plural accommodation and the evolving nature of societies. The primordial God had thrown His unique predicament on His blind adherents. They in return responded to Him with their blood-drenched sacrifices. Bilal and his friends would love to die in His name. He is no longer attached to his family but his traditional-minded parents are tied to him.

Bilal's idealism is linked with the idea of Islam but he hardly has any idea that it would take him back to the medieval era when people were busy in *jihad* and striving for expansion. He is in this war-like situation for an invisible agenda. It is a continuous struggle for political-religious domination against other religions and between the different sects of Islam as well.

Kashmiris, irrespective of difference in religion, faith and creed had stayed united and withstood the loot and subjugations of non-native invasions in the past. But the unity has now vanished because of our own Kashmiri leadership whch looks for reference points beyond the borders. Social cohesion has dissipated and their native thought processes are compromised. They are hardly aware of its ramifications in the form of the loss of social-cultural capital. The willful acceptance of the new package of religious-political mix has made youth euphoric about the changes which were deviously imported in the last two decades, from dress to language, but these changes remain in conflict with the traditionally evolved social formation. It is failing to strike roots. Instead, it is disturbing the natural patterned structures of centuries tearing apart the bonds and weaves of fabric that can never be glued again. *Battas*, for Bilal, are the 'other', an annoyance, an impediment.

Engrossed in his own contemplations, he jogs an old photograph of the family elders resting on the bookshelf and it breaks into pieces on the floor. 'The past is dead', he thinks philosophically instead of feeling guilty.

The night is in its last phase. Rashid desires some fresh air and opens the slit of the sealed window to peer at the big chinar tree that has been a part of their courtyard for many generations. This chinar was his childhood confidante, to whom he whispered his wishes, failures and secrets. In the past, the scene from the window of the room always lifted his mood. However, it does nothing to ease the melancholy he is feeling right now.

He finally falls asleep, exhausted, when the morning birds start singing. He dreams of a grey, aged person wearing a white *phiran* and crimson turban. They are in a thick jungle and the aged man is gathering wood and beckoning him to collect the chinar leaves so that they can light the fire for the eternal sacrifice.

The sound of knocking startles Rashid. He hastily gets out of bed to open the door. With the greeting '*Assalam Aleykum*', Muza enters the room with a smile and asks his cousin whether he slept comfortably.

'*Walekum Salam*', replies Rashid, 'How is the day?'

'It's a sunny morning, a little chilly. Get up and wash your face. They are waiting with the tea', urges Muza.

'I went to bed late. Perhaps, the changes in the room didn't suit me. I was struggling with my memories and worrying about Bilal', confesses Rashid.

'We shall talk about it when you join us', Muza says. He goes downstairs while Rashid rushes to the washroom to freshen up. As Rashid is walking down the stairs towards the dining area, he hears Uzma telling his father about Jawahar Baker closing his bakery shop. Rashid comes and sits at the dining table near Uzma. Pouring steaming tea from the samovar into a cup, he asks Uzma why he is talking about Jawahar Baker first thing in the morning.

Uzma responds, 'Uncle, it is rumoured that Jawahar Baker is involved in militant activities. His house is in the vicinity of the new building behind the old mosque where young *mujahideen* usually gather on Fridays to conduct secret meetings on the pretext of saying namaz. It is his job to gather boys and girls for stone-pelting in case the police raid the area so that the those participating in meetings safely escape from the building towards the forest.'

Muza comments that Haji Masjid, as it is known, indeed has a strange topography. It is close to the three houses owned by Jawahar Baker and his cousins. As the main locality is across the stream half a kilometre away, people do not know much about the new building behind the mosque. People assume that it is a *musafir khana* (travellers' inn). Uzma says Jawahar Baker has been given the contract to run a restaurant in a newly constructed building at the far end of Bandipore, near Jamia Masjid. It is big news for Muza and Rashid.

'Jawahar shifted to a new house he bought recently and opened another bakery shop only six months back. Where did he get the money to invest in the restaurant business?' asks Muza.

'I don't know exactly what the truth is. Rahim's older son, Jawahar Baker's nephew, was talking about the family behind their back. I heard all this when I went to buy freshly baked *lavasa* (bread) from Rahim Baker's shop', replies Uzma.

While they are talking about Baker's family, Zoya interjects, 'This is the time of people of easy virtue. In one of the marriage ceremonies, everybody was surprised to find Jawahar's wife Khalida laden with gold jewellery from head to toe. All those who knew her well were shocked, as they had never seen her wearing so many gold ornaments. There is a story of mysterious gains surrounding the family's sudden affluence and money. I fear that these young boys-turned-militants are so seduced by her charm that they bring her riches and ornaments pilfered from their own homes and fill up Jawahar's house. They also allow their daughters to roam around and mingle with the opposite sex freely. Zaib, the younger daughter of Khalida and Jawahar Baker, told Razia that Bilal often visits their place with his friend Asiq Lone. Zaib's elder sister Sharifa has an enormous liking for Bilal. She always hints to Bilal about getting divorced and marrying him. I am certain that Bilal, in his right mind, would never visit this disreputable family. The Baker family has done *kala jadu* (black magic) on my son with the help of Gulzar Pir of Lawarpora. We are ruined, *Kahnov,* save my Bilal.'[5]

Uzma does not utter a word in response. He cannot say that Jawahar's house has become a hub for the newly recruited *mujahideen* to gather after the Friday sermons. He knows it is a centre for scheduling plans and activities

5 Kahnov is a local deity.

for these young boys. They would gather here, have fun and make videos about their agenda of *jihad* against the army and police.

Instead, he changes the topic and says excitedly, 'Maybe we can meet Bilal next Friday during the afternoon prayer. A boy in the neighbourhood told me yesterday that *mujahideen* plan to visit the mosque to announce shutdown for a week on account of those recently martyred'.

This has Muza worried; he knows that the new young maulvi (priest), who is not a local, gives fiery speeches against the police and the army which mostly lead to sudden violence in the form of stone-pelting, gunfire and death. He hopes his son will not be there. He asks Uzma agitatedly, 'Why does this maulvi choose Fridays for announcements and hate speeches which instigate mobs to resort to violence against the army and the police forces?'

Uzma replies, 'It is not easy to explain. It is written in Quran that Jumma (Friday) was chosen by God as a dedicated day of worship and attending Friday prayers alone is equivalent to an entire year of fasting and praying. Therefore, attendance is highest on Fridays. As Friday prayers are followed by sermons, it becomes easy for clergymen to address the masses and manipulate them from the high moral ground of religion for their international agenda of *jihad*. I think this is the reason why the maulvi also delivers hate-filled sermons on Fridays. But it is not a one-man show. For the youth, it is an emotional meeting for continuing the fluidity of the shared reality so that the different groups with divergent views about rituals and practices within the faith are united for their confrontation of the Indian state. Also, these meetings are held to give direction to youth for the next week's Calendar and to assess the ground situation in order to ensure smooth functioning of the cause of *jihad*'.

The picture portrayed by Uzma sounds dreadful, appalling. Muza is very worried and questions, 'Uzma, how do you assume that your brother will come next week?'

'Well, Abbu, the meetings are generally held on Friday in the new building behind the mosque where young boys and girls take oaths for *jihad*. It is rumoured that the chief whip of this meeting is a new militant who is very qualified and trained. It is a secret mission. I have a hunch that *bhaijan* will attend the meeting', replied Uzma.

Grasping at this clue to her brother's whereabouts, Zoya looks at them teary-eyed and says, 'All three of you go together, look for Bilal and bring him back home'. They nod, eating *lava*s and sipping tea. She addresses Muza, 'Why don't you go and seek Razz *Babb*'s blessing for Bilal's safe return?'

Hearing this name for the first time, Rashid asks, 'Who is Razz *Babb*? Is he a new Pir? Does he predict the future? Or is he like the new Pirs who are rich and very different from traditional dervishes. Wearing rich robes and commuting in cars, these Pirs enjoy the luxuries of a good life. Mostly middle-aged, they have beards, long hair, wear colourful caps and rich clothes and bring religion even into general conversation. They keep youths engaged in violence in the name of religion while they live in posh dwellings. Uncertainties have made faith a convenient refuge and these Pirs catch our attention as if they can change our plight and tell us when our dear ones who are either missing or already dead would come back. They are easily sighted in each locality of our city and are now mushrooming in towns and villages also. They are growing in strength while institutions fail to deliver', Rashid comments.

Uzma says, 'Uncle, you are mistaken. Razz *Babb* is very different from this new type of Pir. He is a vegetarian dervish and had come to this place after *Batta*s left their homes. People say that he used to live in a Bandipore temple before the *Batta*s left. He is in his late seventies and lives modestly in a one-room cottage near the big chinar tree at Putshay mountain given by a rich man, Hazir Parrey. His youngest son Ahad Parrey who was Rashid's classfellow was killed by some unidentified persons near the chinar tree. The rich Parreys then built this rest house where Razz *Babb* now lives. Perhaps the elder Parrey before his death requested Razz *Babb* to come to stay in this room.

'Since then, the cottage has taken on a surreal appearance. The branches of the tree have embraced the cottage completely and it looks like a dwelling of an ancient civilisation. He is often seen talking and mumbling to himself. He knows how to write and speak English, Sanskrit, Persian, Urdu and Kashmiri. He writes poetry, which he recites when in a good mood. He does not interact with women except for Salim Parrey's mother, who brings food and *kangri*[6] for him regularly in the afternoon and evening. Salim Parrey takes care of his hookah, for this Pir smokes.

'I have gone many times to meet him and seek his blessings. I like his conversations, which are a little indistinct, but I feel as if I am suspended in time. His company is refreshing; when he talks it seems that the past is meeting the future and the present is lost in his storytelling. He always wears a dark-coloured *phiran* which looks shabby and torn, as if it had not been washed for years. It is rumoured that he never uses soap for bathing. Winter or summer, he goes to the bank of the stream and runs water up and down with his right hand while mumbling something for an hour. Amma Lal, who died last year, used to say that the old *Batta*s also did the

---

6 Kangri is a portable wicker heater fired by coal often carried under the *phiran*.

same thing with fresh water early in the morning.

'Everyone in the neighbourhood either fears him or is in awe of him. The *mujahideen* also treat him with respect, they do not mock him. In fact, they ask him for blessings, which of course he never gives', states Uzma.

'Muza, why don't we meet him? He seems to be a sensible sage. Inshallah, he will tell us everything will go well. We should spend some time with him', says Rashid.

It is already past nine. Uzma urges his father and uncle to make a move before the stone-pelting starts, otherwise it would be difficult to even cross the road. Uzma decides to go to Jawahar Baker's house while Rashid and Muza head for Hasan's house.

It is past ten and the sun is high up in the sky when Rashid and Muza finally start walking towards Hasan's house. On the way, they notice that the greenery in the locality has withered. The yellowish sunshine is glittering unevenly on the high snowy peaks far away, separating nature from the unnatural. Concrete constructions encroaching on the forest give intimations of scandal. Strangely and sadly, the abandoned *Batta* houses which have turned to ruins and are lamenting their prime years, bring striking memories of the past to the passerby. Emerging patches of green amidst the ridges and ruts of these houses mock their predicament and bring discomfiture.

'*Assalam Alleykum*', Rashid and Muza say in unison the moment they see Hasan waiting on the street near his house.

'*Walekum Salam.* You both have finally come. I have been waiting here for the last one hour', says Hasan.

'Sorry, Hasan. We are late because of Rashid. Living in the city has made him lazy. He slept till 8 in the morning', Muza replies, looking teasingly at Rashid.

'Come, we shall have tea and then decide what to do',

says Hasan as they walk towards his house.

'*Yaar*, I have decided to extend my stay here to help in finding and persuading Bilal to come back home,' Rashid tells Muza and Hasan while entering the house. Hearing this, Muza's face lights up with happiness. He exclaims that he is glad for the support.

Hasan then asks Muza, 'Did Uzma get any clue of Bilal's whereabouts?'

'Uzma says he has a hunch that Bilal will come to the meeting scheduled next Friday in a new building behind the Haji mosque. He has gone to Jawahar Baker's house to get some detailed information. I think we should also go to the mosque near Jawahar's house for the afternoon prayers', replies Muza.

Hasan's wife Aamna enters the room and says, 'I have already prepared the food. You all go for namaz after having lunch'.

Hasan nods. 'Of course, we have enough time to even rest before going for namaz'. They talk for a while, eat lunch and then go to the other room to rest. They wake up late and therefore head for the nearby mosque instead of the Haji mosque. After namaz, Hasan suggests a visit to Razz *Babb*'s cottage, which both Rashid and Muza readily agree to.

Razz *Babb* lives alone. A stray black dog often sits near the cottage as if listening to *Babb*'s murmurings.

The door remains open and any visitor can clearly see him even from a distance. It is away from the main path of the village in the shadow of the hill. The sun gazes at the chinar tree from the far end of the sky and the tree in turn spreads its rays on the cottage, exalting Razz *Babb*'s presence. The place no longer looks like an ugly darkened ruin but a beacon of hope of life and light in Razz *Babb*'s presence.

Razz *Babb* is serenely sitting with his street dog, listening to the unremitting hiss of the leaves that still cling on to the majestic tree.

'Look, he resembles Ahad *Babb*', says Muza.

'He looks like Parash's father, Ved Lalji', Rashid responds. Hasan nods his head in agreement but Muza says irritably, 'I wonder when the two of you would get over the *Batta* hangover. He is an old Pir. Why should we bother who he resembles and who he was? I wonder why people try to find out whether he is a Muslim or a *Batta*. I know that he has the capacity to talk in Kashmiri metaphors that can be understood in the subjective interpretations.'

'Muza, you should sometimes go with what your heart feels and what your eyes see. Look, his *phiran* is a long one, the type *Batta*s used to wear and he wears a Kashmiri winter cap too. His nose is pointed and his grey face along with parallel wrinkles on his broad forehead reveal extraordinary longevity. The big, bulging eyes are full of light. He is not an ordinary fellow', Rashid comments.

They reach the cottage and sit down, paying *Salaams* with their heads bowed. Nearby, Salim Parrey is busy preparing a tobacco hookah for *Babb* and inclines his head when he sees them. Salim has been looking after *Babb*'s needs for the last two decades. He knows his language and can easily understand his smallest gesture.

'*Babb*, boys are missing and families are being robbed of their peace of mind. Mothers are sick and daughters are scared. *Babb*, will our sufferings end?' asks Rashid.

Babb looks at him, drops his gaze and replies, 'Where is the path and where is the chase? Since the day incidents of braid-chopping started, we have been lying. We are chopping the braids of our sisters, blaming Indians and spreading the news beyond the mountains even though we know that it is a lie. No braid-chopper has been apprehended so far. But many innocent people have become victims of our collective criminal behaviour and Kashmiris have humiliated their own women. We are only helping those people who want to paint us black. We are in disastrous moral descent and are left with no one to even argue against us, let alone argue in our favour'.

Hasan feels restless hearing this observation. He says, '*Babb*, braid-chopping is a reality: thirty cases have already been reported'.

'Telling lies and creating ghosts out of fear have become our new behaviour pattern. It is coming out from our homes, unlike in the past. Initially, we lied to strangers but now we lie to ourselves too. Braid-chopping must be a reality but it is a reality based on a lie, which is being mystified'.

Muza is puzzled and asks Salim to explain what *Babb* was talking about. Salim understands what *Babb* is hinting at. While *Babb* is drawing on the hookah, he explains, 'Over the months, I have seen *Babb* repeatedly talking about the destruction of our Kashmiri language. He thinks that we have killed our language and replaced it with non-native languages. Initially, we did it in schools and offices but now we are doing it in our homes too. *Babb* says without mincing words that repeated denigration of our mother tongue and mothers are the root cause of our sufferings. Our grandparents were our custodians: Hindu or Muslim, they knew only this language. Now they have been deprived of the right to converse in this language and hence there is generational disconnectedness.'

'*Babb*, when would our Bilal come home? We are all in pain. Every day we hear news of *mujahideen* getting killed. They say it is all-out war against India', says a desolate Muza.

Babb has become pensive by then and is mumbling something. Dragging a long *kash* (inhalation) from his hookah, he states, 'We are not able to talk to our children but we want to have control over them. Our children move in and out of relationships without accountability. Multilateral relationships are based on the feint that self-interest and self-involvement would be protected but, as a matter of fact, they remain exposed and unprotected. The levers of control lie somewhere else. Therefore, it generates suspense and insecurities. You may buy anything else but you cannot buy trust. Its prerequisite is honesty in relationships. Market is another version of falsehood, it can distract with many options but with no control. Bilal is floating in this realm without accumulating any socio cultural capital. He will come back. He will be disillusioned, with huge insecurities but he will come back for sure.'

Muza quickly adds, '*Babb*, we are worried that he does not visit us but he goes to that Baker's home. It is rumoured that he is having an affair with Baker's elder daughter Sharifa. It is true that many before him, who frequently visited Baker's house, got killed subsequently.'

'You should not blame Baker or his girls. The fact is that the boys give their personal information to others and make themselves visible and easily traceable to all those who want to chase them. That is how they facilitate their own elimination. Technology is a seduction which entices these youths through social media platforms like

Facebook, Instagram and Snapchat. Selfies and self-construed videos are in abundance. Their availability has not only intoxicated youngsters but wired the elders too. Social media has given space to each one to introduce themselves to the world the way they want. Social media platforms enable us to show the best of ourselves without any nervousness or reservation. Youngsters are especially vulnerable. They think they are alone in secret places entertaining themselves but all their activities are stored; it is easy for the intelligence agencies to extricate whatever information they want. Entertainment which comes with invasion of privacy in this glamorous digital world becomes part of their dream world. These young children thrive on fluid relationships and are confused and unstable all the time. They are seduced, caught and then destroyed. Social media platforms carry their biographies along with pictures and their movements; they willingly display their address to unknown people and blame others for being informers.' *Babb* looks pensive as he put his hookah aside.

Rashid is astonished by the way *Babb* is tackling their queries. It proves that he is a very informed person, up-to-date with modern technology and not a lost wanderer.

The evening shadows are lengthening. The chill of November is penetrating their jackets. Muza's mobile is continuously abuzz. They decide to take leave from

Babb with mixed feelings of hope and anxiety; the hope of getting Bilal back safely lifting their mood but *Babb*'s warning about the increasing vulnerability due to Internet making them fretful and restless too.

Razz *Babb* has made such an impression on Rashid that he decides to visit him again before leaving for Jammu. He feels that *Babb*'s words had clarity with deep insights.

Hasan does not go home. Instead, he goes to Muza's house along with Rashid and Muza. Hasan informs his wife Aamna that he is going to spend the night with his friends. It is not safe for Hasan to walk back home all alone to the other end of the town after ten at night.

The moment they reach home, Zoya rushes towards Muza and asks desperately, 'What did Razz *Babb* say about Bilal?'

'*Babb* was not in a good mood but he did mention that Bilal would be back. He indirectly warned that Bilal should not move with groups which are active on social media and must not expose himself by posting his pictures', says Muza. He then laments, 'The biggest worry is how we are going to stop him or warn him when we don't know his whereabouts.'

'Oh, my Mukadam Saheb,[7] save my Bilal and give him the wisdom to stay away from danger', cries Bilal's

7 Prayer to a local deity.

mother. She adds, 'Poor Uzma too has gone to search him. He has informed that he will be staying with Altaf, his friend, as it is difficult to come out on the main road in the evening. In the past, we invoked divine spirits like Kahnov, Dastigir Sahib, even Parbat goddess for the welfare of our families and children. We had faith even when the Divine was not a human being but an unknown pious spirit. In the present times, the unknown is human agencies which are invisible but interfering and controlling all the time without giving us any sign of their character and intentions. This contradiction between the past and present has led to these difficult times. In the past, the invisible was sublime, subjective and helpful. In the present, the invisible pretends to be divine but obstructs rather than illuminates us. This is brazen madness', Rashid thinks.

Their concerns are deep-rooted and everyone is perplexed by the changes in their lives. They have dinner and then go to the room upstairs to talk.

Once they settle in the room upstairs, Muza asks, 'Rashid, what do you make of the recent braid-chopping incident? Rumour mills are at work. The incident has caused panic among the people and rumours have spread across the Valley like wildfire. It has been followed by severe unbridled public frenzy which has made it a perceptible reality. Despite suggestions that the cases are fabricated or fuelled by hysteria, the consequences are all too real. The elders are worried and the young ones keep drawing meaning from such sensational news'.

I think Razz *Babb* was right', says Hasan. 'In the past too, Kashmir witnessed sensational incidents like the '*Dayan*' episode, 'Children missing' and '*Burqa Walia*'. In the mid-1990s, when militancy was at its peak, 'Six feet tall ghosts' used to scare people in the night hours. My friend Imtiyaz who is an engineer told me that the braid-chopping incident is similar to the *bhoot* (ghost) phenomenon of the 1990s.

'There is method in the madness of both the incidents. Imtiyaz had discovered from a hard-core

Hizb commander that in the 1990s, when the army was searching for their hideouts during the night; their think tank had introduced this sensational 'night *bhoot* mystery', so that society remained vigilant and kept guard in their neighbourhoods. This stopped the army from raiding hideouts and *mujahideen* would sleep well at night', Hasan adds.

They sense that these aberrations would continue and they want to know what would happen to them. Why are stories and sensational narratives made out of small incidents to help people play victim and enjoy destructive manifestations? The braid-chopping phenomenon was reported in other parts of India as well but in a way which did not cause any panic or sensation. It was simply a deviant act and was handled by the police. People there have faith in law and order agencies too.

In Kashmir, the psychology of victimhood is widely prevalent and manifests as a mystified trepidation. Distrust is deep and has caused uncertainties all around. It is a willful collective suicide. In some cases, the same person plays dual roles of culprit and victim. The police fail to find valid evidence. Innocents are treated as braid-choppers and are beaten and humiliated. Next day, the same innocent people become culprits. It is a strange vicious circle.

'As if common people like us would ever dare go out after sunset', says Hasan sarcastically. 'The tragedy is that we know the truth but do not speak about it', he continues. 'In the past, during the rule of monarchs, when we were ruled by non-natives, we used to cry and laugh at ourselves in our own native cultural realm and draw sustainable strength to move to the realm of certainty and predictability with the help of our common divine, *ziyarats* and pilgrimages. Religion was fused with the non-Kashmiri realm and used by political elites and rulers for our subjugation. It was a different type of plotting which induced inferiority in our collective consciousness and made us believe that Kashmiri culture is sub-standard and Kashmiri people are subservient to the non-native. The new generation fell in the same trap: non-native touchstones are an illusion, political ideologies are bankrupt. We are back to the the pre-1930s.

'Youngsters hardly know that the Quit Kashmir Movement in the 1930s was an uprising against this duality to change the two realms and make them one sustainable realm. Nehru and Abdullah knew it well. After experimentation with the elite bubble, Abdullah went back to Nehru's realm of understanding—that pluralism and secularism in a representative democracy is best for Kashmir, rather than the Islamic Republic of Pakistan. By then, Nehru was no longer alive.

'These half-truths and half-lies have robbed Kashmiris of their peace of mind. There is madness in creating disinformation and inflicting suffering so that there is no discontinuity in the agenda of creating estrangement. The flow of sensationalism has been propagated since the time of non-native subjugation but the unknown factor which caused sensations was divine—that is, sublime and benevolent—and gave us strength to bear the tyranny of natural and unnatural calamities. Now, the element of the unknown to give us peace is worldly. It is conniving and malevolent. It is constructed to escalate the feeling of hatred and revulsion and suppress logical thinking. Fear and mistrust is a part of our psyche since the deceitful exile of our native king, almost five centuries ago.[8] It is as if we need to create these scary commotions synthetically for our survival. It has become our routine to live in wariness and suspicion.'

Muza enquires, 'Why is it different now? India still rules and we have no order in society; the moral fabric is in pieces.'

'This is our cultural poverty,' replies Hasan. 'Disillusioned by a remote referent, we have now become sick. Had we been allowed to live the way our leader Abdullah had decided, we would have not only become one of the leading states of India but would have come out as a well-respected community in the entire world.

8 Yusuf Shah Chek, the first native king whom Mughal emperor Akbar had captured by deceit and imprisoned outside the Valley.

But we were not allowed to do so. We are tagged with this moth-eaten Pakistan that continues to weigh down our culture as poor and brand us as victims. Our mindsets have thickened with the illusion of pure religion whereas it was altogether a different story there. Those in power were our people but they too did not reveal the truth. They had to lie, mystify their agenda and blend it with the alien Islamic ideal to remain in power. The moment to act came with the end of the Cold War, when western ideologies had proved bankrupt. But we wasted the opportunity. Western modernity was in search for supplementation whereas we tried to erase modernity. The real remedy lay not in refusing modernity but filling up the gaps—lost pragmatism and identifiable lived plural traditions which can only be provided by an evolved culture and not by codified religion. And now codification itself has collapsed.

'In order to reverse the journey, we had to jump backwards, which was impossible. So we fell into the pit of primordial discourses, a space pre-modern and post-Islam. This is not religion but a bunch of interpretations of men of lesser knowledge. We are now hitting our heads against the wall, killing our own people, degrading our religion and bemoaning culture.'

Muza reiterates, 'How are the academicians explaining it?'

'Who listens to them? Some commentaries come

from Islamic scholars. They find that Muslim tradition subsumes reason within revelation. It has given in to subjective interpretations and emergence of militant and radical groups who are in the race of capturing resources, so that intellectual base is shrinking further. Look, for the last two decades what is happening to us is a reflection of what has happened to Pakistan. See what the Pakistan columnist Khaled Ahmed in his *Dawn* write-up explained: The increasing sectarian divide uses Christian theological terms, dubbing the Barelvi school of thought as 'low church' and Deoband's Ahle Hadith schools of thought combined as 'high church'. He depicted sectarian violence and attacks on shrines as the confrontation between the 'low' and 'high' churches.

The recent rise of Barelvi activism can also be seen in the same context, which is not an intellectual or reformation attempt but a response to the growing influence of the Deobandi school of thought. The establishment of the MML (a radical Islam outfit) can also be seen as an effort by the Ahle Hadith School to dominate, which indicates further sectarian proliferation. The 'low church' is building upon Sunni Asabiyyah and the 'high church' is widening its political and ideological appeal. If you ask me, I would say it is the spread of traditional animosity of 'Arab and Ajem' (non-Arab) across the Muslim world. These radical groups are flourishing on the generous charity of state and non-state organisations for the supremacy of their own radical wings. Saudi Arabia and Iran command the bipolarity of the Muslim world', says Rashid.

'I feel that nobody knows any more who is in control of the movement. There are many organisations at work which are aided by both internal as well as external sources. I recall my son telling me about his hostel cook Rahim. That man, after Haj in 2013, did not resume his job. It was rumoured that he was unwell, hence on leave. But he never returned. A couple of years later, we came to know that he had established two colleges in his name on the outskirts of Srinagar. When my son and his friends did a little research, they found to their astonishment that it was *zakat* (charity) money openly given in Saudi Arabia for the victims of Kashmir which he had invested in these colleges. Many individuals use this type of aid for personal benefit. For the last three decades, money poured into Kashmir like monsoon rains. Subsequently, the money which is drenched in blood brings untimely death to our dear ones', Rashid bemoans.

'Who cares about morals and values? Who listens to the elders? With changes in social demography, moral policing has become a thing of the past. Today, our actions are centred on our own vested interests and our disparate ideologies. We ignore the larger picture i.e., the ramifications of our actions on society. For youth, this is the new normal', says Muza.

'We have seen a different era when we blindly believed in everything our leaders, both political and religious, said. Since then, unprecedented changes have taken place and nothing is in its rightful place. Our own *Batta* neighbourhoods have become desolate enclaves of ghost houses. These standing skeletons of bricks covered with dusty roofs and dark spots on their countenance look like paintings of suffering done by grief-ridden tribes. The stream across the field is beating its chest and heaving sighs emerging from the whirlpool of circles; it was clearly lamenting the loss of past glory repressed in the pallid present. The remains of a cluster of half-ruined buildings are not a welcome sight.

'In our childhood, relationships were lasting and bonds were strong. Coming from the same lower middle class, studying in the same school and hailing from the same neighbourhood, we did not need any apron. In our time, caste, class, rank, title and religion were merged into a single universe which was like an extended family. There was only one established higher secondary school in town and we all studied in that school. People were genuine and honest. We had freedom to express our opinion without fear. I can never forget Parash, my childhood friend. I truly treasure our friendship and would have to erase my entire life to erase his memory,' says Hasan.

'In the past, we were stratified, but today we are divided', Rashid says. Then continues, 'I know that both of you think I am fortunate to have a cosy home in a posh locality, enough money to send children out of the Valley for pursuing professional courses and a working woman as a wife. It is quite true that I have everything but I remained fragmented, lonely and scattered since the day I left Bandipore. I crave to have meaningful conversations which can bring respite from the disconnection I feel from my day-to-day life. This is true for everyone displaced from their roots—voluntarily or involuntarily. The sense of belongingness comes from peace, love, care and meaningful conversations and not from gaudy and materialist things like bungalow, car and costly mobile or extravagant lifestyle.

'Earlier, the community was our unrecognised institution where children evolved naturally and were not raised. We understood the world around us. Affluence of others did not bother us but we had desires and dreams too. Everyone pursued their goals in a linear fashion. We now undermine our social, cultural and symbolic capital which is invisible but cumulative. It is as important as our economic well-being. Economic capital alone cannot illuminate our path. We never should have run after affluence alone, ignoring our social and cultural capital.

It only blurred our vision. Our life lacks meaningful, quality conversations. Money cannot purchase happiness. It is our familiar surroundings and communicative interaction which generate a sense of togetherness and joy within which, in turn, give us enough social and cultural capital to sustain ourselves. Migration for the last two decades has made localities segregated. Always compared with 'Sheher Khaas' downtown, a new layer of stratification has been created that has ramifications on day-to-day life. Peace is elusive and has paved the way for uncertainties and unpredictability with intolerance suffusing interactions. It is exclusively economic interests that govern us and our interests and the social and cultural bond is disconnected from it. The market is not a leveller, it is a divider. If you lack purchasing power, the market excludes you.'

The night is taking strides but the trio is engrossed in heartfelt conversations. Muza points out that if they can get freedom from India, perhaps their hardships might end. 'This is what our leaders want us to believe. It would be a miracle if we are left to fend for ourselves', responds Hasan.

Their ignorance incenses Rashid. He quickly responds, 'The dream of *azadi* is a mirage which our leaders and Islamic organisations are exploiting for their own vested interest and agenda. For the last three decades, international journalists have come to report our movement formally as well as informally. A few are known to me through our common overseas friends. You would be astonished to know that most of these overseas journalists got disillusioned and were at a loss to comprehend us. They then turned into theoreticians in order to analyse us in the broader category of "Muslim worldview of post-colonial Cold War dynamics" and "Muslim world in the representative democratic countries". Christopher Snedden's analogy about Kashmir is in vogue.'

Rashid shows them the report posted online from his mobile: 'You know Hasan, last year in July, I went without a haircut for three months. It was strike and stone-pelting season and our barber, who is from Uttar Pradesh, had gone back until the close of autumn. People have become lazy and don't want to do anything on their own. They have money now. It is from both genuine and fake sources. The youth do not have proper engagement. They have funds without jobs. Recreational engagements deprive them of status and dignity. It has caused identity crisis with moral decay. The chaos suits everybody.

'What is our fault? Why are we suffering? Are we not humans before we are part of the larger entity like religion or nation? Geographical boundaries are given priority over human life and peace', laments Muza.

'You are looking at the current scenario from your

narrow perspective', Rashid responds, adding, 'Genocide in the name of religion is no joke. We lost our chance at peace when we forced our minority *Batta*s to leave. Misled by people from across the border, we inflicted violence on our own people in the name of purity of religion. We forced them to leave but in the process, we have dug our own grave. At least *Batta*s are peacefully living in other states of India. For us, even peace is elusive. This is our punishment for betraying our native people in the name of religion. In the 1990s, we added fuel to the fire which was already there due to decisions of our leaders'.

'What are you trying to say? You mean our leaders Abdullah and Nehru were wrong? How are they responsible for what is happening today? You sound like a BJP spokesperson', Muza says with distaste.

Rashid laughs, 'I am not saying that they are fully responsible for the current situation but their decisions did affect us in the long run. We would have been reconciled with the accession to India if not for the ceasefire command of the UN. As Nehru and Abdullah were in harmony, things did work for some time. But in their absence, there is lack of mutual trust between Srinagar and New Delhi which further deteriorated the situation in Kashmir. The final blow came in the form of the genocide of Kashmiri Pandits in 1989'.

'What is this Nehru-Abdullah conundrum?' asks Muza.

'Ah! Nehru, Abdullah had the same ancestry. Two-and-a-half centuries ago, had they belonged to same generic pool of Kauls. Nehru, the hero of the national freedom movement, identified Abdullah in Aligarh Muslim University to launch the Quit Kashmir Movement to dislodge five centuries of non-native rule in Kashmir and end the monarchy. This joint sustained commitment since 1930 saw emergence of the National Conference, denial of the two-nation theory as well as affront to Jinnah in Kashmir and a common struggle against Dogra monarchy. If not for Nehru, Abdullah would have not been dubbed Sher-e-Kashmir and he could have not survived the wrath of the monarchy. They had devised a plan how to remain together and grow in a dignified way in a plural nation-state of India.

'Before they could settle down to transform the lives of their people, the Cold War dynamics of a bipolar world played the trick. The West made Pakistan a formidable strategic asset against an ascendant communist Soviet Union. Hence, a tribal attack on Kashmir by Pakistan in 1947 to snatch Kashmir by force. Through Mountbatten, Britain persuaded Nehru to take the case of Kashmir to the United Nations. Nehru believed that Pakistan would be declared aggressor. Instead, the UN kept Kashmir on the boil and converted India and Pakistan into two warring neighbours for the contestation of Kashmir. Its resolution on Kashmir put the onus on both countries to meet its preconditions before plebiscite could be held. The unrealistic resolution had conditions which could never be met by two estranged neighbours.

'In the 1950 Delhi Declaration, Abdullah swore by Nehru and requested complete merger, which Nehru cleared. In 1953, when Jinnah had died, Liyaqat was assassinated; Abdullah was pursuaded to back Nehru for the crown of Sultan of Kashmir by Adlai E Stevenson, shadow foreign secretary of the US, a promise which was never fulfilled. During the Cold War, Pakistan was seen as providing strategic depth to the Western power bloc against the Soviet Union. In the bargain, Pakistan had asked for the settlement of Kashmir in its favour. It was Anglo-American craftiness to create religious satellite states to serve their own interests to keep India trapped and Pakistan wishful while Abdullah was encouraged to dream of the crown. Bipolarity was used to keep conflicts unresolved and international diplomacy on the UN resolutions was a tool to balance the interests of the superpowers. India will not give up Kashmir, Pakistan cannot take Kashmir and our leadership continues playing sides from time to time for their vested interests. We have become a trampled lot', Rashid explains.

There are certain questions in Hasan's mind. He wants to know why the Muslim Conference founded in

1931 had to be dissolved in 1939 and why Senior Pir considered it a historical blunder by Abdullah. He puts the question to Rashid, who does not give a bookish answer, as he has developed his own opinion about it. He states, 'Judgments in retrospect disjoint time with space and structuring. You may have been told otherwise, but the fact of the matter is that Kashmir Muslim League was controlled by non-natives of Kashmir who were primordial in their approach and orientation.

'If permitted, they would have submerged us as subjects of Azad Kashmir (PoK).[9] Not only would our distinctness have vanished but we would have been left as a bunch of illiterates with a thin section of dominant elites too. Who would have been then the transforming agency for the vast majority of illiterates even if the state had wished for the eradication of illiteracy? Nehru's company guaranteed Abdullah active state support and the backing of *Batta* minority, the traditional educated lot, well spread all over the Valley at the time. Take away the interventionist centrist state (Nehru's India) and the agency (the *Batta* community) and we would have been akin to Swat Valley inhabitants, a primordial tribe of Kashmiris. Nehru's welfare state programmes, along with free education and development funds, extracted value from forests, tourism

9 Pakistan calls the portion of Kashmir 'liberated' from India during the tribal incursion of 1947 'Azad Kashmir' while India calls it Pakistan Occupied Kashmir, or PoK.

and handicrafts to produce a new rich class, an alternative for regenerative politics. However, that class remained mystified and caged in the imagined referent of pure Islam and believed in the era of closed boundaries. I certainly feel that Abdullah (and the National Conference) were for a progressive linearity whereas Maulvi Yousuf Shah was a primordial reluctant siding with the monarchy'.

Hasan knows that the past was not wasted. He supplements, 'It was a historical segment, before the close of the twentieth century, a dreamy social world, where illusions of the pure Islam, a synchronistic *Batta* minority, stable neighborhoods with clear-cut transfer of land to tillers without a price via land reforms, cheap public schooling and quality medical facilities which could have made our lives and our world perfect. The processes of development and democratisation, even if in distorted form, generated a new Muslim educated middle class which had a chance to go for the progressive modes of existence. We somehow lost our way'.

Rashid intervenes, 'We were made to enjoy the benefits of modernity and to live in the realm of anti-rational mode of existence. Subsequently, the politics of bipolarity in Kashmir was used to galvanise the Muslim world against the Communist Bloc. One of its ramifications was that Abdullah turned into an exclusive leader of Muslim Kashmir and the other two regions—

Jammu and Ladakh—were willfully ignored. There was no socio-political awakening in these regions in the absence of developmental measures. It was as if only three districts—Srinagar, Baramullah and Anantnag—existed in the entire state of Jammu and Kashmir. Along with political and religious mystification of Kashmir, the developmental lag between the regions also amplified rancour among the people of the region against each other, cutting across religious lines. We could never talk in a favourable manner about Rajouri, Poonch, Kishtiwar or Badrawah Muslims. They are graded inferior to Kashmiri Muslims. It has split our voice in political discourse'.

The whole interaction is being recorded by Razia, Muza's daughter, for she is in search of new insights and a new awakening about the past full of details which never surfaced before. The story might have been told before but in fragments. Discourses beyond 'Nehru promised plebiscite' were never permitted. Sleep has escaped their eyes. They are immersed in their discussion of Kashmir's estrangement, as if they have to submit a report to a university professor next morning.

Muza goes to the washroom and on his return, changes the direction of the conversation to Bilal's estrangement. In a straightforward manner he asks, 'What should we do to get Bilal back? In case we fail, the family goes down and we may lose Uzma as well.'

Hasan reacts, 'It has to be a three-pronged endeavour. Rashid will talk to his friend Nassir, a friend who is a police officer, that police should not impede our efforts to bring back Bilal. Uzma, if he meets him, should continuously interact with the girls and if possible, try to convince Bilal to come home for the sake of his mother and sister. Above all, we should pay visits to Razz *Babb* for his blessings. Tomorrow will be another busy day. We need to get some sleep before the sun rises.'

'*Yaar*, Hasan, after ages I have talked freely without any reservation and filter between my mind and tongue. In the city, I interact with my relatives and friends without my heart in it. In Srinagar, I am a familiar stranger moving around with formal gestures and symbolic expressions, so that nobody knows what I want to say. There is neither predictability nor certainty about what the next moment would bring. People instantly sever the contact if the conversations do not match their ego level. Relationships are maintained for material self-interest. It is because the shared past in our professions or in our new locality lacks childhood innocence and self-reflective interactions', says Rashid.

Muza prepares beds for Hasan and Rashid on the carpet and bids them '*Allah Hafiz*'. It is the fag end of the night. As they lie side by side, Rashid continues, 'I regret not taking genuine interest in Muza's life all these years. He is stuck in the past but I have moved on. I feel sad that I did not even stand by his side in his good and bad times for support and assurance as his elder brother. I recall all those moments when my wife and children humiliated him at my place and he silently ignored their taunts for my sake. All these years, he requested me to visit Bandipore but I never came. My wife never wanted to pay a visit to this place. When I now reflect on this, I suffer guilt pangs. Until now, I was caged by circumstances. I could never confess the truth even to myself, although I knew I was unfair to him and his family'.

Hasan replies, 'The estrangement of relationships is common these days. Relatives have become strangers now. Except the rare phone conversations on special occasions, we seldom call or visit one another. Where has the idea of joint or extended family gone? Its inherent tacit roles are now openly managed by new alternative agencies which lack cultural and social capital. Carefree, genuine, holistic and natural flow of conversation and informal expressions are rare now. These things remain confined to biographies and narratives of the distant past. Rashid, try to catch some sleep and do not torment your mind. Morning is almost here. *Khuda Hafiz.*'

With these words, Hasan closes his eyes and falls asleep but Rashid is still awake, in a state of agitation. Only when the morning breeze taps at the windows does he fall asleep.

Rashid is woken up by Uzma's call in the morning. Muza's number is out of reach so Uzma asks him to inform the family that he would come after breakfast. Leaving the bed silently, Rashid goes downstairs after freshening up to inform Muza and Zoya.

Muza is talking to his wife. 'Zoya, the thick darkness of the night has gone into my heart and I feel restless all the time. Although I am unable to think beyond Bilal and his safe return, we cannot simply drop or ignore our work. We need to look after our crops too. Look at this spell, the weather is also moaning and there is no sunshine. Where will we dry our crop? There is a long queue at the rice machines due to the frequent electricity shutdowns. We need to process our dried paddy before December. The chill has started and it may rain'.

Rashid interrupts, 'Muza, Uzma called to inform that he will return after having breakfast with Salim, a university friend of Bilal's, at his place.'

Muza nods, saying apologetically, 'I guess you woke up so early due to his call. My number must be out of network or switched off if Uzma called on your number.'

'It's alright. I only wish he gets some information about Bilal and Bilal comes back soon. It will bring peace and order to our lives', replies Rashid.

'Uzma keeps insisting on handling it alone. He thinks that our direct involvement will make them suspicious and expose our intention to get Bilal out of their clutches. I feel frustrated by my helplessness. In the effort to get Bilal back, Uzma has gotten himself entangled in the mess and I sometimes fear for him. It is affecting Uzma's life too', says Muza.

'Uzma is trying his best to bring Bilal home. With the blessings of Kahnov, our bad days will soon end. I too want to confront Baker's wife Khalida but Uzma has stopped me. It is better to trust Uzma. He will do the right thing. He mingles with young people of his age and he is in the know about *mujahideen* activities', says Zoya, before going to the kitchen to prepare tea.

Meanwhile, Uzma goes to his close friend Salim's place to talk about Bilal and persuade him to help in the search for his son. Salim is a close friend of Bilal's. It is common talk that in 1994, when cartons full of cash were distributed among middle-rung Hurriyat leaders in Kashmir, Salim's father Sunna and his cousin Sikandra, a Jamaat-e-Islami member, had a verbal brawl near Nishat Park mosque for a share of the pickings sent for recruitment of *jihadi*s.

Since then, the two cousins have become bitter rivals. Sunna says that his cousin Sikandra flourished on that wealth. Sikandra got his two sons established in business; his daughter Safina was married to a junior engineer in Sopore. On the contrary, Sunna lost a beloved son, older than Salim, in the bloody 1998 Sonawari armed encounter. His children are still not settled.

Safina has also come to meet Salim but the visit is related to the mission. She knows that Jawahar Baker was involved in conscription of young boys and his house is used as a nodal centre to communicate instructions for newly recruited *jihadi*s.

She had met Bilal on Saturday in the same building to clear the names of girls who would like to go to universities outside Kashmir for higher education. Their names for this *jihadi* assignment were cleared by an overseas Kashmir mission and endorsed by Junior Pir from Muzaffarabad, capital of PoK.[10]

Uzma is surprised to see Safina at Salim's place. Uzma and Safina still share a warm relationship because of their common connection with Bilal.

'*Assalam Aleykum*', Safina greets him warmly.

'*Walekum Salam*', replies Uzma.

---

10 India believes Junior Pir is Salahuddin, chief of the militant outfits operating from PoK.

'How are Chacha, Chachi and our dear Razia?' asks Safina.

'They have become old before their time. Nothing seems right since *bhaijan* left home. *Mauj* has become restless and Abbu has become mute, relying on Rashi Chacha to help us out. Poor Razia is confined to the house,' replies Uzma.

Safina is a little perturbed by Uzma's answer and her eyes become moist. Before Salim joins them, she gently says, 'All will be well with Allah's grace.'

Salim takes Uzma to the backyard of his home which is surrounded by a big boundary. With tea and *lava*s, they settle down for a chat in the cloudy dry morning under the apricot tree that is devoid of leaves and flowers. Salim's mobile rings and he excuses himself for a minute. Sitting alone under the tree, Uzma sips the tea and looks around. The late morning air is not refreshing. It seems as if the sky is holding back tears at the sad sight of forlorn trees. The soil, visibly upset with the barrenness around and pile of pale reddish leaves thrown in its lap, is asking the sky to veil her shame and bring her poise back. Late autumn has turned mischievous. Uzma thinks that Mother Earth will soon be laden with snowy chill, and spring will soon bring buds to continue the cycle of plant life.

Salim ends the call and looks at Uzma, lost in his own thoughts. 'The phone call was from Hamid. It's strange, he's come here without any prior information. He must have some urgent information to convey.' Salim opens the gate and Hamid joins them in the backyard.

Hamid is a stocky man with a flowing orange beard, dressed in a black *salwar kameez* with a black waistcoat. He has recently come from across the border and his body language seems very assertive and aggressive. He has brought the directive that they have to be more ruthless in explaining the real Islam. After the greetings, he says, 'The army has launched an all-out war against us. We need to sustain our movement with a new recruitment drive. A couple of Razakar maulvis shall soon join as preachers in the mosque. School children along with boys and girls in our private college need to participate in waging the war. There is no choice other than the complete *jihad*'.

For Hamid, it is a fight for occupation of territory which he regards as a divinely ordained duty. Uzma is taken aback by Hamid's assertion and is curious to know details about Muzaffarabad from him. Although Hamid does not discuss much with Uzma and Salim, he reveals that there is a new plan which needs to be implemented in letter and spirit. 'It has to be all-out participatory *jihad* against pro-Indian mainstream politicians who speak about *Kashmiryat, Insaniyat* in order to please Delhi.

Democracy and secular politics cannot prevail in the *umma*. It has to be Islamic Shariat law', he adds with vehemence.

'China will support us if we make it completely indigenous on Islamic lines with new slogans. Anything happening in the world should not bother us and as per the wish of China and the West, we should delink ourselves from Middle East terror outfits.'

Uzma reacts with anguish, 'But there will be more blood on the streets. India will not let us go and Pakistan cannot snatch us. We can do nothing other than killing ourselves while the whole world becomes indifferent to us. Should we allow the death dance to continue? There won't be any solution, Hamid.'

Hamid too gets worked up. He retorts, 'Martyrdom is our motto; *Milat* (Islamic solidarity) is our soul and Nizam-e-Mustafa is our agenda. Kashmir is the beginning of Islamic domination. It is a long-drawn battle, so we have to give our blood for the *deen*.'

Before Uzma can reply, his phone rings and he sees his father's number flashing on the screen. He excuses himself and steps aside to answer the call. After assuring his father he will be home soon, Uzma decides to change his plans. Because of Safina and Hamid's presence in Salim's house, he postpones his plan to take Salim to Jawahar Baker's house to find about Bilal's movements.

Salim approaches Uzma and says softly, 'Hamid has brought a new blueprint from Junior Pir for the ensuing months which he does not want to show to us. His sudden dropping in here has a purpose. He has come to meet and talk directly to Safina alone, on directions from an unknown power. Safina has some message from the Bai-ul-Mujahideen. But Hamid will not discuss anything in your presence, especially after your outburst a few minutes ago'.

Uzma laughingly says, 'I have anyway decided to go home for now'. He bids farewell to Salim and Safina. Before going home, he heads towards Razz *Babb*'s cottage in a desperate bid to calm himself. Uzma is perturbed by the very idea of young girls participating in stone-pelting by design. They are being led into the mission of *jihad* where they fall prey to the passions of youths.

The killing of Abu Dujana of Lashkar-e-Tayyeba and Khalid of Jaish-e-Mohammed were the result of their involvement in multiple relationships with Kashmiri women. 'One of his partners, on discovering that his interest had shifted to a new woman, decided to take revenge by helping police track him with the help of messages they had been sharing via social media'. It was in the newspapers that 'a tip-off from a local Kashmiri woman led the J&K police to track him down and kill him'. These honey traps had been deployed for the first time in Kashmir, masterminded by those nodal centres.

'*Salam Babb*', Uzma greets Razz *Babb* with respect. The sage, draped in a long *phiran,* is smoking his hookah. He looks at Uzma with his bulging eyes and nods his head disinterestedly.

'*Babb*, what will happen to us?' Uzma asks.

Babb does not say anything. He simply mumbles, '*Kham oas bulbul, moat ghav rangas* (The immature nightingale was possessed by the colorant)'.

'*Babb*, we have another martyr.' Uzma reads aloud from the newspaper he has brought: '*A pall of gloom overwhelmed the family of Aashiq Ahmed Bhat, 24, of Palhallan, as they received his body. Aashiq was killed in the encounter with government forces at Handwara in north Kashmir on Monday. He was the fifth member to have fallen to bullets of government forces in the past two decades.*'

'*Babb*, one Majid has also gone missing. His mother is crying, look what the paper has to say about the family's plight'. He starts reading again, '*Come back...come back and kill us (parents) then go back. Whom have you left me for? Majid, come as fast as you can...for the sake of your father who is ailing*'.

'*Babb*, it is a desperate situation. Bilal is also missing…', his voice trails off sadly.

Babb looks up and unexpectedly says in his thunderous voice, '*Kaath raven gaye waath raven*' (Loss of conversation means denial of common direction). Then with a faraway look in his eyes, adds gently, 'Our barbers are from outside, our harvest secateurs are from outside, our carpenters and workers are from outside, our maulvis and preachers are from outside and our discourse and language are also from outside; we are left with only the silence of our graveyards. Listen to the silence and find how untimely they have gone.

'You live on, well into the nineties and get checkups after every week and say, "We should remember their unlimited sacrifices". We first take their brainpower and seduce them with unproven yarns. We then take their lives while ensuring our own longevity and preach to others to follow the righteous path which we ourselves never traverse. This is not *jihad*. This is politics of power, based on fraudulent and seductive narratives. Allama says, "*Yeh dekhne ki cheez hai isey baar baar dekh*". (This is something to look at, look again and again.) This empirical world should be lived to the full. Death has to come, once the time is ripe. The mythical promise, after all, is for disciplining your own self and not for killing and getting killed.'

Babb closes his eyes and falls silent. Uzma is alarmed and gently says, '*Babb*, bless us, so that we get Bilal back, alive and healthy'. *Babb* raises his hand, as if asking him to stop and then tells him to go home.

Safina goes to Jawahar Baker's house from a back road through ruts and ridges. She is in her mid-thirties but looks young in her short green *phiran* and loose pink *salwar* with her head wrapped in a colourful *dupatta*. The piercing chill strikes against her cherry cheeks. With her deep black almond-shaped eyes above a sinewy pointed nose and a radiant distinctive face, she looks like an angel descending from the sky. She heads towards the entrance of the double-storey house and slips inside without any hesitation. The front gate leads to the road towards the mosque and the back gate to the fields. From the entrance, she sees Bilal waiting near the door of the first room. Bilal is seeing her after a year. He is awestruck by her beauty, his tired gaze riveted on her. He does not voice his thoughts but simply puts his hands on her shoulder and guides her inside the room. The room has a beautiful bed with two chairs and a table, some books, a couple of paintings on the wall along with framed Arabic inscriptions. The window is closed and the lights are on. She takes a chair near the room heater in the corner for warmth. It is a relief after the outside chill.

Safina wants Bilal to relax and not talk about business at first. 'Come a little closer. You are sitting too far', she says softly. Bilal brings his chair closer to hers. In his white Pathan dress and black pullover, he looks exhausted. Internal conflict is written all over his face. He says, 'You look like a flowery peach tree in the early spring'.

'Well, we are meeting after a long time. You too are as vibrant and ardent as you were in the University', says Safina. For a moment, Bilal is taken back to the university days of romance and innocence. He deliberately changes the topic and asks about her husband Naba.

'As usual, he is busy in his own world', Safina says without eye contact.

Bilal knows she is hiding something because she does not look him in the eye. 'Is everything alright between you and Naba?' Bilal asks with concern.

'I don't know what is going on in his mind. He wanted me to be associated with the *tanzeem* and I did it against my own will but he has become more critical about me over the years. You have no idea how often Naba demeans me and my family. It has become a pattern with him. If I appreciate anything, he immediately criticises it', says Safina sadly. 'This bitter experience has taught me one thing: in loveless marriages, women are always at the receiving end of criticism and suffer incessantly.'

'Maybe he is jealous and he feels insecure when you

praise others. I guess he wants your appreciation to be directed towards him', Bilal says to mollify her, although he knows Naba is not a doting husband.

'*Achha*, leave my marriage aside. My situation is never going to change', Safina says in a dejected voice. She looks at Bilal and adds cautiously, 'I met Uzma yesterday. He sounded troubled and upset'.

Safina is trying to create a proper backdrop to convince Bilal to return home. She states, 'Violence will not get us anywhere. How long will we remain in this state of perpetual conflict? The entire Valley is hemmed in by bunkers, curfews, shutdowns, frequent encounters, internet bans and in the mosques, the same repeated assurances and sermons. People desire dignity and justice. Do you know that Majid has come back home? Prayers and appeals of his wailing mother and an ardent request from his father finally compelled him to surrender before security agencies on Friday, a week after he had joined the Lashkar-e-Tayyeba terror outfit.'

Bilal does not react to what she says and swifly changes the topic. 'We need to hurry. Jawahar Baker's family has gone to their new house from where they run their restaurant. When we leave this place, I am supposed to leave the key in the mosque with Maulvi Ahsen. Anyway, Hamid wanted me to meet you regarding the mission. Did he give you the details?' Bilal asks hastily.

'Details?' asks Safina.

'Yes, I want details about the few women who were sent to Delhi. They have now become double agents. They worry about their parents and about the *tanzeem* as well. The new recruitment has to be well thought out. They should be picked young from madrassas, trained in colleges and then sent to the plains for the mission. The old experiment has not yielded the expected results. I am supposed to identify the girls to be sent to Indian universities. It has to be done very quickly, before the beginning of the new session in Delhi, Hyderabad, Lucknow, Bangalore and Varanasi. The application forms have already been received from these universities, which are with Iqbal, who will hand them over to specific operatives. You are supposed to help me in this mission', says Bilal.

'I am at your disposal and I will tell you everything about the mission. But before I forget, I need to tell you what I heard from Naba's business partner Rahim. He was in Muzaffarabad for a month. According to him, this movement has entered into multiple trajectories: economic and power distribution, cult doctrines and ensuring safety for a certain class of people. We hardly figure in it. The meeting he attended was held in Muridke campus after the death of six *mujahideen* in Hajin. As usual, the core group of Difai Pakistan along with ISI top brass have deep contempt for Kashmiris.[11] They claim that our Sufi form of Islam is corrupt, an evil practice which will definitely be eliminated in future. They feel that unless Charar-e-Sharif Dargah[12] is destroyed completely, Kashmiris will remain tied to their traditional narrative. According to the resolution passed at the meeting, their fight is for a pan-Islamic caliphate. In fact, one of the top commanders hinted at eliminating the whole population engaged in living and advocating the Western way of life.

They have distanced themselves from Hizbul Mujahideen chief Syed Salahudin for his inability to make all Kashmiris 'Islamic madrassa *tablighi*' (preachers). The reports of maulvis from the mosques of Kashmir are typically anti-Kashmiri. They want us to shun modern education and take the new generation out of their homes to madrassas at the early age of four. This will detach them from their family and they would be ready for *jihad* by the age of twelve. Therefore, the plan is long term. Grants are allotted for the process of Islamisation away from the boys 'homes and families. They will be primed for whole-hearted participation with slogans and attacks in multitudes.'

Bilal says in a hollow voice, 'Our maulvis are from outside, from UP and Jung. They always report that we

---

11 ISI is short for Inter Services Intelligence, Pakistan's surveillance agency.
12 Tomb of a native Sufi saint.

have not been able to follow them. Hamid informed me that grants have been linked with the participatory *jihad* of our children. I do not know how to convince our illiterate leaders about the importance of social and cultural roots going back centuries which are not compatible with the monolithic madrassa ethos. Gulam Qadir with his doctorate from JNU failed to convince Pakistan to keep the *Azadi* Movement local and was killed.

'We also might fail in convincing them that the *mujahideen* from across the border were caught young, detached from their families and sent into *jihad* camps and madrassas where the only conversations are about *tabligh* and martyrdom. Of late, these Tablighi are from different countries—from Indonesia, Turkey, some Iranians and a few from Kazhakastan. They are being dispatched in groups to the different mosques in Uttar Pradesh, Bihar and other states where they can change the mindset of the people. I think the day is not far when you will find participatory Tablighi movement planting its feet firmly on the Indian soil. We are resisting it in Kashmir but other Indian Muslims are bound to get swayed. For the Kashmiri Muslim is different from other Muslims of the world. He has that ancestral cultural chip in his mind that makes him more comfortable as a native Kashmiri, rather than anything else. No wonder, Hurriyat and mainstream leaders keep up the anti-India tirade.'

Safina says that Rahim was clearly told to burn schools and convert the buildings to madrassas for children taken from their homes. For this, they had given a period of six months i.e. spring to autumn.

'This is the kind of instruction we can expect from them', says Bilal sarcastically. 'There is no doubt that we face a schism. There is an ongoing debate about what Islam is and what these *mullahs* preach to retain their power. Truly, if we forget time and space, erase the modern era, the scientific revolution, the rise of European hegemony and centrality and the Enlightenment, then everyone is a *kafir*. The irony is that our Pirs do not refuse the comforts made possible by science and technology. Yet, they preach to us to accept madrassa life for our children.

'It would have been acceptable if not for the atrocities inflicted on the young children in madrassas. The increasing number of cases of child sexual abuse is alarming. The excerpts of the interview of a grieving mother in a leading newspaper reads:

> Saima Khan struggles through tears as she remembers the blood-soaked pants of her nine-year-old son, allegedly raped by a religious cleric. Each time she begins to speak, she stops, swallows hard, wipes her tears and begins again. The boy fidgets with his scarf and looks over at his mother. 'Did he touch you?' He nods. 'Did he hurt you

> when he touched you?' 'Yes', he whispers. 'Did he rape you'? He buries his face in his scarf and nods yes.

Sexual abuse is a pervasive and longstanding problem at madrassas in Pakistan, an Associated Press investigation found. But in a culture where clerics are all-powerful, it is seldom discussed or even acknowledged in public. 'I am at a loss when I hear such disheartening cases', says Bilal despairingly.

'Bilal, why have we become sceptics? Islam is dear to us, so is modernity and its values', states Safina. She swtiches to a personal note. 'I am really upset with the deteriorating health condition of Zoya Chachi. Muza Uncle has also grown thin and silent. Uzma has become a wanderer looking for clues to your hideouts. Razia is confined to the home all the time. Their conversations are all about your safe return. I think you should think about people who love you and want you to be with them. Your mother, whether awake or in dreams, prays for you all the time. She has swollen eyes. At any moment, she might turn mad in grief. Like Majid's mother, who was declared mad by *tanzeem* functionaries for making media appeals to her son to return, she would be declared insane.'

Her appeal makes Bilal contemplative. His eyes are half shut. He gently touches Safina's hand and says, 'It is a long drawn battle. Please give courage to Mother. My return is not easy and my job is not what you perceive. I play a different role here but I have to be dedicated. I thought you had come with some message and we had to decide a role for you. Why do you look so feeble and indecisive? Hamid told me that the identification of girls to be taken out from Kashmir for anti-India tirade in the universities will rest with you. Admission and accommodation are already taken care of. The only thing is to find out whether they are up to the job or not'.

Safina holds his hand, longing for a respite. She looks directly into his eyes with blatant hunger. Instantly, the old spark rekindles and they kiss with a passion that sweeps them off their feet. Bilal's fingers clasp one of her breasts, feeling the iron-hard little peak straining against her clothes. 'Come here', he says throatily. Pulling her into his arms, he picks her up and carries her to the bed. Their fingers are trembling but somehow, they get rid of their clothes and continue their exploration of each other's bodies. 'Oh!' she gasps, the moment he enters her. With urgency, he thrusts deeper into her body and Safina moans with pleasure. He feels her buck beneath him and then he too is lost in the mindless bliss of sexual fulfilment. Afterwards, they remain motionless for a while, their minds blissfully devoid of any coherent thought. Reality returns with the slowing of their heartbeats and after a swift kiss, they stand up to put on their clothes.

On the table, she sees Mir Khalid's *Jaffna Street*, a book in demand. She finds that some paragraphs are underlined. 'Have you read this book? I found it too terse and difficult,' she says to defuse the sexual tension in the room.

'Yes, it is a difficult book but portrays the absurdities wherein we have caged ourselves', replies Bilal. There are details on the ramifications of the war cry '*Hum kya chahte: Azadi*' (What do we want? Freedom!), especially gang wars, death and destruction, which allow the Indian state to monopolise full power to curb the insurgency. A passage in the book goes:

> The inter-Tanzeem feuds started quite early – before and after the counter insurgents started their killing forays in the first winter of insurgency. At first juncture, proponents of various ideological hues limited their derision to spewing vitriol in the vernacular press where the insurgents voice held sway through coercive tactics.

Safina says softly, 'I have to go.'

'Don't worry. You can go after fifteen minutes. Somebody will drop you to your place.'

'Okay but we did not speak about the chore that we were supposed to discuss.'

'But we were serious where we had to be', smilingly replies Bilal.

'No, I was told to relay to you the issues of the last recruitments and find out why those youths are not unified. There are reports that youths are distracted, they have forgotten their basic agenda for which they were financed to fan out from the Valley. We are supposed to discuss these issues and send a report about the persons who deviated from the cause. I am deliberately leaving behind these concerns because I am more interested in your safe return to your parents. Do I need to say that I want your well-being?' asks Safina.

'I assure you I will not pick up the gun. I can take care of myself. At the moment, this is what I have to say. *Khuda Hafiz.*'

'I'm leaving but I hope you return to normal life in your home. I desire to meet you again and again,' says Safina.

'*Khuda jane*, the car is awaiting outside to take you back.' With moist eyes, Safina glances at Bilal before leaving his transit house. She waves at him after she gets into the waiting car and leaves with mixed feelings.

She did not find Bilal as effervescent as he used to be. His answers to her queries did not satisfy her. But she cherished the sharing of his bodily warmth where she found him focused and full of intensity. 'He was not sad but thoughtful. He was not loving but lustful and he was not where I had left him. He clammed up and it was difficult to know his agenda. Possibly we are not on the same track now', she thinks.

Uzma does not bring any good news for his family. However, he is not disappointed with his efforts. He has a feeling that Bilal has not become a militant. He is escaping from home and reality. If rightly persuaded to change his ways, he would be back, he feels.

The failure to understand their own predicaments and the current political situation has left everyone bewildered. Rashid has to go back to his family in Srinagar but before that, he has to talk to Muza about his own conundrums. Besides Bilal's absence from home, he has to share something very confidential with his cousin.

It is a murky afternoon; the dim light seems pugnacious as its warmth does not give encouraging vibrations. It is difficult to broach the subject but after all Muza is his brother. He has not changed much over the years; it's Rashid's migration to the city that has made the whole difference in their relationship.

'Muza, since 1989, the social landscape and geography has played a definite role in changing our language and thinking, especially of those born after 1980s. We are bound by their diktats and are being groomed and moulded by them. They make judgements very quickly and also reverse them as quickly. We remain disillusioned, stuck between what we desire and what we have.'

'But why do you talk like this? Has anybody been uncivil with you? Has anything untoward happened?'

'No, nothing has happened to me. I was taken back to my childhood memories and the life experiences we have had. *Batta*s have gone, good for them. Our children and leadership expect us to believe that their exodus was the first prerequisite for our *azadi.* Could be, I don't know. There seems to be an unusual excitement about it, invariably in the rural areas, where *Batta* land has been taken over. However, the traditionally privileged elite miss them.'

'The privileged have migrated to the city,' protests Uzma. 'It is no longer a memory with us. Other than those dilapidated ruined houses, some elderly women or men speak with fondness about them. The young are fed with a different discourse. It is a discourse that calls them kafir. This has gained currency gradually.'

'Yes, it is a debilitated social and cultural landscape. The transition between 1989 and post-1990 has deep ramifications, which this generation cannot comprehend. We have dismantled the superstructure laid by our evolved *Reshi* culture and driven out the agency that could have sustained it. Look at this, money has become the reference point and religiosity and *azadi* instruments to secure it at the cost of civil, social institutions. Neighbourhoods have changed and Kashmir's cultural capital has vanished. Earlier, the family itself or the village elders upheld moral values but now moral policing is done by militants. Our children have become directionless. There is no communication among members of a family.'

Muza retorts, 'What have we given them except directionless assurances along with death and destruction? If our Hurriyat leadership had an understanding of the power of the Indian state, why did they undertake this adventure at the behest of Pakistan? It is an unending suicide mission for our present and future generations. Therefore, there is a deep sense of defeat which is difficult to acknowledge publicly. Privately, people are disillusioned with the concept of *azadi*, hence its very mention is like thorn pricks. The young are indoctrinated, they do not want to retreat from this fight. When the 'image in the mirror' frightens them, they muse on the triumph of *Batta* migration from Kashmir which Hurriyat sells them as a victory. Everything else is wilderness. Look what has happened to our family and many other families like us. Each one has suffered and is fractured. The institutional order has broken down so the new leadership is no longer dependent on the old principles which have failed. They are spared by the masses for their forte is religion'.

'Muza, it is true that *Battas* were driven out. This is the only satisfaction that we draw from the turmoil of three decades. In return, what we got is chaos and uncertainty. Their presence was an invisible capital, symbolic victory of moral order over material goals. Unlike our rich and upper middle class that mostly emerged from apple money in the 1970s, they were the educated middle class for generations. Their value system had a moral core. Therefore, their presence was a connecting thread for building trust. They were a functional minority, the core from which we have parted. They say that our agenda is *azadi* and it is a prerequisite to wipe out all traces of Indianness from here. It is now proved that we are naive because the agenda is not ours. It is the agenda of a section of the powerful elite in our neighbourhood, which itself is fractured and in disarray. Our referent is blurred and defeat is a fait accompli'.

The conversation exudes pensiveness. Rashid barely manages to say what he wanted to say to his brother. He suggests the two cousins to go to Razz *Babb* to seek solace and sort out some dilemmas. 'Muza, I shall leave for the city tomorrow. Is it possible to take blessings from Razz *Babb* before I leave? I am full of anxiety and I need some solace.'

'Alright, let's go before it is time for *digger* (evening) namaz', says Muza.

In the hazy afternoon, very few shops are open. They do not come across any acquaintance on their way to Putshay to meet Razz *Babb*. A few years back, even strangers whole-heartedly greeted one another, a practice that has dwindled over the years. The Valley is now just a scenic land with wispy streams, sickly grass and insipid sunshine struggling to get through; even the breeze is too piercing for comfort. In the far corner of the main road, on a mound, are some army bunkers which were put up in the 1990s; a few still remain with gun-toting soldiers to safeguard their convoy when it passes through the Bandipore-Sopore road.

'Muza, autumn was not like this in our childhood. There are no ducks in the cold streams nor is there a single bird on the naked trees. Even the happy sight of men and women gossiping on the roadsides until late evenings have vanished now', laments Rashid.

'Militancy has changed it all,' responds Muza. 'Death, destruction and displacement have alienated our ambience from us. It is difficult to recognise our own place and people.'

Rashid quips, 'All over the world, people are interested in their own material welfare and good of their families but in our state, we have a burden of this *djinn* from Pakistan that haunts us. It has taken our children from us, caused disintegration in our families and changed our neighbourhoods. In short, everything has altered; we feel estranged and everyone is worried and exhausted.

We have been living with this cob-webbed mindset for many decades and are unable to shake it off because those who lead us are ruined by their own imprudence. They are pulling strings from across the border and we are paying the price. It is neither retreat nor progress. These gnarled trees, shrunken streams and grey mounds are watching the funerals of our children and witnessing the displacement of the locals.'

When they reach the cottage, they see an elderly gentleman everybody calls Wali Sahib talking to Razz *Babb*. Wali is a retired principal of a government degree college, well respected and scholarly in his conversations. '*Salam Alleykum*', say Muza and Rashid to the two older men. Razz *Babb* nods his head while Wali replies, '*Walekum Salam*'. Wali whispers in the ears of the cousins that *Babb* has been continuously talking to himself since morning and has not even addressed him.

'Yes, he is *mout* (insane)', Muza replies. '*Mout* but *tout* (insane but searing)', says Rashid. '*Babb*, say something', urges Wali.

Babb gives a wan smile and sings, '*Araeshe Jmal say Farig Nahe Honuz.*' (It is journeying and journeying, circles overlap till they mingle.) Roots are where leaves come out. It is all within you.'

Rashid is mystified and blurts out his own anguish. '*Babb*, we are worried for our children. Bless them so that they are safe.' Other than his worry for Bilal, it is clear Rashid is agonising over some other problem as well, which he has not expressed to anyone. Muza cleans the *chelum* of the hookah and *Babb* suddenly utters some astonishing words. His eyes wide, he intones, 'If estrangement from work is alienation, what then is attachment without engagement? It has to be frustration and that is why all of us are perturbed.'

'*Babb*, please explain. What do you mean?' asks Wali. '*Kya* (what) Muza, you all weep for your children day and night and are attached to them but have you ever engaged with them? It has to be attachment with engagement, only then will you be in a position to question them. Otherwise, this divorced relationship which should inherently be a holistic one, would always keep you sad and moaning. Attachment with engagement is bliss, whereas attachment without engagement is loss.' *Babb* still seems lost in his own world.

'Where are my Herath *dooyn* (walnuts)?' he suddenly bursts out. 'It has been a long time since I had some. I really used to love them. Well, what can I say, we get what we get. Crows peck them out from our trees.'

Rashid is surprised that *Babb* would remember Hareth, a *Batta* festival of yesteryears, which was usually celebrated in late February. Just then, he sees a crow with a walnut in its beak.

'*Babb*, why do you feel like this? They have gone along with their Shiv *watuk* (worship)', says Wali. 'In this journey, we are in the process of creating dualities all the time. Binaries are not contradictory, in fact, they emerge from the same point, a pivot which ensures that the signifier and the signified are in motion and not fixed. Attachment and engagement, security and freedom, power and problems are all welded together. The state guarantees it. A repertoire that would give freedom with security has the power to solve problems. In fact, politics is all about solving problems. We have kept politicians apart from the core; hence the boundaries among co-travellers. The boundaries of time and space are connected with linearity of time and space, in a circle of continuity.'

Rashid, Muza and Wali are amazed at these utterances, filled with collective guilt. The original sin was perennial but the other sins are worldly, imposed by construed boundaries and constructed in time and space by everyone.

Abruptly, *Babb* speaks again, 'Unless you inherit supremacy in holistic form, you cannot solve the problems of existence, hence Allah is supreme. *Battas*' Shiv and Shakti are one. No dualism, duality is complementary.'

Rashid wonders why *Babb* always brings *Battas* in his conversations. He is perturbed instead of getting any solace. '*Babb*, why can't we stop talking about them? They are gone. We need to think about ourselves and our children.'

Babb glares at Rashid, and says, 'The source of suffering is alike for everyone. Their referent has given them deprivation and your referent has given you a sense of defeat. It is better to be yourself than pretending to be something you are not.'

'*Babb*, why is peace elusive?'

In response, *Babb* quotes Emerson, "What lies behind us and what lies before us are tiny matters compared to what lies within us." 'The glaze of the market on money and material has chased away the memories of peace and happiness you experienced in the village. You try to find solace in the memory when you are in the city but here it is dimmed and you again became a wanderer. Everything seems diminished and covered with muck. The glaze of the city blinds you. It fades when you stay away from your childhood home. You cannot disconnect one and find other elements to create harmony.'

'*Babb*, please be specific. I am at loss to understand the sins that brought us bad luck.'

A man in his late twenties arrives with *noonchai* and *telwoor* (Kashmiri tea and baked bread). *Babb* sips the tea and is now in full flow: 'Morals and material were inherited in that order but they are divorced from each other because of the market. Instead, we now have a new language of half-truths and half-lies. Parents and the elderly in general decry morality of the young, while the young bemoan lack of material things and put the blame for their miseries on the shoulders of their elders. We have turned into a lot which is engaged in blame games with self-pitying notions. Moral values have vanished and material hunger has amplified. Hence, there is a crisis in the social order. The elders blame the youth for their moral bankruptcy and the young think the old are non-productive liabilities. The social order had a point to direct and manage the boundaries. That notional core cannot hold the boundaries any more with the same rhythm. Hence, splitting has caused dualism. The disjunction causes fluidity and trust deficit'.

Babb takes something out from his *phiran,* gives them all some *nabad* (offering) and says dismissively, 'Go, you will get late.'

There is a real nip in the air by now. The chill is biting. Rashid and Muza, along with Wali, get up and salute Razz *Babb*.

Every neighbourhood in the good old days had its saints. They were holy persons but eccentric in their behaviour. They would say things at times that would bring miraculous changes, surprising the entire community. Their weirdness was evident in their unpredictable, sometimes crude sayings and their physical raggedness. Children would be afraid of them. They indeed were uncommon persons but godly and remarkable in their simplicity. Their words worked wonders. The people had huge faith in them—*Battas* as well as Musalmans. Unlike the fashionable cult *gurus* and religious Pirs, these *Reshis* and saints, commonly known as '*Babbs*' were the epistemological connect which is missing in the new social order. People would go to them for restoring faith in their own existence. They would act as a bridge for humans to Nature and the Supernatural that would give existence its purpose and would do away with the individual puzzles of day-to-day unpredictability.

On the way back, Rashid decides he would talk to his brother after dinner about his worries. They are soothed by the open-ended conversation at *Babb*'s place. *Babb* has played well his role of a mystic sage connected with the divine.

Two days ago, Barkat had come to Razz *Babb*'s cottage to escape the police. *Babb* did not try to dissuade him but the communication between the two was very limited. *Babb* was lost in his own world, talking and mumbling all the time. Still, he was not totally absent-minded, for he always gave the main share of his food to Barkat. *Babb* did not cook for himself. A few families of the neighbourhood served him food in turns, insufficient for the two of them. In *Babb*'s company, Barkat felt peaceful and had no inclination to leave. *Babb* reminded him of his life before he joined militancy. Although *Babb*'s piercing gaze felt like he already knew everything, Barkat felt an uncontrollable desire to confess everything to him. But throughout the day, the cottage was crammed with visitors seeking Razz *Babb*'s blessings and advice. On the third day, Barkat woke up early, determined to have a heart-to-heart conversation with *Babb.*

Babb is already awake, absorbed in prayer. Barkat waits for *Babb* to finish, prepares tea and sits with him to talk.

'*Babb*, I want to stay here with you', Barkat ventures.

Babb looks at him questioningly, 'What about your

gun? I cannot accommodate you with your gun.'

'*Babb*, I threw it into a cavernous spot in the rivulet yesterday. Bless me, *Babb*, I am weary of the world and wish to find comfort in your company here', Barkat replies in a defeatist tone.

'It is not easy for you to leave everything behind. They might come for you and disturb me', *Babb* exclaims.

'Yes *Babb*, You are right. But I still wish to be here. My life has been full of disillusionments. I want to confide in you and clear my conscience. I can only hope that they do not disturb you when they come for me. My two *Babb*s must be turning in their graves because of what I have become. I feel ashamed of myself for wasting all the efforts they invested in me.'

With moist eyes, Barkat continued, '*Babb*. I am an unfortunate person. I was abandoned at Mughalsarai railway station where Rahat Bhai picked me up. Baba was a handicapped beggar who never allowed me to beg. When I was nine years old, he got me enrolled in a government school. I did not take studies seriously but Baba made sure that I regularly attend school.

'In the evening, I used to spend time in Khan's garage where I learnt basic mechanics of car repair along with driving four-wheelers. Everything changed when Baba died. I still remember the day, it was Basant Panchmi. The whole area was in a celebratory mood and I was weeping bitterly. With the help of other beggars, I buried him at the railway colony graveyard of Mughalsarai. Baba left fifty thousand rupees for me. It was his lifetime savings. Like most beggars, he died at an early age—he was only fifty years old.

'He was sick for ten days before his death. During his illness, he told me about my parentage. He told me that I was an abandoned child like him. Baba raised me and gave me my name, Barkat. Baba was born with a physical disability. My Baba was an affectionate and God-fearing person.

'I was all alone at the tender age of thirteen. I stopped going to school and started working full time at Khan's garage. I worked there for three years before I was recommended to a travel agency by my boss. In these three years, with money in hand and no guardianship, I indulged in all the bad habits: smoking, tobacco, pursuing agreeable women and drinking.

'My life as a driver was a little better. I started drinking less because of the nature of the job and had little time for pursuing women. Driving gave me a chance to meet new people and see new places. One day, I drove a professor from Allahabad University to Varanasi. He was a nice person. He gave me five hundred rupees as a tip too. Two days later, the agency asked me to go for a two-way journey from Varanasi and Lucknow. The client was the same professor travelling alone. He asked about my life and experiences. There was something about him that persuaded me to open up without hesitation.

'I ended up telling him I was an orphan. Throughout my taxi driver tenure, nobody conversed so affectionately with me as this professor. He smiled and said, "I am surprised that you did so well on your own. In my life, I have seen people with privileges doing far worse".

'His words moved me and I confessed, "My Baba wanted me to become a school master. I regret dropping out of school after he died. I wish to resume my studies but I don't have any clue where to start."

'He thought for some time and then said, "I will find a way to help you after reaching Varanasi".

'When I drove him home, he introduced me to his father whose gaze was so divine and ennobling that I automatically touched his feet. The moment the professor told him about my wish to study, he asked me to come to him from the next day. I grabbed the opportunity with both hands. My new life started with him. He was a scholarly and pious person. I went to his place every Sunday religiously for the next four years and studied under his tutelage. I passed my 10th and 12th exam with his help. Everyone in his family used to treat me like a part of the family. For the very first time, I closely saw a normal, decent family atmosphere and realised how significant it is to have a good family for the socialisation of a child. It completely transformed me and I gave up smoking and drinking. I started learning prayers. I even started going to Sankat Mochan temple on Saturdays. It was a turning point in my life.

'*Babb* was very happy with my progress and insisted that I continue my studies and become a graduate. Money wasn't a problem as *Babb* took care of all my study-related expenses. I also joined computer classes in the evening after the results of my 12th exam. I continued working as a taxi driver but reduced the working hours substantially. My life had found its rhythm and I was happy and content, so long as I could study as well as drive the taxi.

'But the moment I cleared my 12th exam, I looked for new friends, boys and girls; I started feeling the competition. As my circle expanded, I became keen to seek attention and acceptability. I would sometimes hide my identity and could not be comfortable in new company. My straightforward truthfulness gradually changed. I started exaggerating about myself. I remember, I might have even lied to my Teacher *Babb* that outside, I stood out in the competitive group. I was piling up falsehoods, for I did not want my past to come between my present and future. Somehow, it remained an unsatisfactory socialisation process. I felt a sense of deprivation and starting envying all those who were ahead of me in my age-group in worldly conduct and social skills.

'My only refuge was my Teacher *Babb*, who had huge expectations from me—but at times that too would make me nervous and restless. Masterji's family became my inspirational referent. They were originally from Bandipore and were driven out during the 1989 Kahmiri Pandit exodus. But they never complained about their Muslim neighbours of Bandipore. In fact, they missed them and remembered them fondly.

'Masterji was my second *Babb* who gave me dignity, pride and reason to have faith beyond religion. My first Baba helped me survive physically and the second one gave meaning to my life. Razz *Babb*, I believe that you are my third *Babb* and the final one. I beg you to help me, *Babb*. I am precariously placed on the crossroads of my life and desperate to know its meaning. I lost my ability to smile the moment I left my second *Babb* in Varanasi.'

Babb listens to Barkat's story with great interest and asks, 'Why did you leave Varanasi? What happened after you left your second *Babb*?'

'I still remember the day, it was 17 August 2005; I met a middle-aged man in the computer shop who told me that he would give me stable employment in another city. He offered me a handsome salary of twenty thousand rupees for teaching children in a primary school of Kanpur. I remembered how my Baba wanted me to be a school teacher. The stranger wanted me to decide quickly.

'The manner in which he was rushing the matter troubled me and I went to Masterji's place to ask for advice. Unfortunately, the family had gone out of town and the house was locked. I thought about the teaching offer and the salary and felt like opportunity was knocking at my door. Ignoring my earlier apprehensions, I decided to go with the man.

'I left Varanasi on 19 August for Kanpur where I was given a room in a locality similar to the Mughalsarai slum. The institution in which I was to teach was a madrassa, not a primary school, and the children were seven to ten years of age. Initially, I did not mind the misrepresentation as they paid the salary he had committed. In the evenings, I had to join religious discourses. These were the directives of the management.

'After I had spent a few months in the set-up and my initial excitement of having a stable job diminished, I realised the trap I had walked into. My Baba had not wanted me to become part of such an ethos. I remember the time when madrassa men at Mughalsarai had come to take me when I was seven years old. He had cursed them and refused to give in to their demand. After they left, he said, "These madrassa people are always in search of abandoned children above four or five years of age. They take them from those who raised them with blood and sweat in their early years and give them a small amount of money for their silence. These children never come back. It is a big industry where politics, religiosity and power are in nexus at the cost of human lives."

'Blinded by my own ambition, I forgot what he had told me and I willingly walked into this trap at a mature age. I had no choice but to do my job and learn the religious verses which were mostly about *jihad*. The emphasis was on 164 *jihad* verses. Young minds were thrilled with K 4:089-091:

> And reckon not those who are killed in Allah's way as dead; nay, they are alive (and) are provided sustenance from their Lord [meaning they are enjoying their 72 virgins in heaven].

'Since they were not profound scholars but agencies to give the kind of interpretations that suited their purpose, it was difficult to question them. They called us "God's children on Milat's way". I was brainwashed and became totally engrossed in *jihad*. I continued to work in Kanpur for six months. After that, I was sent to Pakistan through proper travel documents. I stayed in Pakistan till 2013 at a stretch.

'I once met a scholarly Islamic person in Pakistan who explained that verses need to be explained in proper context, time and space. *Jihad* can be against anything that is anti-human. Meanwhile, my identity papers were altered. My name was changed and I became Abu Tasleem. In December 2013, I went to Syria, where I worked till I was called back to Pakistan in December 2015. I am at present deputed to Kashmir for *jihad*.'

'Who else knows your story?' asks Razz *Babb*.

'I had told my early life story in full to my Teacher *Babb*. He kept it a secret, not revealing it to his family, not even to Mataji, his wife. The only thing they knew was that I had lost my parents and was groomed by different people. The distressful, unforgiving act on my part was that I did not take his permission for the next phase of my life. He must be wondering why I went first from darkness to light and then into total oblivion. I feel sad that he, my angel-teacher, must have searched for me. He was at that point my only well-wisher. I owe him a huge debt of gratitude for opening my mind to all the possibilities that life offers. I was in a hurry to take flight but he would tell me that I should be patient, which I could not do. I unnecessarily made my life complicated, blurring my two selves: what I was and what society should know of me. I failed in that articulation of my identity and lost it for an easy escape. The sense of deprivation spoiled my destiny. Education and knowledge brought me out from that bliss of ignorance without any reflective, endurable experiences. I lost my childhood, my closed world in the new awakening of limitless choice and open competition. My failure in the world did not match the dream set by my old Teacher *Babb*. I wish he had come into my life when I was born. He came late in my life and I ended up in complete darkness, loneliness. I do not dream now and my urges are dead. I have only remorse and exhaustion.'

'You had a woman companion who dropped you here. Where she has gone?' asks *Babb*.

Barkat does not reply. 'Why is *Babb* asking that question?' Barkat wondered. Perhaps *Babb* did not want disturbance in his daily routine. He had never wanted or liked women to visit him—for that matter, not even most men, who would of their own accord, without any specific purpose, come to see him. Perhaps *Babb* was keen to know if he could associate with Barkat without any outside interference.

Barkat evaded his question and said, '*Babb*, I shall be back in the evening. I must go to work. It is ten to eight.'

Babb gave him a sharp glance and turned to his books on philosophy. Barkat came out of the cottage. He had shared everything with *Babb* except his wish to marry a girl named Tahira who had lost her husband in 2015, in Syria's war. Barkat had met Tahira for half an hour only a month ago. Barkat had heard about her from her husband Moen Abu Mosad, who was with him in

Syria during the war. Moen died in the war while Barkat somehow survived and returned to Pakistan in December 2015 and was eventually sent to Kashmir for the big mission of participatory *jihad*.

The wintry darkness with its piercing chill fills Rashid with a sense of dread. After an early dinner, he and Muza sit down to chat. There is no electricity and Muza switches on the inverter which is now found in every household. Rashid remembers that during their childhood, they used oil lamps and candles. Electricity supply was nominal, hardly a couple of hours a week. It was a matter of grave concern during the winters.

Things have changed altogether since then. There is no dearth of facilities and goods in the market and in homes. Markets are full and the general masses have sufficient purchasing power. The passing years had left their imprint. Despite militancy and no employment opportunities, money had flowed in, Rashid thinks, 'We are a unique community which is losing its young men without knowing what they really want. Youth has lost all sense of direction. The moral chord that bound people together had come from long associations in families, neighbourhoods, localities and institutions. Now it is kaput: the lack of interaction with youth is visible at all levels. The social mirror has broken to pieces.'

It saddens him that there were wars of words within families, triggered by the slightest argument.

'Muza, close the door and listen to me', says Rashid.

They settle down for a conversation. 'Muza, you know our cousin Javid who did his Master's in Economics and joined the police force. He got married to my wife's sister Ruby. I happened to be instrumental in that marriage. They have two children: Husna and Altaf. His job has made him a different person altogether. He hardly visits anyone and has severed ties with his cousins. He is not happy with me as well.'

What happened to him?' asks Muza.

'It is a sad story of their marital lives. He started doubting his wife. In fact, he was even critical of her relations with us. They hardly ever come to see us. That was alright but soon after their daughter Husna was born, he did not accept her as his child and accused his wife of adultery', replies Rashid.

'I knew that they always used to quarrel, but perhaps the situation was far worse', Muza replies.

'Yes, Javid was posted to Kokernag. This further estranged them', says Rashid.

'Yes, the nineties of the previous century was a dreadful decade. In fact, since then we are not at the right place in our moral sphere. For the first time, our private spaces which were so sacred became profane and transgressed. First, these boundaries were crossed by the militants, and then by the army and simultaneously by us as well. Public became private and private became selective without any transparency and accountability. Collective restraint is gone. With moral constraints weakening, the collective will has no meaning. Our youth are going astray, the aged becoming helpless, women vulnerable and children anomalous in their socialisation. This has happened because we let ourselves play the music of others, who know nothing about our culture. Instead of peace, we are given violence. The elements of strength and sustainability in our culture were in dialogue and understanding through mutual interaction. That abruptly died. Javid was an introvert; he must have become suspicious of his wife under such circumstances', responds Muza.

'True, it was a decade of collective confusion. We had new illusions. The vacant spaces were filled with random intrusions. Unpredictability of the individual realm and despotism in a public sphere caused humiliation and disappointment. We became helpless. Surveillance lost its meaning. Power was wielded somewhere else. In a moral morass, we start doubting everything. Human relationships become full of suspicion and vulnerability. Javid always had arguments with Ruby. One day Husna came to know that her father did not consider her his legitimate child. It further disturbed Husna's personality which was already in bad shape because of daily arguments between her parents', says Rashid.

Muza is pained to hear all this. He had heard similar stories of his acquaintances where patriarchal structures became repressive amid the tumult. He asks, 'What happened then'?

Rashid gently replies, 'What had to happen? Ruby came closer to us when Javid was away from home in South Kashmir for years. He did not care for his family. Their communication was minimal. Ruby quite often dropped Husna at our place. She grew up to become a very beautiful girl in her teens. Bilal met her at our place when she was in college. Like cousins and friends, they shared things and became fond of each other. Javid came to know about it and was furious, accused us of spoiling her. Once he was back, he started wooing and poisoning Husna against her mother and us. They stopped coming to our place. We did not mind and were happy that the family was again unified but knew little of what was happening in their house. Ruby, despite knowing us well, was also easily influenced by Javid. Husna did her Master's and left for Delhi against the wishes of her father. It seems her mother had given consent'.

'So what is the problem?' Muza asks.

'Muza, they want her to come back and she refuses to

return. It seems she is pursuing her PhD in JNU. She got admission in MPhil and then registered for PhD without clearing NET or JRF.[13] She is not getting any fellowship. Her parents have refused to support her research outside the Valley', Rashid says.

Muza enquires, 'How is she managing her expenditure?'

'This is our main concern. Her supervisor is supporting her research and stay in JNU. He is a famous professor of political science, a divorcee and a non-Muslim. It seems that he has become very close to her. They have been traveling together to different places in India', answers Rashid.

'What is there to worry? In research you have to travel with your supervisor in order to attend seminars and conferences. It is a close relationship', Muza states in confusion.

'Muza, their relationship has turned intimate and it has caused chaos in the family. Ruby dissolves into tears at the slightest provocation. She has been ill for the last three months. Javid says that Bilal was instrumental in sending her out of the Valley. It has become a family quandary, steeping each one in bitterness', states Rashid.

---

13 Fellowship tests. NET: National Entrance Test. JRF: Junior Research Fellowship.

'Keep heart, have faith in Allah. All will be well', Muza assures.

'Right now it is difficult to believe all will be well. An enraged Altaf wants to kill his sister. He has turned rebel, a Wahabi, who blames everyone in the family, especially his mother', Rashid explains with concern.

'Why do they not try to bring her back?' asks Muza.

'They have been trying but have failed so far. In fact, Ruby went with Itika to meet Khamsi maulvi of Faizabad. They say that he makes *tabeez* (good luck charms). He gave one for Husna and instructed that she wear it on the upper arm in order to stop her from leaving home. Ruby told Husna that the *tabeez* was for her health and education but she became more irritated and argued even more with everyone in the family. Ruby said that she kept talking to her professor during her last visit home. It is a real family problem that might bring shame on all of us. Altaf has slapped her several times because of her affair'.

Muza becomes restless and enquires, 'How is Bilal connected with this? Why is he being accused?'

'Javid and Altaf brought this story that beautiful young girls were being sent to Indian universities with the agenda of creating a socio-political movement against the Indian state. This has been decided in Pakistan—a complementary role for our educated women and bright boys to study outside the Valley for enriching our cause.

They had to cultivate young teachers and powerful voices in these identified universities. Since JNU is the prime university and liberal in its ethos, it would be easy to create this new consciousness against the Indian state and spread it in other universities. Husna, according to them, is a part of this project', Rashid replies.

Muza is shocked. 'I don't think this can be the case,' he exclaims. 'Before going missing, Bilal sometimes talked about Husna. He thinks she is a gentle, pretty girl and very emotional. Since they had a chequered family life, she was always eager for friendships outside her home. Recently, she was keeping company with some of the bad boys of her neighbourhood. Bilal had perhaps advised her to relocate to a better environment for her personality growth and studies. I am sure that they know it and just want to hide their flaws under the carpet of blame games', Muza replies angrily.

'Muza, I understand that he might have given her the right advice, but it has turned out to be a nightmare for all of us. Bilal is missing from home and Husna is going astray and turning into a rebel. This is a bad phase for our family. It is rumoured that both Husna and Bilal belong to a *tanzeem* that has been trained and radicalised. They can even ruin their homes to achieve the agenda. Their handler is somewhere in Norway. We are really a cursed lot', laments Muza.

'Rashid, kindly request your friend Nashir not to harm our Bilal. He will be back. He alone can bring Husna back on track. It is still possible to bring them back. Since January this year, seven boys have returned from militant camps to their homes. Their mothers have been vociferously making appeals and requesting them publicly to return. I think our womenfolk have to make perpetual pleas for our children to live normal lives. Only women can bring them back and save our ruined homes', Muza says.

'Yes, we do not have any other choice. It is best to trust in God', Rashid responds. He adds, 'I want to go back to Srinagar tomorrow. Autumn has turned to winter but we have made no breakthrough in Bilal's homecoming. I have told you everything about Javid but keep it to yourself. After all, talking about it is painful.'

Next morning, Rashid pays his respects to Razz *Babb* and in the afternoon leaves for Srinagar.

Tahira has been on Barkat's mind from the moment he met her last month. He is baffled when Razz *Babb* asks him a question about the 'woman who accompanied him'. Razz *Babb* has not seen her physically. But she is always lingering in Barkat's thoughts, leading him to reflect over matters of the heart which are beyond reason and logic.

He is in a hurry to meet Tahira. They had planned to meet in a Bankoot forest hut. Barkat's first impression of her was that of a mature woman who is worn out, robbed of the joy of life. He knows Moen was not sincere about the marriage. For Moen, she was not a partner but a means to an end: a mediator in the locality. He treated her like an object to satisfy his sexual needs, among many others. She often became an informant for him and brought whatever he needed from the local market.

The wintry morning is like a foggy evening. The sun is in the sky but is invisible due to the dark clouds which are threatening rain.

Tahira is already there with a black leather bag slung over her shoulder. '*Assalam Aleykum*', Barkat greets her at the entrance. She softly replies, '*Walekum Salam*'. They enter the cottage which can sufficiently protect them from the chill as well as people's gaze. Bashir, who is at their service, moves to the kitchen in the side room. Both Tahira and Barkat have serious expressions on their faces.

'So, you are off from the mission nowadays. When are you going again?' asks Tahira.

'I would probably go after a few days. What about you?' Barkat enquires.

'I have taken voluntary retirement from my nursing job. I am enjoying my time at home.'

'At such a young age, you are free from struggle and get pension as well', Barkat says.

'Yes, I live comfortably with my relative's son until I go back to my village. It is a small locality, five miles away from Kupwara: Dardpur. I don't have much time. Please tell me all about Moen. How did he disappear? Why did he leave me?' she asks.

'Please settle down and sit closer to the fire. I'll tell you everything Moen shared with me. He was basically from the far-off locality of Sindh. His father had come to Pakistan from Rampur in 1974. Moen had no fond memories of his childhood other than the cries of his ailing mother. His father worked in Karachi and had another woman there. He rarely came home to meet them. Moen, nicknamed Abu Mosad, was taken to a madrassa in Karachi at the young age of nine. After a few years, he was sent to Waziristan for arms training. After that, he was sent back to Karachi on a mission. He became the area commander of a group called Fauj-e-Nabi before he was sent to Kashmir in 2005. He was in his early twenties at that time', Barkat says. He asks her when she met Moen.

'I met him in 2006. He came to our house with my brother. My brother too had gone to the other side for arms training in 2005. He died while crossing the border in 2008. My father had already been killed, we were left to Allah. Nobody supported us. The local Pir recommended to my mother that she meet the Senior Pir in Srinagar. To our shame, Pir Sahib did not even meet her but after a long wait outside on the verandah, a person gave her an envelope with five hundred rupees in it. My mother had already spent two hundred rupees in reaching Pir Sahib's residence. It was then I decided to take the help of Moen', Tahira says.

'What happened then?' Barkat asks.

'Moen was very famous in the Valley. The agents of all parties used to send their *salaams* and praise him in privacy. He was a dreaded militant with seven boys in his team who were well trained in weapons. He told me that he was raised in the gunbattles of different *hujra* (camps) in Karachi. He had fought with the different groups in

Orangi, Baldia town and Kalakot. He often talked about his friends in Kalakot when he was here. He became a big support to us. He would give us money whenever we needed and would provide us with medicines too. My mother got cheap and timely treatment from Saur IMS.[14] But I had to pay the price. He would use me to satisfy his lust and at times I had to buy drugs for him. It was a strange relationship where I had to woo a Major for getting bottles of alcohol for him. I thought that after marrying me, he would settle down either in Pakistan or in Poonch. He lied and left me', replies Tahira.

'Did the Major know about him?' Barkat asks.

'Of course not', Tahira replies.

'So, you were a double agent?' Barkat asks again.

'No, I worked for him only. He often asked me to go to the officer for his bottles and if possible, get information of army movements. I did everything for him. I did get some information by allowing the Major some minor sexual favours. In Moen's company, I too got addicted to drugs. After a few months, he asked me to shift to Shopian, south Kashmir, for helping boys to get their drug quota. My mother was bedridden and had no one but me to look after her. I could not leave her alone and go anywhere, so I refused. He did not sympathise with my circumstances

14 Institute of Medical Sciences.

and kept on pressuring me to come with him. One day, he got angry after I repeatedly refused to go to Shopian, slapped me, abused my mother and left. He never returned after that fight.

'A few months later, my mother also died and I was left alone. It was a very difficult time for me. I regret wasting my precious time and emotions on such a person... Anyway, how did you meet him?' she asks Barkat.

'I knew him through my network when he was working for the *tanzeem* in Karachi but I met him in Syria. He had a dislike for Kashmiris, men and women alike. He said that Kashmiri Muslims are compulsive liars. They pretend to be homogenous for public consumption. In his opinion, Kashmiris are highly individualistic and motivated only by material interests. They hardly bother about concerns of the *umma*.[15] They pay lip service in abundance when it comes to talking about religion in public. He warned me to be careful about their mockery and humiliation of non-Kashmiris. He said that Kashmiris have no respect for their mother tongue, they speak in broken English and their Urdu pronunciation is bad. They use their own language when talking of non-Kashmiris, especially in abusing them and deceiving them for petty profit. They are united in downgrading others.

---

15 Muslim community worldwide.

Kashmiri Muslims are a suspicious community who look down upon the Muslims of the sub-continent. Only celebrities in politics and cricket charm them. They are a divided community on many levels: rural/urban, *maraz/kamraz* (North/South Kashmir), besides class and literacy divides, creating binaries all the time while pretending to be pure Muslims in conversation for material gain. Their guilt over conversion and syncretic culture have made them a completely different community. Moen even said that Kashmiris are hybrid in culture and are affected by several social forces over the centuries. They are not to be trusted but can be used for noisy misinformation.'

'What it all means is that he never liked me and only used me,' Tahira concludes sadly.

'In new Islamic practice of emergent *jihad*, women in the *tanzeem* are treated as inferior to men and are a usable commodity for their sexual fulfillment', Barkat tries to explain, to make her understand Moen's psyche. He adds, 'Kashmiris are middle and upper middle class people but are segregated among themselves on rural, urban and linguistic parameters. Srinagar Kashmiris of the downtown area think that they have the final word. They think that after the city's *Batta*s were driven out, they alone speak Kashmiri in its finer form. They do not follow any leader and laugh at them in private conversations because they have no faith in the success of the movement. They treat this movement as a business which has many stakeholders. They are an argumentative lot, like Bengalis, as if they know everything under the sun. For them, Senior Pir is only a resource and not a referent. They pray for his longevity, so that he suffers all the problems of old age. They treat him as a bargaining chip to scare the Indian government and approach Pakistan for money and material. Otherwise, in their private conversations, they call him village con, crude maulvi and backward zealot, one-man army and murderer of thousands.

'Therefore, Moen did not leave with a good impression of the sustainability of the movement in Kashmir. After coming back to Pakistan, he told the Difai Council that Kashmir should be punished for its half-hearted participation and insincerity. The present lot needs to be destroyed in order to write a history with Pakistan on a new slate. Their socio-cultural structure has to be dismantled. Their memory and history have to be erased. He emphasised that Kashmiri *mujahideen* should fight along with their families and live in their localities so that their villages are wiped out by the Indian army as well as us.

'Kashmiri Muslims are different from normal Muslims. Kashmir's *mujahideen* never live in jungles and eat herbs. They want to live with their families. They swear by the holy Quran all the time. Our Prophet would never wish a true Muslim to live like them. They are lethargic by disposition but motivated by individualistic interests. They are not mad for sex but obsessed with girls of their choice. They can be informers for money and to pay for their vices. They cannot become a homogenous lot for *jihad*. Moen was disgusted with Kashmiri *mujahideen* and volunteered to go to the war fields of Syria himself. He wanted to leave Kashmir.'

'He should have been truthful to me', Tahira bursts out angrily. 'He should have understood our helplessness. How can he be right? We have given thousands of our boys for this *jihad* which they have brought to our peaceful Kashmir. For the sake of Islam, we have made all possible sacrifices and he thinks that our boys die for entertainment?'

'The goal of Kashmiri *jihad* is affluence now. They are vociferous about it but celebrate the bereavements. It is a strange syndrome where every week they want public curfew and shutdowns, so that they can do multi-tasking at home and outside. Their monthly salaries remain unharmed. Initially, it was faith and common shared competition, now it is faith, entertainment and collective escape also. Note, in these thirty years of the movement, not a single son of the prominent leaders has perished. The boys in rags have turned out to be members of the new rich class. The commanders have become economically well off. *Jihad* in Kashmir has become a strange industry which has many stakeholders and no genuine freedom lovers. Rather than fighting for the faith, it prospers on the greed of profit making—which is because of weakening family ties and vanishing of social policing. The young join it for new identities with the help of money and resources. Kashmiri participation in *jihad* is fluid, whereas we come out from the stable structures of *jihad* and our mindset is firm', Barkat comments.

'You have no idea how much the Kashmiri women like me have suffered. Our boys were not meant to perish in their youth and still you pass judgement that we are not pure Muslims. Moen played with my emotions and you are justifying it. How could he leave after marrying me? A Kashmiri would never do something like that. I know you despise us. Moen's relationship with me was a means to an end and when I was no longer useful, he dumped me like trash. We too find you inferior to us in manners, education and in overall Kashmiri distinctness. I hate him for treating me as if he bought me by meeting my family needs. He often passed me onto his fellow *mujahideen* for the *jihad* ransom. He considers women as property and claimed, "What the *jihadi* chooses to do can't be considered rape",' states Tahira.

'Well, he died while squabbling with his commander

who was of higher rank in the organisational structure and was given preference for promotion. His commander, a Sunni *salafi,*[16] shot him dead. I think you should forgive him. *Innaneillah inne rajuh,*[17] Barkat says to Tahira.

'Anyway, I have come to meet you here for a very personal reason,' Barkat adds.

Just then, Bashir comes to inform that the meal is ready and requests them to eat in the kitchen. 'What do you want to tell me? Talk about it first, and then we'll have our food', Tahira says.

'Let us have our food first,' Barkat insists.

'I don't have much time. I have to reach my place before sunset. I'll go immediately after my food.'

They have their meal in a serene atmosphere. Not far from their hut, the river Madhumati is making music, its crystal-clear green flow seems to be dancing and striking against the stones to produce white shining trinkets. Nature is smiling and the darkness of the forest is thinning down. The thoughts in Barkat's mind remain unspoken.

16 Follower of radical Islam.
17 Islamic prayer for the dead.

Rashid is back in Srinagar after a month's stay in his native village, Bandipore. He had gone there with a purpose: to find the real narrative about changes in Husna's life.

The uncertainties caused by the era of militancy for the last two-and-a-half decades had brought structural changes in Kashmir. The middle class is upwardly mobile but a chunk had got rich without any justifiable rationale. They were traditionally associated with religious political parties. Their control over the masses was thought to be derived from their ethical capital. The youth thought of militancy as a unified force. It would have been an integrated strength if it had been successful in making Kashmir completely primordial, pre-modern. It could not make the change holistic, for the socio-cultural core of Kashmir had already split in many parts. The symbolic culture manifested in uneven distribution. It was hegemonic in unequal spheres, well differentiated in time and space.

Rashid's wife Itika is eagerly waiting to hear everything about his travels.

'This time I think you are right in ridiculing village life. It is where it was, but misplaced. Encroachments overlapping concrete buildings reveal affluence. However, the blackened spot resulting from the abandoned houses of expelled *Battas* has cut off Nature from it. What I cherished in childhood is missing. The familiarity between people, cultural homogeneity, certainty and predictability of day-to-day happenings was part of my village universe; they are now dismantled. Earlier, I could identify with the surroundings and neighbourhoods of Bandipore. That connectedness which was our pride has been severed. I was full of memories of the mountains, gardens and streams along with collective sports and lively discussions in tea shops on the streets that was a part lived history until I revisited it. The image of my childhood days in Bandipore are now shattered; my stories are in pieces like a broken mirror.'

Itika is surprised to hear this from Rashid, who always eulogised Bandipore. The revisit to his native place there seemed to have disillusioned him. She asks, 'What happened to Bilal? When will he be back? Is there any connection between Husna and Bilal's stories?'

'Bilal has left home but we are sure that he has not yet taken up the gun. It is rumoured that he is handling a job in the movement which is connected to Husna also. They are part of the project to bleed India through participatory *jihad.* The blueprint of the project has come from across the border. Our boys are engaged without any attachment to life's essentials. I think Bilal and Husna do want to live glamorous lives in affluence but they do not want to face the competition. Therefore, they have chosen to escape and have found an engagement which leads down a perilous path', replies Rashid.

'What else did you find about them? How exactly is Husna connected with Bilal's job?' asks Itika.

'It seems that these young girls who have been to colleges and universities in different states of India somehow are connected to one another. They are in communication for a cause. They say that Jawahar Baker's daughters play double-edged games. They entice young boys towards militancy and sometimes inform the police too. Bilal also visits their place. Muza fears for Bilal's life and he thinks that those beautiful, cunning girls might put his life in danger. Young boys also use our girls for different jobs like carrying information and entertainment. They even carry drugs and money to predetermined places and persons.'

Itika is dismayed to hear all this but Rashid has not finished. 'Husna has come home after two months. She has refused to even discuss the marriage proposals that came for her. She says that she would not marry anyone. Her family is in troubled waters. They do not want her to marry the Hindu supervisor from JNU. Javid, who retired last month, is perturbed. Do not tell Ruby about Husna's connection with the movement and Bilal when she visits us with Javid. If Ruby talks to you about Husna, listen to her without loosening your tongue. Even her son Altaf has joined Al-Hadis, an Islamic organisation. Ruby and Javid must be distraught as both their children have gone astray. Nowadays, children do not care about the consequences of their actions or how their parents will be affected. I pray for God's blessings on our children. Looking at the directionlessness of youths in Kashmir, I get worried for our children. I wish they finish their studies and come back home without getting distracted like Husna and Bilal,' Rashid hopes.

'Don't worry. Our children would not join the fringe, by God's grace. Let them stay outside the Valley. What will they do over here? The movement might turn bloody again this summer. In Bandipore, I got to know that young boys from radical madrassas meant as cannon fodder for *jihad* are trained in the cadre-based training camp in Bahawalpur and are ready to mix with our boys and live in the safehouses of congested localities. They condition our boys for *jihad* in local mosques and schools, expecting our women and elders to shield them from army and police when raids occur. It is done in order to achieve total participation with the help of mind-changing religious discourses and *tabliqh*', responds Itika.

'Yesterday, thirteen *mujahideen* were killed. Kashmir has become a killing field. There seems to be no respite. Have you heard Shaheb's conversation with his *mujahid* son, who died while fighting? It has gone viral. This is the first time we have heard something different from a Kashmiri father', she adds.

'What did he say?' asks Rashid.

'The father did not request his *mujahid* son to surrender or reform but instead encouraged him to continue in the movement and promote the spread of *jihad*. It surprises me that the death cult in Kashmir is now being encouraged by parents in the name of martyrdom. It is a reality which reflects on the failing of a distinct Kashmir view of humanity. It is a step towards a religious monolithic. Even if this viral conversation is spread in a planned move, it is a strong plea to plunge Kashmiri into an era of *jihad*. It is an extermination of traditional Kashmiri worldview, an annihilation of the sustained resource and representation of cultural, social and religious capital. This is a colossal loss; a plunge into the darkness.

'Yes, it has become a fluid *jihad*, changing its stance every now and then but contributing to violence and deaths without any break. We are a complex lot when it comes to our love for protests. Our obsession comes in streaks. Our history has revealed that we live parallel lives; we have reverence for distant cultures and languages and follow the western referent for life chances with passion and zeal but still believe in the native worldview for togetherness. This has caused intellectual bankruptcy.'

'What did your *Babb* say?' asks Itika. Rashid had already told Itika about Razz *Babb*'s mystic personality.

'*Babb* was positive but thoughtful. He said that Kashmiris were very fluent in their native language and were also open to learning English and other languages in the past. It was our window to the world and it made us bold and confident. The situation is quite contrary now. He said that we are too naïve to believe our leaders who are calculating and engage us in the utopian agenda of *azadi* for their vested interests. The hypocritical face of our leaders is clearly visible to him. Children of the elite class are settled in the big cities of India or in western countries. This duplicity has been passed down to the young generation as well. We are engaged in anti-India and pro-Pakistani agenda but attached to our material welfare and settling our children. Those who sacrifice their life are the excluded lot, even before they are labeled as martyrs'.

'How come, on one hand, Hurriyat and government want *Battas* to come back and on the other, they tacitly support the continuation of terror and turmoil?' Itika wonders.

'You are naïve. People talk well about *Battas*, but they don't really want them to return and claim their land and properties. They feel that their displacement was a reward for *jihad*. It is all lip service. Each passing day is tainted by new tragedies with religious colouring. Muslim rape, Hindu rape, Muslim lynching, Hindu lynching—it is being sensationalised through media and social media without a whimper. Hindu-Muslim rift is on the increase. Times are hard and choices are difficult.'

They heard the creak of the compound's main gate. Itika looks out of the window and sees Javid and Ruby. 'But they were supposed to come tomorrow', she thinks. Immediately, she says to Rashid, 'Ruby and Javid have come. Please be polite and simply agree to whatever they say. Don't give your opinion or contradict them.'

Itika opens the front door and invites the couple into the room. They both greet her.

'*Assalam Waleykum.* Is everything alright'? asks Itika.

'Yes. We came after we heard about Rashid's return. What is the news from Bandipore? How is everyone?' Javid asks Rashid anxiously.

'Bilal has gone missing. Nothing seems to be in its rightful position. The whole family is worried and agitated but there is nothing they can do', Rashid replies.

'The big plan to bleed India did not work, even though it has become an all-out war from our side also,' retorts Javid. 'Pakistan feels that it can directly defend us; we have to defame India in terms of child abuse, rape and communal rife of Hindu India. We have to formulate issues which would be supported by our media and subsequently raised in Indian universities by our boys and girls so that our diaspora frames India in cases of human rights violations and puts it down to Hindus being exceedingly communal, subjecting Muslims and women of Kashmir to humiliation and indignity. We have told Husna to play her role even if she has to stay for another year in JNU', Javid states.

'You think that Husna is mature enough to play her role without getting trapped?' asks Rashid. Ruby intervenes, 'Allu (their son) also asked to bring Husna back from Delhi and get her married, for he cannot tolerate the thought of her interacting and moving with Hindu boys. I have been insisting that Javid force her to come back. Otherwise I don't know what is in store'.

'Husna will come back. She has promised us she will be back after completion of her doctorate. Let her do her PhD and then she would agree to marry anyone we choose for her', Javid tells Ruby. He turns towards Rashid and says, 'I am worried after the recent development between Husna and her supervisor. I want her to complete her mission and return to the Valley without any emotional attachment to her target. I now fear that she will go astray and marry that Hindu professor. In case things do not go according to the wish of the high command, the hidden hands who hold the strings obviously will not let her live. She would eventually get exposed.'

Itika goes to make tea for everyone. Ruby goes with her to the kitchen while Javid and Rashid talk in the guest room. After tea, they excuse themselves and leave for home.

'Itika, what did Ruby say when she went to the kitchen with you?' asks Rashid.

'She said that Husna has become very aggressive. She has refused all the marriage proposals and does not interact much with anyone. She has even refused to take money from her father. She told them that she would not marry anyone. Ruby has warned her not to move with the *kafir* (non-believer). It seems they met him when he came for some academic project in Kashmir. She said that he was a nice person, but she does not want Husna to go with him. The atmosphere in their house is least affable', replies Itika.

'I think they should first try to put their house in order. Javid loses no opportunity of blaming Ruby for all the misfortunes of their family. I don't think Ruby should have covered up his wrongdoings for such a long duration.'

'What else could she do? She is his wife. She had no choice but to carry on the relationship. She deserved a better man. He humiliates her all the time in front of everyone and has made her miserable. I am really afraid of talking to him', Itika replies.

At that moment, a group video call comes from their sons and they both forget about Ruby and Javid.

Babb and Barkat have developed an amicable chemistry. *Babb*'s gestures on seeing Barkat are positive and welcoming. *Babb* states, 'So two more boys have died in Pulwama.'

'Yes, *Babb*, Sameer and his accomplice were killed yesterday afternoon.'

'What have they said? I mean what did Hurriyat say?'

'Their objective is to continue until the last one goes to the grave. The leadership said that those sacrificing their life put a huge responsibility on our shoulders to honour their sacrifices and take the movement to its logical end. *Babb*, it is an industry that flourishes on these corpses. They have been trained to continue with this wreckage. For the common masses, there is deprivation and death. This is further deepening the gap between the rich and the poor. The western world and our elites are living with the riches of life, moving freely and going anywhere they like while we, the destitutes, are all set for collective suicide. *Babb*, I have nothing to gain from this industry. And I feel sad, dejected with the gameplan for the suicide of Kashmiris which their leaders relish in the name of *azadi*. They will realise their mistake when it is too late to comprehend the loss of life, loss of social capital and trouncing of symbolic capital. Whatever little is left, they will lose it once and for all. Things are moving in that direction.'

Babb curiously intervenes, 'How do you know all these things?'

'*Babb*, I have wasted my youth in militancy. First, I experienced *jihad* in Pakistan, then Syria and now in Kashmir. My experience as a militant has thought me all these things', Barkat replies.

'I am exhausted and disillusioned in the uncertain realm of my mid-life. Your cottage is a haven for me where I want to be reborn as a new person. I no longer wish to live the life of a militant. I do not want to take anybody's life now. I have wasted a long period of my life in the name of *jihad*. I now realise the futility of the movement. The common people are scared while the elites have an interest in the continuation of this movement. The state is also propagating this religious mixture of patriotism. We do not want it; God does not need it. It is an artificial construct, this nationality and religiosity', he concludes.

'I can see you are coming close to your inner self. Would you be able to cut yourself off from the life you have been living for the last fifteen years? Would they allow you to live if you turn your back to the gun?' asks *Babb*.

'*Babb*, I don't know, nor do I care. I have turned into a lonely person seeking solitude. I know that I have limited options. In any of these situations, death is inevitable. However, I shall follow whatever path you guide me to take. When I decided to take this path of destruction, I had no clue that I was getting trapped into a vicious cycle of meaningless violence and deaths in the name of religion. Bereft, lonely, with little social acceptance in my immediate neighbourhood, I wanted to erase the past. I chose the option of belonging to a group which gave me honour and dignity, the means to become rich quick with a dose of adventure and fight for the cause of God as well. But it was not what I presumed', confesses Barkat.

'Why do you want to give it all up? Death is inevitable in any case', *Babb* questions.

'I have realised that social plurality is more significant than collective comportment. There should be honour for each of Nature's creatures, who are evolving. Killing does not give you peace, however high the stakes. Sharing of wounds has to be for humankind, not for one group, or one community or one nation. My mind is filled with hate, darkness and loneliness. I lose sleep when I remember Muslims in Pakistan, where I was taught and groomed in *jihadi* culture. Majority of them are nervous wrecks, illiterate and living a subsistence existence. Except some parts of Lahore, Karachi and Islamabad, the majority live only for *jihad*. They do not understand that this life should be lived well. The tragedy is that they believe that the Muslims of the non-Muslim countries live below their standards. In comparision to them, Kashmiri Muslims live a lavish life with big cars, costly mobiles, rich cuisine and expensive clothes. They have no dearth of basic necessities. Their choices are limitless, be they religious, cultural or professional. They abhor non-natives, look down upon *mujahideen* like us in private conversations and get all types of services from migrants. It is Biharis in their fields and orchards, it's tourists who fill up their pockets and it is Pakistan and other countries which fund their properties. And it is we who fight at the cost of our lives. *Mujahideen* get disillusioned here. Whatever we were told does not match reality. We are rated inferior with no social acceptance', Barkat complains.

'But Kashmiris have their own people killed in gunfights and operations.'

'*Babb*, it is not religious zeal or the *azadi* mantra that motivates them to join; but adventure, fun, escape from this life to find meaning in group existence and desire to become rich quick. They have grudges against their friends and family, have been jilted in love or isolated by society, dropped out from school or were caught in some misdemeanour. It is their compulsion also. The Hurriyat, an umbrella organisation of illiterates with their sham media statements provoke them to run the show of *azadi*. It is actually their mothers and families who miss their children, mourn them day and night, weep in corners and then, consumed by these tragedies, slowly fade away', Barkat says.

'Do you have any idea how these killings can be ended?' *Babb* queries.

Barkat replies, 'I see it as a confusion of agenda. Therefore, the gun does not lead us anywhere. The youth may perish only to keep India and Pakistan at each other's throats. This is to sustain the power elite in Pakistan and maybe political elite here in India too.'

'I wonder what we gained by forcing *Batta*s to leave and occupying their lands. The cost was way too high. We lost our children in the name of martyrdom', says *Babb*.

'Engagement of our youth in the violent industry is a well-thought-out strategy to run the ideology of nationalism. Normally, they should have been a part of the political process, questioning political moves and creating headaches for the leadership. But they are on the verge of untimely deaths and in turn strengthening militant discourse and relieving politicians from their accountabilities and responsibilities. Our resistance leadership is a coalition of people who hardly have any exposure beyond the walls of India-Pakistan, that too in closeted, monitored groups of maulvis. The movement needs identification agenda, not vague interpretations. Their *azadi* means to hate India and fight the Indian army. This in turn bleeds us day and night. Hurriyat has become insensitive towards the future of Kashmir', states Barkat.

Babb asks, 'What is the view regarding Kashmir in Pakistan? They don't realise the futility of the movement and we are paying the price with the lives of our own people. We are surrounded by violence, death and instability'.

'I learned only one thing in Pakistan: The Islamic Republic is least bothered about Azad Kashmir. Kashmir serves as a window of opportunity for them to bleed India. 'Ghazwa-e-Hind' (Islamic India) is its final project approved by its army along with some political and bureaucratic elites. It is the domain of the belligerent ISI leadership along with some political hawks in bureaucracy. This has been happening since 1990. The only change is the shift from active state participation to tacit support. Finally, they have handed it over to a non-state agency for its continuation, which receives condemnation and faces the brunt. It has been like that since 11 September 2001. The two sides of militancy, i.e. state role and non-state participation, have become curved lines, emerging from the same source of *jihad* against India. It is a failed strategy which is sustaining itself with the help of funds from madrassas. Kids as young as five years old are bought from poor parents of tribal and peripheral areas, and are trained for the cause of *jihad*, 'the total war'. Kashmir is one of its main targets. Here it is a changed strategy. It means the ratio should be two commandants and eight Kashmiris in each group of militants. The local Imams, who lead namaz, have been identified by the militant leadership and commanded to find safe places in localities besides a hideout in the nearby forests for these armed boys. They would be supported by maulvis from outside Kashmir, Imams and a section of intellectuals in the name of violation of human rights against state intervention. It is well proclaimed by the umbrella leadership here and from PoK as an indigenous movement through shutdowns and closures of institutions. Pakistan as always would play the diplomatic music for it. Since earlier experiments have failed, there has to be total participation of the local populace, especially women and the children. That will spread in the towns and in the cities. Supply of arms is to be managed by Pakistan through the porous boundaries of different states of India. Women and children should come out to protect the *jihadis* in large numbers if they are traced or cordoned off by the Indian army. The People's Democratic Party (PDP) gained power through latent support for separatism in south Kashmir which has been taken as a battlefield as its soil is conducive for carnage. There is no way to end this carnage unless Kashmiris themselves reject this', states Barkat.

Babb pauses for a moment and then says, 'What do you wish to do now?'

'*Babb*, what are my options? I feel agitated and keep questioning my identity. Am I a *jihadi* or just a useless being who was just thrown in this world? I wonder if God wishes me to do away with these worldly religions and politics and be with him without any religion. When I reflect on my past, I feel as if a new aspect of my personality unfurls at each turn; be it the case of being thrown near the garbage bin and raised by a Muslim beggar or being guided towards a dignified life with education and social acceptance by a Pandit family. I regret turning my back on them and instead listening to the maulvis of the madarassa I taught in. In the evenings, they persuaded me and many other young boys for *jihad* and religious way of life through their manipulated speeches and sermons. They created a collective euphoria for the religious cause which mysteriously conditioned our young, ignorant minds. I lived a life of uncertainty attached to *jihad*, wandering in darkness from jungle to jungle and place to place in search of killing fields, hidden and isolated from the people and gradually getting lost in the wilderness with regrets and remorse. The euphoria faded and I have once again become a lonely person full of uncertainties', replies Barkat.

With a faraway look in his eyes, *Babb* says, 'The Pandit who took you under his wing was one of our professors, teachers and doctors who perceptibly dominated our offices till 1970. They made us to go to school when we refused to be educated. Before 1947, we were illiterate and poverty-stricken in villages as well as in urban centres. *Battas* launched the movement for our education and empowerment. Non-native rulers and elites were against them but could not ignore them for they were functional. They were with us like our soulmates. Sheikh Abdullah was instrumental in forming a team and launching the movement for our education with the support of Nehru, thereby ensuring our empowerment. There was hardly any non-*Batta* in those transforming teams because hardly anybody was educated in the 1920s. New setups like Jabri school phenomenon, was one such transformative programme.[18] Nobody will tell you this, nor is it documented or recorded. You may hear this real social history of Kashmir from some elderly people in the family who are in their eighties or nineties. *Battas* gradually diminished in number when we became qualified for these positions. They were driven out in 1990. They were scattered throughout the Valley. Though

18 In 1935, the administration had forced illiterate masses, mostly Muslims, to attend these schools, where Pandits were teachers.

less in number, they were functional in all the spheres. They were peaceful and educated and had the capacity to create moral and social mores. They were engaged in these professions with attachment to their noble objectives and established norms. Therefore, we miss them as able teachers and efficient doctors. The maulvis who took you to dark forests for hiding and shooting, told our people that they (*Batta*s) should be segregated and their role in education and professional institutions should diminish. They created the rift and altered the social landscape of the Valley. It was their decision that we should part ways with *Batta*s. We only approved it with silence and sighs. Their existence was the symbolic core of engagement with attachment. Hence, it was a mediating moral presence. Since then, we have built boundaries and only multiplied them. These encroached spaces owned by the new leaders of the nation were once free fields, common parks and open pastures with no boundaries. Education linked to formal degrees lost its attachment with academics, a new boundary. *Mast kalandars*, *Reshi*s diminished and new cult gurus and Pirs replaced them to tell us about the infidels. Morality was taken out from the religious codification. Our East is bad and non-Muslim, while our West is mystified. Had there been an educated leadership or *Reshi* guidance, youth would have had a passion for life instead of a love for reaching the grave early. They would never have romantically eulogised death to block the tears of our women who weep for the untimely departure of their children. Kashmiris feel caged in these manufactured uncertainties, just like you. I wish those who claim they love their own people could take note of it. It is not too late to confess that they did not know what they wanted for their children and for future generations. They were mistaken and falsely led into the present conundrums. The logic of martyrdom has made Kashmir empty and it seems to be the final nail in the coffin. What happened to our political acumen? We thought that we were wise people, but sadly, we are not. Our insights do not go beyond our theological discourses. Those who know it well mystified it and caged us. Those who led us were myopic, knowing nothing beyond Kashmir and mythical notions, told and sold. The rest who could have been trusted have no say, they pass by with silent sighs and hidden narratives. For we parted ways with Lal Ded and Nund *Reshi*.[19] Kashmir is cursed by Zoon and by the pain inflicted on our mothers and our daughters, our women.[20]

19 The two great saints of Kashmir who are revered irrespective of faith. Lal Ded, a woman, gave Kashmir its sense of identity and Nund *Reshi*, who brought the Sufi tradition to the Valley.

20 Zoon was a local queen whose husband was taken away by Mughal emperor Akbar. She abdicated her throne and turned into an insane wanderer. She is believed to have put a curse on Kashmir.

'If not today, tomorrow surely posterity will pass the judgment that the two components of the Kashmiri core were broken and divided, one defeated and alienated, the other driven out and deprived. In the process, Kashmir is completely destroyed'.

Abruptly, *Babb's* expression changes and he thunders, 'Get Bilal back if you really want this endless violence to end'.

Barkat sees the rage and challenge in his words and says, 'Bilal will not pick up the gun. He is in a different type of cell. He has to bring homogeneity in *jihad* by embedding religious zeal in college students, identified girls and boys. He leads the team that plans visits of religious scholars in schools and mosques for *jihad* so that they teach Salafi Islam, create messages, manufacture information.[21] His team manages the print, electronic and social media as well. He is also the selector of girls who are sent to different Indian universities for propagating *jihad*. I know in a couple of cases it was difficult to manage. He had to explain it. He is well into it.'

'We want him back to his family and you have to help him', *Babb* commands.

'*Babb*, I shall try, but I would not be able to do it without your blessings.' *Babb* takes out a few walnuts and gives them to Barkat, who takes his leave.

21 A radical Islam outfit that does not tolerate non-believers.

Bilal has been away from home for over six months and is disturbed by the new spate of killings in his own district. Murders by slitting of throats and chopping off of limbs, unheard of in Kashmir earlier, is rampant. These are primordial methods of revenge. Above the serene dense forests of Deanshur in the lap of high ranges of Bandipore, snowy melting peaks nurture the bubbling fresh chilled water streams gushing through the locale of Chhandeej and other villages of Bandipore to the final destination, Wullar Lake. Bilal has found his safe hideout in this covered, guarded ridge amidst the forest.

Barkat finds his way to this warren. He is an asset identified by secret agencies of Pakistan and it is not a big deal for him to meet anybody associated with *jihad*. He can monitor, guide and take reports from any of the outfits engaged in Kashmir.

Early in the morning of 25 May 2018, Bilal and Captain Masood are waiting for Barkat in their den. Capt Masood had spent half of his life in *jihad*, which he learned in the jungles of Murray and Waziristan. He was given army training and then a position to command

and train the passionate boys ready for martyrdom. He came to Kashmir with a purpose and mission to make Kashmiris participate in this war against India.

'*Salam Alleykum*', they say.

'*Walekum Salam*', Barkat replies while Capt Masood shows the way in. They settle down for a conversation.

'This is a perfect hideout. Ridges are narrow and the clusters of deodars darken the surroundings and make it safe. I once stayed in this forest for a week but that was on the other side of the river', Barkat tells Bilal and then asks him, 'Who stayed here before you and how many people have come here to meet you?'

'Some Gujjars come to give milk and meat. No one else knows about this hideout. Capt Masood has been living here with me for a month', replies Bilal.

'Bilal, I think social media and the print media is deviating from the line. Mark my words, I can't sell hope when there is no hope around. My mission lies in the lives we save, not in the lives we lose. I beg for life and if that means defeat, such defeat I celebrate as a self-proclaimed victory,' says Barkat. 'The spirit of *mujahideen* will be dampened when these types of statements come from a popular and influential columnist. Martyrdom of boys should have flared up the sentiment and thickened the participation of women and children. Instead, participation is thinning, diluting. The boss is worried and angry. I have to report everything to him. What should I tell him?'

Bilal pauses for a moment and then says, 'Barkat Sahib, time is moving fast with unexpected developments here and across the border. We have no control over the beams coming down from the shadowy trees. Three-time prime minister Nawaz Sharif blamed his own army for the Mumbai blasts. This has buried our cause deep into the earth. Where is Ghazwa-e-Hind? Both common people and *mujahideen* are alarmed with his statement. Was it not enough to mock us that we should have a public sermon from a retired spy chief and a general of Pakistan telling us about the money trail and payrolls of our leaders? Through his book, he even elaborated how they worked with our sworn enemy. Do you think that people should rejoice at the unfolding of these incidents and ridiculous statements? I am burnt inside and find thick smoky darkness around me. A prime minister is blaming and exposing his army and the general is divulging things that should put us to shame. It indicates disgust and ruin.'

Barkat responds, 'Should we lament over it again and again? Do we have any idea what is happening over here? Look at the incident of Tanveer Maulvi who was a firebrand impressive speaker. He was picked from a *dargah* and was trained in a madrassa[22] for eloquent

---

22 Schools which impart only religious instruction.

mind-altering addresses. People used to close their shops at noon to ensure they got space in the mosque during his sermons. His job was clearing the dust of *kufur* (the traditional way of life) and bringing boys to the way of *jihad.* He did what his peers have been doing since 1990s, serving their self-interests. They succeeded in visiting the kitchens of the families. The high command applauded it. Today, we hear that Shafi was killed by his wife who was collaborating with Tanveer Maulvi in a carefully thought-out plan. During the course of investigation, it came to light that "Asifa and her paramour Tanveer Maulvi, a prayer leader at a local mosque, had killed Shafi after giving some tablets to him", the newspaper stated'. Capt Masood was in a rage and wanted to kill the maulvi along with the woman.

Barkat again interjects, 'Have patience. How would you bring life to a cadaver when it has been drained completely? It needs fresh blood with vitality of fresh reformative social-religious consciousness that you lack'.

'What do you mean? Should we tolerate it? We are living such a hard life in jungles and they are making fun of it. This is not acceptable', protests Bilal.

Barkat looks at Bilal and says, '*Jihad* needs complete devotion and complete submission. It is not just for Kashmir. We all know that Kashmiris hardly lack anything other than their sanity. It is a mistaken *jihad.* Majority of the Kashmiris enjoy their lives in big bungalows and move in luxurious cars. The poor do not have this lavish lifestyle: They join the *Azadi* Movement to get rich quickly. Our boys, mostly from poor families and dropouts or failures in technical colleges, join us for the *hoor*s and fun of this world and those who are in salaried jobs support us to get paid without doing work. They might seem like soft-spoken people but they are soft in their homes and tough in the offices, playing mind games for their vested interest all the time. They live in two worlds: one for their immediate kith and kin and the other for outsiders. They are divided in multiple realms but capable to convert the parallel lines into one big line with their strong campaigning and capacity to engage in deceptive discourses. They do not know the real agenda of *azadi* and therefore experiment with the help of the agencies.'

Bilal is taken aback with these revelations. He sighs, 'Our elders were naive and illiterate and were easily lured by those mythical stories. Since 1930s, this narrative ruled the minds and hearts of our people in order to build an Islamic edifice which Pakistan symbolised. We had notions of an enlightened Pakistan. In reality, it is an uncivil, divided and primordial feudal mass of land where tribal patriarchs, westernised army, elite and feudal lords run the show. There was no internet; the countries were divided by impenetrable wire boundaries. They showed only Lahore and Karachi on their television shows and we believed its literary, sweet Urdu content and got caged in a seductive imagined country. We were more jingoistic Pakistani than they ever were. The golden decades of 1960s allured us and we were seduced by those mythical notions and messages of green Islamic richness. We wanted to be a part of that richness and presumed that it would complement and enrich our evolved culture. We were mistaken. The real Pakistan was completely opposite to the one we adored. We loved peace and our shared peasantry universe. We appreciated our institutions and civil urbane existence was our ideal. We wanted to be linear in the process of development and accommodative in anything that came from reason's triumph. We loved faith which enhanced our intelligence and rationale. We accepted whatever we were told in the name of Islam. Our leaders deceived us. Our emerging educated middle class was given the wrong impression about the ground realities in Pakistan. Kashmiris were fed on the lies hatched by Azad Kashmir Radio. Our leaders knew it, but they betrayed us in order to retain or replace the elites in power structure. This also kept them in a position to bargain with India. It was a political game played to kill the cultural and moral strength of a community. If peace and development had been given a chance, Kashmiris would have prospered with dignity.

They had intellectual capacity and an accommodative temperament. The community had the physiological features of an advanced race and mental acumen with contentment and cultural richness to evolve on the finest traditions of interfaith accommodation. We were broken, divided, displaced and deprived to become parallel lines, striving independently for our destination, without any common agenda. The *azadi* mantra is seductive, a notional and primordial slogan which is divisive in nature. In contrast to this *azadi* mantra is our *Reshi* culture which is ever-evolving and accommodative. It is commingling of reason with faith filled with the desire to quench the thirst of humanity to fulfill its own potential. It is a different story now. The youth does not understand that tradition due to their caged minds which are dispossessed of socialisation. They still support Hurriyat, the so-called last saviour, which attaches uncertainty with religion to mystify Kashmir politically.'

Capt Masood steps in. 'I had suggested that our first target should be pro-Indian mainstream politicians and not the army. We did succeed in driving out Kashmiri Pandits who supported India, but not in eliminating the pro-India elite politicians. It is necessary to eliminate them first. It would make a big difference. Unless we completely erase the past, we will not succeed in making Kashmiris pro-Pakistan. It is about time the *mujahid* commanders follow late General Gull's advice to go for *jihad* regardless of the moral costs—only then can we wipe out the *Reshi* culture to fulfill our agenda. It is impossible to believe in the *Reshi* culture as well as follow the primordial mode of thinking preached by the radical Islamic organisations we blindly trust. There is no turning back, now that we have arrived at a crucial phase of our movement.'

'That is the myth Pakistan has been nourishing in their mind. ISI thinks that that it can erase memory and history from the mind of Kashmir with the help of Difai Pakistan. Despite Big Pir's claim, even Hurriyat is divided on Habba Khatoon's narrative. Some Hurriyat leaders do not want Kashmir to accede to Pakistan, others want it to be independent. Gilani, the Senior Pir, wants the Valley to be part of Pakistan and other Jammu and Kashmir Liberation leaders want it to be an independent state. This is where Kashmiri Muslim is different from other Muslims of the world. In Kashmir, Hurriyat and mainstream leadership are synonymous with anti-India tirade. There is no doubt about it. The only difference is that while Hurriyat is visible in expression, the mainstream parties of Kashmir are gaudy in language and act as a shield. Neither Hurriyat nor the mainstream political parties want absolute Talibanisation of Kashmir, as it happened in Swat Valley or Afghanistan. We realise the value of development as well as our cultural repertoire but somehow end up contributing towardds ISI's agenda of Talibanisation of Kashmir. That has made the agenda of the movement meaningless and *azadi* a notional misnomer. It is a strange mixture where the political elite do not consider our stone-pelters or *mujahideen* as religious or communal. They address us as secular. This has made the BJP-PDP alliance possible where the BJP has given in to PDP for the sake of grabbing power. Kashmiris know it. Hurriyat understands it and mainstream politicians tacitly approve it. Neither can a Pakistani comprehend it nor can we explain it to them. Therefore, many *tanzeems* are at work in Kashmir', replies Bilal.

'There is an element of truth in Bilal's statement. India, Pakistan, Hurriyat and mainstream politicians of Kashmir are the four parts of the one heart. The more Hurriyat shows dissent and protest, better opportunity it is for NC, PDP to gain from India. Similarly, more the prominence of mainstream parties, the greater role for Hurriyat to enjoy proximity with ISI. The game in Kashmir is the engagement and attachment of India and Pakistan for their nationalisms. In this rhythmic circle of seasons, we suffer day and night. This is a new normal and we are seduced by it', states Barkat.

Masood, a little upset by this statement, speaks. 'We have not gained much success in the last two decades.

We think that the young men and women in private institutions and media circles passively support us. But, in reality they are diluting our movement with their half-hearted involvement. They are more attached to their families than our cause. Those who are involved in *jihad* should not care about international opinion. High command is not happy with this passive lot who carry our misinformation campaign of each one being at war in Kashmir. We need open support to Jihad Council to create mayhem. Either they are with *jihad* or they are not. We do not fear India or Indian army, but we need complete surrender of Kashmiri elite and leadership for our cause. We have to take the command. Otherwise, we would not die the way that would please God and do any good to Muslims. Our beginning was wrong. You cannot go on elegising Kashmir on one side and on the other, eulogise its culture. We have to break it and make them feel that they were inferior to us. They have to be cut off from their history and memory. Instead, we have made them feel superior to us by allowing them to enjoy lives with their families. They think the *mujahideen* are foolish. They look down at us in their private appraisals. They regard us as a rejected lot. Their opinion about Islam in Pakistan is the same. Should we go with it?' asks Masood.

Barkat calmly listens to him and then argues, 'Masood, I have been to Syria, Pakistan, Kashmir and also to the plains of India. Even after all these years of fighting in the name of religion, I am unable to find out whose war are we fighting. My experience has made me understand that it is not God's war. God is merciful and He loves humankind. I had no understanding of the preciousness of this world clearly before I met a maulvi in Pakistan who explained that God loves this world and tries to coordinate with Nature for its beautification. *Areshe jamal say khali nahe honuz...*'[23] (Death and destruction are not His priority). It is peace, it is order and it is tranquility in a holistic way. Religion is not for division. It is a message to live together, along with Nature. He said that Islam is practised more in the western countries than in South Asian countries.

'Do you see the messages on social media? Read them. Hossein Askari, a writer of Iranian origin, suggests that Muslim countries have miserably failed to follow Islamic values in different walks of life. This may not come as a surprise for many who have seen the situation in Muslim countries go from bad to worse. What is surprising, though, is that New Zealand tops the list. The best-ranked Muslim-majority nation is Malaysia at serial number 43 while the only other Muslim nations in the top fifty are UAE and Albania at 47th and 48th ranks

---

23 In luqman 31:11 in Nalm: 27:88 and in Gafir 40:64, Altin: 4, and other verses also.

respectively. Saudi Arabia ranks number 88, India is at 90 while Pakistan lags behind at 137. In Morocco, I learnt that when Islam came to the West before the tenth century, it spread the message of peace to the divided infighting groups. They got easily converted. Now they spread war and inflict violence on the peace-loving communities of the non-Islamic countries, so symbolically the *jihadists* are no longer Muslims by that standard, while in the present times, non-Muslims are more Muslim than the populace in the Muslim countries. God would see peace, compassion and parity rather than violence, coldness and divisions. He is not bothered about tags and names, mind it. Therefore, Masood, it is an era of demystification. We need to understand it and we have to know the interests of our religious and political elites.'

Bilal's restlessness is apparent. He says, 'I had heard from my father that Janab Mama Sahib, the Imam High of Bandipore in the 1970s, used to give speeches in mosques and schools as well that *jihad* was agreeable on illiteracy, ignorance and ill-information that had enslaved the Muslims of South Asia. He further adds, 'Barkat, it is a shame that our maulvis who are receiving so much from us are resorting to such a low level of conduct. Where is the Muslim in them? Look, Danish got everything from his Jamaat-e-Islami background; the elder Pir recommended him to many places because he had a Pakistani wife and acted as a maulvi. He was made a liaison officer in the university so that he could connect the institution and the students to our noble movement. When his conduct with his wife, who has turned frail and ailing, was revealed, everyone found it abhorrent. People are saying, "They take refuge in these long beards, a little Quranic recitation and symbolic dresses with those short pyjamas and in the name of Islam, indulge in anything that suits their interests and lust". The "kirdar cell", a moral policing outfit, is quiet and has done nothing about these incidents of shame.'

'Bilal, since it has come to the surface, you know about it. This is the reality inside the mask. How long should we die for these liabilities? We should finish them first,' Barkat laughs. He continues, 'First, we have to finish non-Muslims, then political Muslim elites and finally the maulvis. Those who are left would be finished by the Indian and Pakistani armies. Long live *azadi*!'

Masood feels as if life has drained out of him. 'What should I say to the high command? That we have not been able to homogenise Kashmir for *jihad*? This was our first task. Maulvis failed to woo women and children, because they wanted women to play subordinate roles. If *Batta*s had not been driven out, we would have not been able to break society's internal cohesion. They had to be removed. The only thing we have been able to do is that we have broken their bonds with the older values. Kashmiris, military commandants have failed us. They had relations and interests with the political pro-Indian leadership of Kashmir. It was their interest that prevented us from Talibanising Kashmir completely. I understood this five years ago when I found that even Big Pir's properties and children are outside Kashmir in the cities of India; others too have properties in plenty in all the big cities from the south to the north of India. They are engaged in *jihad* but are buying properties elsewhere. ISI needs to delink it. In the past, this became a bottleneck and now again it will surface if Kashmiri leadership is taken into confidence. Unless it is done, we shall fail again and again. Kashmiri police is divided, Kashmiri leadership is divided, youth of south Kashmir and north Kashmir are divided, and Hurriyat is divided. ISI alone cannot win this war for Kashmir'.

'True, should we continue until we are eliminated too?' asks Bilal. 'We cannot change the past but we can take care of the present and the future. At present, Pakistan is too weak to take Kashmir from India and the future of Pakistan itself is in the dock. They say Imran Khan as Prime Minister will take a break from the past. The military high command in Pakistan understands that their heydays will not last, so they have given their concurrence for peace with India. Hurriyat might take the offer from Modi Sarkar to come to the table. In reality, National Conference (NC) and People's Democratic Party do not want it, but there is pressure from the public as well. Let us see that we have a dignified break with the past. Take it easy', Barkat remarks.

'Yes, Barkat Bhai, I think each one in Kashmir is exhausted except for the leadership, pro-Indian elements and the Hurriyat. They benefit from it. No doubt, the PDP spokesperson, a sagacious Bandipore person, wise because of his astuteness and experience, sincerely pleads for a dignified peace. I have read his statement about the NC leadership: "The party is convinced that it can survive only by being part of the problem rather than the solution for which post-2002 the entire mainstream has been campaigning in the state." We know that sabotage comes from unknown quarters. It would be too early to speak straight, which would not be in line with the current. We have to see what we can do.'

The sun has gone into hiding under the thick cover of clouds and trees. It is dark at noon. The serenity of the early hours turns into noise as if Nature is lamenting the condition of Kashmir. Barkat, Bilal and Capt Masood share a meal and then part ways.

Barkat has to receive Major Kamal of ISI who wants to visit the Valley to assess the ground realities. He is supposed to enter the Valley through Kupwara sector where the advance party of six *mujahideen* has to sneak inside the Valley from across the border, a week before his arrival. Since all the six militants were killed at the border while crossing, Major Kamal would find it difficult to make it to this side. At the penultimate hour, Barkat persuades Major Kamal to delay his visit.

Barkat's commitment to *jihad* is shaken. These days, he finds peace and solace either at Razz *Babb*'s cottage or in long conversations with Tahira. They have become his anchors in time and space. After a narrow escape at Halmatpora forest the other day where five of his companions are killed by the army, Barkat moves to Batargam's dense forests for refuge. He knows that the nearest village is Dardpora, where Tahira lives with her sister's son. He is restless, seized with a strong desire to meet her. He feels as if the Batargam forest breeze is bringing her fragrance to him.

Early in the morning, he calls Tahira and requests her to meet him at a place of her choice. He is not sure if she would agree but he wants to see her and talk to her again. Tahira is taken aback at his request of meeting after many months. Perhaps, she also wants to talk to him. She takes a deep breath and replies, 'We cannot meet here in Dardpora. It has become a place full of foes instead of friends. Each one is deprived and crushed by the wheel of time. Why do you want to meet me? I am of no use and I have passed the stage of hurry and scurry'.

'I need to meet you. Please, if you could kindly make it', requests Barkat.

Tahira pauses for a while and then says, 'If you are free tomorrow, then come to Dedi *Mauj* Ziyarat at 7 in the morning. It is a shrine in Meelyal. I'll be there to distribute *kheer*. Come alone.'

It is Friday. Shujaat Bukhari, the Chief Editor of *Rising Kashmir*, along with two security guards, are killed by unknown gunmen while leaving his office for 'Iftari' at home. The killings come a day before Eid. The atmosphere is charged and rumour mills at work.

Tahira has been visiting Dedi *Mauj* every year on Eid for the last ten years. Unlike the first time she met Barkat, Tahira is liberated in a sense that stigmas of any kind do not affect her any more. She simply wants to live peacefully with her sister's son. She feels no excitement about this meeting. Barkat, on the other hand, is looking forward anxiously.

Early in the morning at 6 am, Barkat arrives at the shrine and stands at the far end near the stream under the chinar from where he can see people coming and going. An hour later, he sees Tahira coming towards the shrine with a middle-aged woman. For another hour, he observes them from afar and then sees them settled near the Ziyarat, a place of pilgrimage, cooking rice, milk and sugar on an oil stove. There are not many people inside the Ziyarat. But after Eid prayers, a good number of men and women will be streaming into the shrine.

Barakat becomes restive and calls her on the phone. After the greetings, she says, 'We have prepared *kheer*. Come and have it'.

'I am about to reach', Barkat informs her and then asks, 'Who else is with you?'

'I have come here with my neighbour', she replies.

'We need to go to Reshwari. I have arranged a guest house there for us to talk in privacy'.

'First come here and then we can decide', she says.

Barkat looks around and then walks towards them saying, '*Salam Alleykum* and Eid Mubarak'

'Eid Mubarak to you as well', says Tahira, Looking at her companion, she says, 'Maasi, he is Shamsi Sahib, manager of the hospital. He has come to check certain places here in Kupwara. He wants me to accompany him to hospitals in Reshwari and other places. I too desire to visit Khanum who is hospitalised over there. Do you want to join us?'

'No, no, I don't want to go today. You go with him but come back home before sunset,' replies the lady.

They have *kheer* in plastic bowls and then Tahira puts on her hijab to cover her face. Nearby, they board an autorickshaw which takes them to the tourist bungalow of Reshwari. Spring has arrived. The sun is playing hide and seek with scattered wisps of ashen clouds. The clean waters of Mawar river are flowing past bushes and trees in a zigzag pattern and are making music, singing enthralling hymns of Nature. It is a delightful walk in the serene outskirts of the locality. People are seldom seen here. You could talk and walk without any encumbrance. Far in the distance is an army camp.

'That is the guest house. I have booked it through the *tehsildar*. You do not have to worry. Be at ease with me as long as you wish. Nobody will disturb us. I have brought some bread and eggs too. We shall eat and then have tea', Barkat tells Tahira. Sultan is waiting at the front gate with the keys.

'*Salam Aleykum*. Eid Mubarak. *Janab*, this is the key. I have to go for Eid namaz. I will be back by 3 pm. In case you need anything, please let me know, I shall arrange it before I leave. Nissar Sahib told me that you would be here to inspect some hospital in the nearby town', Sultan says.

'Thank you, Sultan. You go for your namaz. We don't need anything. We may leave before you come back. In case you don't come, I'll keep the key under the sandstone near the front gate of the cottage', Barkat says and then gives him some money as *Eidyana.*

Sultan thanks him and leaves. Barkat rushes towards the room where Tahira has removed her hijab. The guest house is small with one room, two side windows, a kitchen and washroom. She sits on the bed while Barkat takes the chair.

'Why did you call me?' Tahira asks right away.

'I want to tell you something', Barkat replies.

'Then please tell me quickly. This place does not seem safe so I want to go back home early', she says.

'It is a safe place and today is Eid. Nissar, the forest guard, has been instructed not to allow anybody here, so relax', Barkat assures her.

'I too have many questions for you. How do you manage to stay safe? How do you get your hideouts? How do you manage these favours and through whom?'

'It is easier for me to remain unnoticed because I stay away from social media. I don't expose myself like newly turned militants. My identity card says I am Shamsi, son of Kabul Deen, working as a manager in private hospitals run by Salliqa. I can go anywhere to check private hospitals. My gun operations are over. I am on the monitoring team to look after injured boys', Barkat says.

'Ohh, this is news to me. I don't know if I should trust you', replies Tahira.

'It's up to you. I am answering all your questions. Here in Kashmir, relationships are blurred and dealings are fluid. You can be an extremist, as well as a healing moderate. You can kill a person and you can also woo his family. You are everywhere and anything in a given time. You can talk Kashmiryat in one breath at a public place and you can speak of Shariat in the mosque and privately. Have you seen opposite and parallel lines meet anywhere? They do here in Kashmir. Hurriyat is as friendly to you as to the Indian state and Pakistan is as much your enemy as is the NC. PDP is as good to you as BJP is good for Hindus in Kashmir. These are all complementary and colliding structures where religion and science have come to finish you and politics does the muddling. Here, we want neither Islamic fundamentalism nor ethnic *azadi*. The mystification of the two has found not only a connection to the politics of resources and power but has made each one of you greedy while consuming religion day and night. Years back, when the mountains were closed, boundaries were tight and there were no visual pictures or social media, Kashmiris used to laugh at themselves and fool others with their lies. Now their lies do not befool even themselves. Therefore, they have lost the ability to laugh at themselves. Others know it and use it to their advantage, be it Pakistan or India, or even their own rivals in power. If there is killing, it does not hurt anyone except the family of the deceased. There is nothing like silent majority in Kashmir. It is noisy preponderance, in which everyone is complicit'.

'You are leaning towards becoming a *kalandar* (foreteller)', laments Tahira. 'You know that children in Dardpora play "terrorist games". *Jihadi* fervour is construed in marriage songs and children's play. *Jihad* is legitimised in public through mosque loudspeakers. Indoctrinated infrastructure of *jihad* is flourishing in schools and mosques; it does not take us anywhere. If you say anything against them, you are labelled as *kafir*. We have lost everything. Our men are either dead or have gone missing. They call us half-widows and look down upon us. We are stigmatised. Our men are killed; our women are exploited and thrown away like trash and even our children are seduced in the name of *azadi*. Our world moves round this puzzle: how to eke out a living to look after young children and how to save them from radicalisation. Most of us have turned mad. Who has done it? We are not indifferent to the source of our peril. Our parents and grandparents have shared their life experiences of a peaceful and happy Kashmir with us. People in neighbourhoods were our own people though they were *Battas*. Now everything has changed. Since 1989, unknown maulvis started coming to newly built mosques and guns were given to our children and men.'

'I know that villages close to the border have suffered immensely,' Barkat says. 'To my utter shock, families are not united against the cruelty even after losing so much. Why do you not unify, at least to put your problems before Muslim organisations and the government? You should take help from wherever it comes'.

'You don't know the story of our village. It had ten *Batta* families, five hundred Muslim Sunnis and five Ahmadiya families on the one side and four Shia families on the other side of the village. Gujjars lived on the mountains a few miles away. There were a good many of them, spread over the ranges. *Mauj* said that until 1989 we all lived happily, hardly bothered about our identities. *Battas* had land and jobs, Ahmadiyas too had jobs and land. We had land, some were teachers and had skilled occupations, while Gujjars had cattle and maize crop on the mountains. Demarcations were without any malice.

'This changed abruptly. Children in school, daily wage earners and people in skilled occupations—like tailors, masons, carpenters and porters—were told that they should go for army training and wage war against

India. They were given huge amounts of money for *jihad*. Islam came to stay and the so-called Kafir Raj vanished. We had two maulvis, one from Kanpur and the other from Shahjahanpur. They persuaded our families to send boys across the border to learn about Islam. Initially, a few *Batta*s were killed. Their sin was that they were not Muslims and they might have been informers. This violence made them flee, leaving behind their houses full of household goods. Then we had *mujahideen* who were more interested in land, marriage and financial matters as per their own laws, which resulted in estrangement and friction in different organisations. There was no government to administer.

'Since the 1990s, the whole social landscape has been changing. First, we had Al Barq *mujahid* (mostly comprising Gujjars), then Hizbul Mujahideen from our locality, guest *mujahideen* from Pakistan, and the Kashmir Liberation Force. They became operational in the area. A fratricidal war between the groups and clashes with security forces killed most of them. Gujjars who were living in the mountains got rich, started taking over *Batta* lands and bought new lands in our neighbourhood too. It became a perpetual war. We remained alive to rue our lot and weep over the deceased. The huge amount of money with these unemployed young people—some Gujjars and some from the plains—altered the stability and tranquility of our society. The number of males started decreasing gradually while women were left alone to fend for their kids and elders. Since Dardpora is close to the Line of Control (LoC), one of the routes used by militants on both sides to cross the border and reach Kupwara was through Dardpora. Our women were exposed to unknown men. Children and old parents have become vulnerable in the absence of men. These unknown men use them for the fulfilment of their lust or for information in exchange for small favours in cash or kind,' says Tahira.

'True, you can think about unity and revolt only when you have your men standing beside you. The burden of responsibilties and economic deprivation has made you weak and divided. We still have a hard time to face. The *umma* is divided. Those whose alms make us fight for *jihad* treat us like slaves. Kashmiris may think that they are superior and sophisticated but if they do not stand up for themselves and respect their ancestry and origin, they will always face this humiliation. Saudis look down upon us. I'll read you the write-up of a journalist who is a Muslim. He writes the same things that Moen and I experienced over there. Let me read it for you:

> Muhammad Bin Suleiman believes that Pakistanis are the slaves of the Arabs. Suleiman is also the Defence Minister of Saudi Arabia. This statement

> proves that Saudi looks at every other Muslim country with the 'converted-Muslim' country perspective. Muslims from India, Pakistan and Bangladesh are called 'Hindu-Muslims' in Saudi. They consider the Muslims from these 3 nations to have converted to Islam from Hinduism. The Indian, Pakistani and Bangladesh Muslims are also called as 'Al-Hindi-Muskeen' referring to them as second-grade Muslims. The differentiation in the system is an open fact. Arabi Muslims are preferred to 'Hindu Muslims', be it any job or top post.

This is the reality. Instead of understanding this inferiority forced by the *umma* upon us, we try to be more Muslim by being more primordial and least progressive. We should have been a prideful community of the sub-continent, living with dignity, but our leaders and political elites have no knowledge about it and they have no international exposure to experience it. They rely on alms from the Arab world, live on blame games and play up their victimisation. It is unending. Besides, the Shia-Sunni split is a worldwide competitive division. I do not know where our leadership is blindly guiding us.'

'You are terrifying me. It means that we are slaves at every junction. In my village, we are slaves of men of the community. Out of the village, they say that we are the slaves of Hurriyat and Hurriyat says that we are the slaves of India and then you say that we are the slaves of the Arab world also. How will we transcend this entire slavehood?' asks Tahira.

'We can try to bring joy to the parents whose sons and daughters have abandoned their homes in illusions of *azadi*. The time has come to save our younger generation, here and wherever they are in the world', responds Barkat.

'What about our sacrifices? On a daily basis, our young boys are being eliminated. Will Hurriyat take back its march of martyrdom? I wonder if we have any way out. Shujaat (Bukhari) raised the same questions and he was silenced. In future too, whoever raises these issues would be killed. It is better to be in oblivion and be directionless because all the paths cage us and put us in the queue towards the realm of uncertainty', Tahira says.

Barkat stares at her beautiful face and is impressed with her insights. He desperately wants to confess his feelings for her but does not dare. They eat the bread that Barkat brought and then call the autorickshaw driver who had dropped them here. The driver says he would reach in fifteen minutes. In between, Tahira goes to the washroom to put on her hijab. When she comes back, Barkat musters the courage to look into her eyes and confess his feelings. Before he can utter a word, the driver honks. The moment is lost and he moves to open the front door but Tahira pulls his hand back. She kisses the back of his right hand and says, 'Whenever you wish, call me. This is my number. I like your company and our interactions. *Khuda Hafiz.*'

Her gesture fills Barkat with happiness. He tightly embraces her, then kisses her forehead and said, 'I shall soon call you. Do come to meet again. I like spending time with you.'

Barkat opens the door and Tahira sits in the auto-rickshaw. Barkat gives the driver some money and instructions to take Tahira safely to her place. Barkat looks after the vehicle till it is out of sight and then moves towards his abode in the jungle.

Parash is amazed to see Husna and Shankar together at the Amritsar conference. All the time, Husna clings to Shankar like a midsummer shadow. She is unmindful of the gaze of those around her even during dinner in the club. There are Muslim students noticing her but she is willfully exhibiting her colourful glass like a rose spreading fragrance in the party. She is extraordinarily beautiful and Shankar is basking in her lovely, vibrant company.

They have invited Parash to accompany them for a visit to the Golden Temple. During the pilgrimage, he interacts with Husna and is convinced she has the mettle and intelligence to cope with any situation. Out of curiosity, Parash asks her why she openly drank during the dinner when it could land her in trouble. There were a few Muslim students who were observing but not participating in the cocktail party. Her reply is strange: 'I want to show them that I am a rebel, I make my own choices in life.'

Her confidence amuses Shankar but Parash is not convinced about this open rebellion. Parash knows that Kashmiri society does not approve of this conduct of one of their own. Women cannot do such things openly, violating the rules of religion and cultural norms.

Although Shankar is Husna's supervisor and they have valid reason to be in these academic gatherings, Parash knows that it is difficult for a Kashmiri Muslim woman to travel freely from place to place and university to university with a Hindu man. Moreover, Husna gives every indication that she is fond of Shankar and Parash feels that there is more between them than meets the eyes. He knows that human relationships become visible when they exude an aura of warmth and possessiveness.

A year later, there is an abrupt call from Shankar. He is blabbering, 'What is this Kashmiri mind, Parash? Husna is so indecisive. How long can we go like this?'

'Shankar, I know that she likes you. But in Kashmiri Muslim society, Indians and Hindus are considered *kafir*. Therefore, it is not only the cultural difference that she has to overcome but also the perception that marrying a non-Muslim means surrendering to an enemy. It must be a difficult decision for her to make', Parash replies.

'What should I do? It has been two-and-a-half years and nothing has moved due to her fickleness', Shankar says sadly.

'Wait and see in the ensuing couple of months, something good might happen for the both of you. By the way, where is Husna?'

'She is in Kashmir but she is unhappy. She has informed me that she would come back in the second week of September. She was crying on the phone but is unable to take a stand for herself', replies Shankar.

'Yes, Kashmir has become a strange place. Nothing is in its rightful position. Without a normal life, the collective pain due to misconstrued fear and shadowy uncertainties lead to more suffering. Husna is in a setting where she senses that her relationship with you is meaningless. Other than disinformation and religious primordialism, the observant realities are the individual narratives and the collective misfortune which is against Hindus', Parash states.

'What should I do then, Parash?' Shankar laments.

'You cannot leave her. It would create more hollowness within you. So wait for her to come to a decision and try to understand her. Other than her physical charm, she has a language of uncertainty and dilemma of consistency. It is only you who can decipher it. I can only give you signals and not shall be able to guide you', Parash advises.

'Parash, when are you coming to Delhi?' asks Shankar.

'Possibly in the third week of September', Parash replies.

'Good. Husna will also be here. It would be nice if you talk to her. She respects you', Shankar says.

'Okay. Bye then'.

'Bye, Parash.'

Shankar's family is a typical liberal intellectual Brahmin family from south India. All three members—mother, father and brother—are professors. Both the brothers have striking resemblance to each other. While his brother is happily married and stable, Shankar had a failed marriage. It is a matter of concern for his parents that he is dating a Muslim girl who seems hesitant to commit to marriage. They want him to settle down.

Shankar is about to go for his evening walk when he gets a call from Husna, who immediately says, 'I am walking in the garden because my mind has become blank. Father is retired and mother has become more unpredictable in her conversations; sometimes she loses her cool and at times remains silent. Altaf has also joined the Salafi movement of Al Hadis and the atmosphere at home has become sulken. He does not want me to go to Delhi and insists I should do a school job here in Kashmir. They will not support my studies outside the Valley. I am terribly upset', Husna cries.

'Why don't you talk to your parents and try to convince them about your future plan?' Shankar suggests.

'It is difficult to talk to my parents. They only want to talk about getting me married. They have been approached by a rich family whose son is in the cloth business. What would I do with their affluence?

I shall die if I do not marry a person with intellect and understanding. I clearly told them that I do not want to marry before submitting my doctorate thesis. I just want to run away from this place', Husna says sadly.

'You need to decide what you want to do with your life. When you are in Delhi, Kashmir controls your emotions and in Kashmir you miss JNU and my company. It is you who has to decide about your future. I am always ready to help. You can continue to work in my project. If you come, I shall release your fellowship of two months. You need to take a stand for our relationship too. Nothing is hidden from my family', Shankar says.

'Ok, I see my brother coming, bye', Husna hurriedly says and disconnects the call. The abrupt end to the conversation makes Shankar uneasy. He goes to the living room where his mother is watching the evening news. The TV anchor is giving details about stone-pelting and religious radicalisation in Kashmir. Shankar sits on the sofa and says, 'Ma, the news is disheartening. Husna was also talking about the manufactured problems at home'.

'Yes, the situation in Kashmir is always the same. By the way, what did you both decide?' she asks her son.

'Her family is against us. Therefore, it is difficult for her to take any decision', Shankar replies to his mother.

'I do not have any problem with Husna but I think that she is too fickle-minded. She might not prove a good wife if she does not control and channelise her emotions and conduct. Better take some advice from your Kashmiri friend. I am nervous about it. Despite staying together for such a long duration, she is not ready for long-term commitment. God knows when I would see you happily settled like your brother', his mother says sadly.

Shankar changes the topic. 'Ma, give me a cup of tea, I feel sleepy. I have to finish a book review'.

Back in Kashmir, Husna is alarmed by her mother's words that she can no longer continue her studies, unless she understands her boundaries and mission. She warns Husna not to even think of marrying her Hindu supervisor, who she says would burn her alive after some years. She says they always do it with their brides. According to Husna's parents, the best thing for her is to discontinue her PhD and appear for the Kashmir Administrative Service (KAS) examination.

Early in the morning, when her father and brother go out, she comes to the kitchen where her mother is working and says, '*Mauj*, I have to go back to Delhi. I need to finish my synopsis and prepare for the JRF (junior research fellowship) test too. I cannot work on my supervisor's project forever'.

'You do whatever you want. We are not against your studies but you cannot marry your Hindu supervisor. We want you to marry because your father has retired and is not in a position to finance you for long.' her mother says.

'I want to go to JNU and complete my doctorate. I have no plans to marry now. I don't want to get married unless I find a person of my taste and liking', Husna replies agitatedly.

'You have entered your thirties. Do not listen to these Hindu boys and girls in JNU. Islam does not allow us to keep our girls unmarried. Choose friends among Muslim students,' Ruby says.

Altaf enters in the room. He seems a little disturbed. He ridicules his sister for carrying on her PhD without clearing the fellowship test, NET. Husna does not say a word to him. Instead, she stands up and tells her mother, 'I am leaving for Roena Apa's place. I'll have my food there'.

Altaf retorts that there is a shutdown call from Hurriyat. Since public transport is not plying due to the shutdown, Altaf drops her at Roena's house. Roena's husband is a deputy Secretary in the Jammu & Kashmir administration. Her two sons are in the US and she works in an orphanage. Roena is a resourceful person for the young girls in universities outside the Valley who look upon her as a mentor

'Welcome, Husna. You have been here for the last one month but did not come to see me. I want to know how much work has been done in JNU', she says the moment Husna enters her house.

'Apa, life is tough. We have some friends who assist us in editing a journal where we voice our concerns. Gradually, political support will come. It is a long-drawn battle. We cannot openly launch the anti-India tirade and put our careers at stake', Husna states.

'You career is your mission. Your job is assured with us. It does not matter whether you have a PhD or not. You have to play the role for which you are sent there. Safina will join us soon. Maybe Bilal would also come. Boss needs the progress report for further release of funds. I take it that you were able to brainwash and convince your supervisor to write articles against the oppression and populism of Modi Sarkar,' Roena says.

'Apa, we are trying but we don't have much success. They are against the ruling party but they are not anti-India. They have been toeing our line but that has limitations. The students have to take up careers later. They do not want to join NGOs here or the corporate world elsewhere. I did my bit. But some of them are so nice that it becomes difficult to lie, again and again', Husna replies.

'I know, Husna. You have played your role well. Now you have to make that professor write dissertations of some students who can toe the line. I need not elaborate on it. Let him guide five students on oppression of Kashmir. We will get it published from reputed publishers. This will help us in the long run. You don't have to take part in violent protests. Your mother is worried that you roam around till late hours with him. We are not worried about it. You do whatever you want but do not promise any long-term commitment unless the high command clears it', Roena informs her.

'My heart is full of conflicting emotions,' Husna thinks. 'I am a symbolic representation of the new normal Kashmiri educated woman who has multiple roles, each role contradicting the other and giving blurred signals. In Kashmir, my life is surrounded by fear, shame and veiled patriarchy and I have no individuality; in JNU, I am acknowledged as a liberated woman'

Instead of giving voice to these thoughts, she simply nods her head in agreement and says, 'Yes Apa, I need to participate in more academic activities with him. He is a great orator and his speeches generate public opinion which we can exploit for our cause'.

Safina and Bilal together enter Roena's lavish drawing room. Bilal greets Husna with a broad smile. Safina hugs her and said, 'My God, you have done such a brilliant job. The spark of the protest against India and the ruling government in prominent universities of India is still alive'.

Husna smilingly says, 'We are simply playing our part in the mission to bleed India. But administrations in most of the universities have changed and have become stricter about discipline and dissent. We play word games but there are limitations. Nothing remains hidden in this era of digital maneuvering; cyber surveillance makes it difficult to blur the manipulations. Also, the continuation of anti-India tirade requires huge funding and sustained support which is not sufficiently available these days. Each one of us was expecting a big military intervention which never happened. These people from across the border are trying to save their faces by providing only covert support.'

Bilal agrees, 'We are always waiting for their funds and commands. We are nothing but a means to an end. It has made us lonely and desolate.'

Roena is silently listening to their conversation and does not look happy about its direction. She stands up and brings an envelope from her room. She gives it to Husna saying, 'We cannot rest until we bring ruin to this country that has subjugated us since 1947. You should intermingle with talented academicians, professors and research scholars and gain their sympathy by playing the victim card. You should then try to woo them and spread the canon of "intolerance". We need to escalate polarised clashes and highlight the Kashmir issue in all academic activities, be it journals or conferences. You are part of a mission in which Boss has invested a huge amount of money. Islam does not allow us to rest until the mission is complete. Also, the martyrs' sacrifices call us all the time. They should not go in vain. We have to be sincere and devoted to the cause'.

She shifts her attention to Safina and asks, 'What message have you brought for us?'

'This year, twenty students are ready as per the requirement. They need to have a workshop before they are sent to various universities. Their one-month training course is also over. This time, three universities in the south and four in the north have been targeted. The students know where to go and what to do. Admissions are already sought and all the fees have been paid.'

For the next half an hour, Bilal and Husna talk about their families. Their eyes are moist and their voices low, while Safina talks to Roena about the literature to be handed over to the students going to study in universities outside Kashmir. A carton of papers had come from across the border, specifically to be given to Roena with instructions. Roena keeps the papers away and then they have a sumptuous lunch with red wine. After lunch, Roena bids good-bye to her guests.

In the evening, Mir Sahib comes to enquire about the students' plans. Roena says, 'This time, the children do not seem excited about their roles. Optimism and passion are missing. They are getting weary day by day. If possible, you should try to meet them'.

'Big Pir has given my name to them. I have tried my best to see that their wishes are fulfilled but the movement is fizzling out. In Governor's Rule, one has limitations. We have to be safe also. We are all under the gaze, from "here" and from "there" as well', replies Mir Sahib.

'I have given grants to Husna', Roena informs her husband. She adds, 'I hope you do not get trapped in this'.

At that moment, someone calls Mir on the phone. 'The children should get protection from the state if something untoward happens to any of them outside the Valley," the caller says. "Last time, the boys in Punjab had to wait till we put pressure on you people. Now we rely on you in the new dispensation', the caller says.

'We are with you', states Mir.

'That is better for us. More the deaths, greater the wedge and better shall be the fallout. Peace, harmony, Kashmiriyat should be praised but on ground it should be despised', comes the reply from the other end.

'Sahib, all right, I'll talk to the group. *Salam*', answers Mir Sahib.

Before disconnecting the line, the caller praises Roena for her contribution towards the movement and informs that their agents would highlight the UNHRC report about the 'mass cruelties' of the Indian army.

'Engineer Sahib has been given the task in the public sphere, but you should take care of academic and administration aspects which are its bolts and nuts', he further instructs before disconnecting.

Mir Sahib is not pleased with this sudden call. He says to his wife, 'This Brigadier will not allow us to live peacefully. How should I get out of it? You have been unnecessarily nice to him'.

'You introduced him to me. You asked me to be cordial and pleasing to him. How am I responsible if he does not spare you? He had invited me to Lahore, but I did not go. The children could have not settled in the US without his generosity. We need to show gratitude for his help'.

In 2015, Roena had specially invited the Brigadier to spend autumn with them. After his visit, Junior Pir had facilitated Mir Sahib to qualify for KAS. He was placed in strategic administrative posts and promoted to Secretary level in a short span of time. Roena had relatives in Pakistan, national as well international links, and she had made a difference in gathering the threads of resistance.

Bilal is even more disillusioned and disappointed after leaving Roena Apa's house. He feels that the *Azadi* Movement has become a business where elites thrive with power and position and the unprivileged endure privations day and night, hanging onto the promise of good in the after-world. Like him, many have gone into oblivion and most of them had met untimely deaths.

Their parents wait with moist eyes and sunken cheeks, whereas children of elites like Roena are dear to everyone in a cherished safe country. Their future is bright and their parents talk joyfully about them over a glass of wine.

In his frustration, he calls Safina and says, 'Our networking is perfect and we all are sincere, but our agenda is not visible to us. Are we to live and die for a privileged lot that enjoys life and has power and social positions at the cost of our blood? It has been the case for decades and it would go on for centuries, "for we cannot allow the blood of our martyrs to go waste". It is pious to remember them "for our accounts in the world hereafter" so that our leaders can retain what they have consolidated over the years.

'I felt strange at Roena Apa's house. On the surface, she was kind to us but her instructions were humiliating. She was dismissive about our concerns and her kindness seemed cloaked in steely ruthlessness. I felt as if she was patronising us'.

'You should not think like this. It will make you sad. They have their roles, chosen and given by Boss. Without their positions and power, we cannot survive even for a day. They are our partners. You should not see their big bungalows and luxurious lifestyle. They too are caged. I am sure that, given a choice, they would also like to come out from this mess. We all are suffering in this circle of *azadi*. Do not dislike them. They are living in misery. Some of us have burnt our cards and have to go on like this. We need something that is not in sight, the agenda. Without the agenda, the agencies are useless', Safina consoles.

She asks Bilal to meet her at the same building near the mosque next weekend.

Early in the morning, Barkat is informed that a boy will take him to meet the guest at a nearby place. He is asked to get ready in ten minutes and wait under the chinar tree near the stream so that the boys do not get to know Barkat's hideout. Barkat senses something unusual. He eats a lot of dry fruits, takes his pistol and goes to the tree near the stream. The boy escorts Barkat to Budnambal at Haji's place, amidst the lush green meadows.

The boy leaves and a local Gujjar takes Barkat inside a cottage where Brigadier Kamal is waiting for him. He managed to cross over a few days after postponing his visit. They warmly greet each other and sit down to talk business.

'Barkat, you have been on this mission for ten years. A good part of your life has been spent like a nomad in these scenic meadows. But you are serving the *deen* and the country. We are proud of *mujahideen* like you', says the Brigadier.

'Sir, why did you suddenly want to visit?' asks Barkat.

'Back home, civil is in disarray. Only the boots can draw up the blueprints. We have some gains but also a misinformation campaign against us in the Valley. I would like to discuss some issues with you today and tomorrow. We have a meeting with the Pir's men. I want you to come with me', says Brigadier Kamal.

He continues, 'Barkat, Kashmiris are like Bengalis. They pretend to know everything under the sun and boast about it too. We should never involve them in decision making'.

'We have been able to manipulate the youth in north and south districts, but the city people are now arguing. They bring this dialogue, Sharmas and Sinhas[24] in between the boys and the Pir. This has made the workpad unclean', Barkat replies. 'Kashmiris are greedy. They quench their thirst for money by playing the victim card. They take a share of *zakat* for their families. Big Pir allows it as long as it does not hamper the mission. We have our checks and balances. They are best in making noises. That is why they are given the role of lamenting which is a significant catalyst for forging grounds suitable for our mission.' Barkat adds.

'True, they like mourning and commemorate it with timidity inside their homes. They blame us in their private conversations. The people in the city say that driving out Pandits has proven costly whereas villagers

---

24 A reference to interlocutors sent by the central government from time to time.

are happy with the houses, orchards and lands of Pandits', comments Brigadier Kamal.

'The Kashmiris do not understand that they have no space for manoeuvring the moral space like in 1965. We do not want Kashmir to be a *Reshi* Veer, a place of Sufi saints. The threads of history are torn apart and in return, we have given them the trash of that community, so that in due course of time, the pyramid of stratification would get altered. The glory of Kashmiri Pandits would get erased from the pages of history. We do not oppose their return. They would not be able to revive the so-called glorious culture they boast about. They are now an unskilled lot who are eager to take even insignificant menial jobs. In a few decades, they would become our subalterns. We need them till Kashmir is annexed. It would alter the discourse about Pandits of Kashmir. Therefore, Kashmir Pandits who want to return are not our target. Our target is the so-called intellectuals of our community who behave like Kashmiri Pandits', he expostulates.

'I think Kashmir is hugely divided today, which makes it difficult to manipulate and provoke them against India. The dropouts, addicts and unemployed low-class people are lured by our men whereas the upper class and well-to-do youths of the city ridicule them. The south is different from the north and the city is the centre that does not hold the peripheries. They accuse us and these boys of the south for bringing drugs to Kashmir,' Brigadier Kamal says sarcastically.

'Barkat, we do not want to end this movement. This is our jugular vein. Pakistani army and its Islamic organisations with ISI connections will cease to exist if this movement dies. The drugs cannot stop now. They supply has to be increased. It will only be an incentive, a mechanism to take Kashmiris away from their *Reshi* roots and argumentative potential.'

'Yes, drugs have made the difference. Shujaat's death would have not been possible without opium. The city dwellers and the intellectuals openly blame us. But why would we need to eliminate him'?

The Brigadier seems to change the subject. 'Barkat, where do you live in Pakistan?'

Barkat lies, 'I was taken from the street and put in the madrassa of Bahawalpur. I was given training at a very young age and since then I have been sent for operations.'

'Ok, you are a true Pakistani. You do not know these Kashmiris. We made PDP win elections through our boys. We supported local parties to come to power so that they play their roles in administration and in changing the mindset at the ground level. We never target those who enjoy power in the Valley because they are needed for our anti-Indian operations tacitly or openly. However, some of them try to outsmart us. They became rich and powerful with our help and then they start to betray us. Why would an independent Kashmir be acceptable to us? Should a middle path be their prerogative? Musharraf had to go for this reason. They should pay back for the loss of our three wars, thousands of martyrs, division of the country as well as the money. Then only would it come to an end', says Brigadier.

'Sir, I feel that we shall not be able to take it by force as Kashmiris are too divided to become one challenging group to bother India. We are doing what we can but that too is not sufficient to take Kashmir away from India. What is the line of thinking in this regard?' Barkat asks.

The Brigadier considers Barkat a brave Pakistani who had seen martyrdoms and enemy blood and heard songs of patriotism from his childhood without family, enjoyment or a stable life. He decides to share the reports of the secret files which have been endorsed by ten generals at different points of time in Pakistani history. He says, 'This year, the same issue has been discussed repeatedly in the Core Commanders Meeting. It is a bone of contention between civil and military. All the ten generals who endorsed the report of the secret file agree that Kashmir is a jugular vein. The battle for Kashmir should continue and even the idea of an independent Kashmir should not be acceptable. The birth of Kashmir as an independent state would be a loss for Pakistan.

A part of Kashmir is already annexed by China and an independent Kashmir would end the very centrality of Pakistan as a nation-state. Its ramifications would be costly and the purpose of our army would be defeated. We know India will not leave it. It is a long-drawn-out Cold War between India and Pakistan as wars have lost their credence. Kashmir, in its current chaotic situation, is our strategic asset. There should be no solution to the Kashmir problem. Kashmir within India suits us more than its independence or its control by China, directly or indirectly. Our foreign policy, our economic axis and our consensus pivot on Kashmir. It keeps India in check, China is with us and the West is on our heels. Internally, it gives the army its meaning and centrality and keeps civilian tongue in check. A cursed Kashmir with the sufferings of its people is our asset.

'This is the conclusion of a well-thought and well-researched report that remains at the core of army HQ, as a policy frame for continuation of their line of thinking. The common people cannot understand it. You need army intellect or vision to understand the conundrums of the sustainability of Pakistan. If Pakistan has to survive, Kashmir has to remain like this. The settled Kashmir is problematic for us. We do not want to fight an open war with India.'

'What should be the project then?' Barkat asks.

'It's quite simple. The movement should not lose momentum. Our civilisation is based on primordial values. Since India gave them pen and paper, they became argumentative. Their educated middle class is essentially sceptical, doubting any and every thing. They believe in stratification and emphasise rural-urban differences in daily life. They have marked south Kashmiris as stone-pelters. They are by nature a community without gratitude. We should give guns to them and make them spill blood, then alone there will be homogeneity and the faith shall take root,' replies Brigadier Kamal.

'Sir, how do you know these things?' Barkat asks in awe.

'Barkat, I was deputed to Stanford for two years. I have been working in the Research Cell of Army HQ for the last ten years. My experience of working in this field for such a long duration has taught me everything', boasts Brigadier Kamal.

At that moment, Haji comes to inform about dinner being served in the other room. Brigadier Kamal asks Haji to bring dinner to his room after an hour. He smiles at Barkat and says, 'I like my vodka but I don't want anyone to know. Come to my room which is in another cottage. It would be safe to drink there'.

Evening sprawls over the autumn sky. The dense mountain forest gives Barkat a strange feeling of guilt. A high-ranking officer has opened up to him for the first time. He is so happy with him that he had offered him a role like Roena's and an opportunity to settle down in Kashmir on the pretext of business. Barkat is being given the option to quit operations. However, for another year, he would have do a monitoring job without touching the gun. He remains with the Brigadier till midnight.

In the morning, Barkat gets ready for the meeting and goes to Brigadier's cottage. 'Morning, sir, are you ready?' he asks.

'Yes, Barkat. We will leave in fifteen minutes. There is no hurry. But nothing remains secret here in Kashmir and we need to be careful.'

'Yes, sir. the venue for the meeting has changed because there was an army operation going on since yesterday night at the scheduled place, Tunga Top in the upper belt of Kachama forests. A guest house was reserved today for the District Magistrate's meeting with the locals but the meeting has been postponed. That place is therefore chosen for today's meeting. JKTDC guest house is located near the banks of the Mawar river at Reshwari and is the main place of stay near Bangus', Barkat informs the Brigadier.

'Good. Pir's men do not know who I really 'am. They know us as members of an NGO team from Dubai working for the cause, so you need to use a face mask too', informs the Brigadier.

'Ok, sir. I shall cover my face and silently observe everything from the corner of the meeting hall,' Barkat says.

It is a half-hour walk to the main road and then another half-hour drive to the guest house. Five long-bearded men who seemed to be in their forties are eagerly waiting for the 'NGO activist' with grave expressions in the room. As they enter, Barkat instantly recognises Bilal seated in the far corner, opposite the manager's chair with an inquisitive expression. Immediately, the room is locked from inside.

'*Assalam Aleykum.* You people have been teaching lessons to our worst enemies including who is behind every misery, including killing of our dear friend Shujaat. Islam is the centre of the universe and Islamic countries are the greatest countries of the world. There is no dearth of funds. Today, I am handing over these tickets. This would fetch all the "books" you need for your "students". It should go to unidentified persons. The young boys should move in groups and the old and girls should come out in multitudes to protect them if they are attacked. LeT (Lashkar-e-Tayyeba) has already condemned the killing of Shujaat as a Hindu conspiracy. We have asked for an international inquiry for this crude murder. Inshallah, the truth will come out. The incident need not dishearten you in any way. Imams have been told to speak out about Hindu subjugation and Islamic injunction on us to overcome this regime. There is no need to open the schools. Shutdowns should continue. At least on the first two days, shops should not be opened and construction work should be stopped on Fridays. We are with you.'

He then asks one of the five bearded men to come forward and hands over a bag containing Rs 5 crore in Indian rupees. 'We do not have much time. If anybody wants to ask questions, they can ask directly.'

A phiran-clad person in his late forties stands up and says, 'You really are lucky to be in Dubai. We are grateful to you for your help and concern. However, please inform our masters that the *mujahideen* do not know the difference between *baithaks* (drawing rooms) and kitchens, which should be kept private. They break these boundaries and it has caused shame and disgrace to us. Our boys have also become like them. Of late, we find this drug menace has come to our homes. Its use has gone up. Opium is grown in the jungles and these *mujahideen* do not allow us to destroy these cultivations. They say it is forbidden in Islam. Is it proper to use drugs and make its users lose everything? They have even made our womenfolk prisoners of it. It is a big menace. Kindly help us out.'

'I understand these concerns but these are not questions to be asked until we get rid of the Indian army.

Our boys use it as a medicine to safeguard themselves. Moreover, we cannot tell our boys what to do what not to do when they are in *jihad*. They have been already taught about these things. If they do anything you do not like, you should not criticise them as it must be in line with *jihad*. If the boys visit your homes, what is wrong with that? You have to like them and protect them too. If they are in difficulty, where will they go? In case they forge friendships and become familiar with the locals, boys or girls, men or women, they must not be ridiculed. They are our assets for *jihad*. We are in a different kind of war in which everything is permitted. There is nothing like private and public spaces for these *mujahideen*. Each and every space is sacred for them. Do not discourage them.

'That is why I tell you that you should join *jihad* whole-heartedly and not half-heartedly. We all are there to help. We shall join you at a proper time too. That is all I have to suggest at this moment. Allow our boys to do what they decide, after all they are in *jihad*. *Allah Hafiz*.'

Brigadier Kamal and Barkat leave the guest house. The five men and Bilal remain in the room for another half an hour after the meeting to avoid the public gaze. Barkat sees Brigadier Kamal off at a Kupwara Chowk, where a car is ready to take him to the airport to board a plane for Kathmandu.

Barkat feels uneasy from the moment he sees Bilal sitting in the meeting room. He feels he has to extricate Bilal from this mess. He thinks to himself, 'Pakistan is in no mood to see peace returning to Kashmir. It has become such a tangle that even if India gives up Kashmir, Pakistan might not take it. The survival of its military which has become a mystic realm for its people, rests on Kashmir and so Kashmir should continue to bleed. There is no respite and they will not permit guns to be silent. Nobody in Kashmir will understand it. My Allah, what a world you have created and what a way to interpret your religion!'

Operations and attacks by militants, army encounters or shutdown calls by Hurriyat changed nothing. Barkat has no illusions about the dynamics of the movement. After his interaction with Brigadier Kamal, Barkat clearly understands the ground reality. He becomes sympathetic towards the youths of Kashmir getting wasted for an unsighted agenda. This new normal has seduced Kashmir. Disturbed by first-hand experience of the hopeless situation, he spends a quiet week at Nagmurg meadows, in the upper hills of Bandipore that connects it with Lolab valley. He books accommodation in the name of a compounder. The scenic beauty of the place, lush green oblique meadows covered by deodar trees gives him the feeling of an ancient *rishi* engrossed in *sadhana* (prayer) in order to attain spiritual bliss. The purity of Nature is at its best.

It is not surprising to find *bhang* (cannabis) and poppy being cultivated on hundreds of hectares of forest land near Nagmarg on Lolab side. Their cultivation started with the advent of *jihad* in the Valley. Its allure as a medicine and resource, troublemaker and toxin has become dear to the direct and indirect shareholders of *jihad.* Barkat finds the situation similar to that in the Swat Valley.[25] The Kashmiris have been quick to catch up with them in the race of reverse civilisational evolution.

The lush green grass of lonely meadows knitted with reddish crimson flowers make Barkat nostalgic. He thinks of his second *Babb* who used to wax eloquent about the spiritual bliss of this place. After sunset, his thoughts shift to Bilal. His youthfulness is shadowed by the darkness in the sky. He remembers Razz *Babb*'s command to safely bring back Bilal and decides to meet him with the same motive.

Up above the sky, the dark clouds change form and position and Barkat thinks of Tahira. He closes his eyes and imagines her sitting beside him. The thought of her escalates his desire to be with her in this beautiful place. He craves to make love to her in the lap of Nature. The stillness of the night has enhanced the roar of the flowing streams and the wild cries of animals from the nearby mountain and it adds a menace to the surroundings. Barkat slowly goes into his room, lights the battery lamp and drifts off to sleep.

On the third day of his stay, Barkat picks up his phone to call Bilal. Bilal is taken by surprise and says in a terrified voice, 'Is everything alright?'

25 A conflict-ridden region in Pakistan.

Barkat replies, 'All is well. I want you to come here tomorrow morning for tea but do not tell your companion about the visit'. Bilal senses something unusual but agrees to meet Barkat at his place.

Bilal arrives at 8 am. They have tea, eggs and maize bread prepared by a local man in his kitchen and then go outside. It is not chilly but a bracing autumn morning. Bilal picks up the conversation, 'This experiment of participatory *jihad* has also lost its vigour. We get daily updates of deaths of our boys without causing any effective loss to the army. All newspapers are pointing towards this fact. And on top of it, there is ever increasing thrust from across the border to do more and to bring fresh blood into militant groups.'

'Look Bilal, this has perplexed me for over a decade. What exactly is Pakistan asking us to do? I have come to the conclusion that Pakistan, which is controlled by its army, which does not want to relinquish the unmatched privileges that come with power and position. This is the history of Pakistan. Whosoever has questioned the army has been eliminated, whether in the Valley or in Pakistan. Be it a ruling politician or an established journalist or a popular human rights activist, he or she has to go. This is a reality that you have to understand. Since our hegemonic leadership has put us in their control and allowed them sway over us, they do everything to protect their interests. Our deaths do not matter to them', Barkat responds.

'I was shocked by the instructions from a Dubai NGO in a meeting organised by Hurriyat the other day', Bilal says to Barkat. Bilal obviously did not recognise Barkat there. Barkat does not say anything but tries to make him understand that the military in Pakistan has an aversion to civilians and their elected representatives. He explains, 'There are many things about this internal system that you do not know. This is not a religious war nor a war to claim territorial supremacy, but a war for retaining power and position. For them, it is a sustained business of economics and politics where religion is used as an instrument to give legitimacy for its continuation. Modern networking has fueled the flames of conflict of our inner thoughts. No one is genuinely interested in a solution for Kashmir. Whether it is Imran Khan or Nawaz Sharif, Bilal or any maulvi, Kashmir shall remain like this'.

'What should we do? We have a well spread network of boys and girls all over India who do not have guns but pens, voices, bodily warmth and cordialities. They even put their virtue on the line to supplement our young *mujahideen* in Kashmir. We had a little success too, but with these revelations, all of them would perish. Not instant deaths but by prolonged torture'.

'I think we have come a long way. What we need is introspection. You cannot voice your dissents openly or show your anger to anyone. Faiz has beautifully said it for us: '*Bjuz devangi vaha chara he kya hai...*' (There is no choice other than madness if wisdom and reason are not heeded).

'True, we are facing the death of politics in Kashmir. There is no need to go into its history. However, Kashmir is undoubtedly cursed. Sheikh Abdullah picked up Kashmir from cultural estrangement and put it in the basket of religious separation. This prompted Jamaat-e-Islami to sow the grains of political religion, for which Kashmir was a hostile soil before. This religion divorced culture to make the new religion of militancy which finally gave us guns to kill each other. If India had left us, where would we have gone and what would have happened to us? This is now the subject of conjecture and scepticism. This feeling of estrangement and disillusionment is striking at our hearts but there is no way to move out from it. The escape routes are blocked by drugs and the agencies working for their vested interests', says Bilal.

'This was done in 2006 and then in 2016 too. The same game will be repeated and new boys and girls would emerge with more venom against India and get deep into their disillusionment. The invisible agencies and their established structures have made it a permanent systemic functionality. Neither is India leaving Kashmir nor can Pakistan snatch it from India. India has not abrogated Article 370 to bring about structural change in its present position and Pakistan does not want any solution for Kashmir. The leaders will lie and our experienced *mujahideen* swear by martyrs' blood. It has become a vicious cycle without any end', Bilal says.

'This is not the full story. PDP's Mufti Mohd Sayed had the right intentions and he wanted to break the vicious cycle of disillusionment but electoral politics distorted his vision of the renewal of cultural potential to build a new Kashmir and his idea was never implemented. The greed to grab power made members of his party play foul at the ground level as they wanted to outsmart the opposition National Conference party. They sided with the militants. This resulted in the failure of the project of New Kashmir and the "Healing Touch" doctrine. He died and then Kashmir was back to square one.

'His daughter tried to do the same indirectly but it was too late to make corrections in the structural web of interests and poor Shujaat had to give up his life. This will happen again. Either we have to go into oblivion or we will be branded as traitors or Indian agents.'

'We need to think with logic and wisdom. The best thing we can do is spread the truth in schools, colleges and universities, so that our boys do not get trapped and disillusioned. They need to understand that escape from the competitive world is instant death. They have to go along with the competitive world, have political freedom and now, we need political bargaining. Respite from the present sense of defeat needs change of track. That possibility is there. There are Sharmas and Sinhas to bargain for what is achievable. Therefore, it is our own society that needs to change. We need to be honest. This new maulvi-mufti culture should go. True Islam means compassion and understanding of times and contexts. The chunk of Kashmiri Pandits who are bought back will not add to the diversity. They have no capacity to play the role which was played by Kashmiri Pandits during anti-monarchy movements and afterwards. They do not truly trust us at present. They are with Panun Kashmir which they would take if Kashmir is separated from India.[26] No matter how small in numbers a minority is, they can neither be eliminated nor can be ignored. Their logic will work. If Kashmiri Muslims are not safe in democratic India, how can Hindu Kashmiris be safe in Muslim Kashmir? It is a Pandora's box. It is better to compress the decades since 1989 till date and close it as aberration of history in order to allow new generations to live with dignity and pride. Peace has to come and guns have to go', says Barkat.

26 Panun Kashmir is a political party of Kashmiri Pandits seeking their own homeland.

He instructs Bilal, 'You should take your time and go home using the excuse of illness. Stay at home for a month and start some business. Once you bring your team back, we will discuss new plans.'

'How can I simply leave my team who took oath along with me and go back to my family? What would I tell them?' Bilal questions.

'Bilal, any oath taken in ignorance or by manipulation is not a real promise. Our religion is very clear about it. Instead of enlightenment, we have brought darkness and violence in Allah's name. We have to safeguard the image of Islam which has been tarnished by some ignorant and irreligious people for their vested interest. We have to work for the same mission but, instead of poisoning the hearts of Muslims with the untruth, we can enlighten them with proper religious teaching. Allah will be happy and you shall have peace and a sense of achievement. "*Jahan mai ism Mohmad says ujala kar dey*" (Kindle the light in the world with the name of Mohammad)', Barkat stresses.

Bilal considers the offer seriously. 'Should I tell Husna, Safina and other girls and boys to do what they want to do in future? Should I ask them to take leave from the mission for some time or should I tell them to quit it altogether?' asks Bilal.

'First, you tell your boys that you are not well and you would take rest for some time on instructions from the top. I shall manage that decision for you. Once you are back with your family, you take your time and gradually try to persuade your team to join our mission to clear the name of Islam.'

It is past noon and the two men witness the play of Nature beautifully unfolding itself in the open theatre of sky; sunshine plays hide-and-seek followed by sudden shadowy darkness, rain bubbles and again a bright, clear sky. They both are mentally exhausted and yearn for peace. They crave for home-cooked meals and salt tea, good company and joyful conversations. They both want to go back to their past where there was leisure and relaxation with no urgency. Bilal is convinced he must return and Barkat is relieved and happy about it.

Barkat says to Bilal, 'The best thing is to understand the present and work for the good of your people. We simply need to get away from this dance of death and agony and the business of politics and religion. Kashmiris are lucky in many ways. You are not like the Muslims of Pakistan and India. You have a vibrant educated middle class and existing traditional occupations. The bitter truth is that Kashmiris themselves have brought the Indian army out from its barracks. There is nobody other than Kashmiris in power or in services. There is not much Indianness left in the Valley. India has become ornamental here.'

Barkat wants to make sure Bilal does not waver. He continues, 'Nowhere in the world do citizens use guns and presume that the state will give rewards in return. Look at the umbrella of leadership which gives calls for shutdowns and protests: How many of them have international exposure and understanding of world history? Who knows them outside Kashmir? Even in Pakistan, people in private conversations call them a bunch of morons. Should you have such a hegemonic leadership which throws you in the deep sea to drown? They pretend to be wise and sagacious but the bitter truth is that most of them are the payroll agents of one organisation or the other. You and I only dance on the music of the religious nationalism they have played to seduce us', Barkat says.

Bilal is astonished to find that Barkat knows Kashmir so well. He is able to understand the myopic worldview created by the leadership over the decades which would not lead them anywhere. On the contrary, it would lead them back to medieval times or tribal modes of existence. Barkat had seen factional bloody conflict in Pakistan, travelled to Middle East countries and is now lost in the wilderness of this directionless movement in Kashmir. He can compare Kashmiris with the acumen of the conflicting communities in Muslim nations and is extremely sad for the fate of a community misled in the name of 'pure' religion.

In a late night conversation Barkat says, 'Bilal, you do not have to struggle for the basic needs of life like us. We risk our lives for food, shelter and clothing. Your problem is psychological. The restlessness of the youth of Kashmir is being manipulated by the affluence of the hegemonic class. It has given dynamics to traditional culture and the new-found religion which tasted sweet in the beginning is now a vinegary medication causing identity crisis', states Barkat.

Bilal understands that Barkat is not a typical *mujahid.* He asks in astonishment, 'How do you know all these things? For a *mujahid* who has spent a significant part of his life in war, you know way too much'.

'I was introduced to books in my teens. Since then, as a tribute to my Masterji, I try to read as many books as I can. My habit of reading has made me more analytical. A few years back, I stayed in Daryya, a damaged suburb of Syria, for 18 months. In that war-torn area, I read more books than I had read in the last five years from an underground secret library established by an engineer named Anas. He used to collect books from houses destroyed by bombing. It is there I read *Hamlet* and *Othello*, Rumi and Tagore. I like poetry too. Urdu *ghazals* fascinate me. I was amazed to find out about the reading habits of the young children there. Imagine setting up such a library in Kashmir. Kashmiris are living in an imaginary world with the realisation that it is not real. Still, they are not bothered because they get material affluence without working for it', replies Barkat.

'What would you do if you quit militancy'? asks Bilal.

'I want to go back to the place where I came from and work for orphaned children', Barkat replies with a smile.

'Will they allow you to leave everything and live independently'? asks Bilal.

Barkat smiles wryly, 'I have been working in this system for a long time and have crossed the age for that kind of restriction. I can quit anytime and restart my life anywhere in Pakistan, Bangladesh or even India'.

Husna is back in Jawaharlal Nehru University. JNU has changed from what it was in its halcyon days. In the first ten years (1975-85), there was no regimentation, allowing the flowering of a vibrant, intellectual ethos where even the diffident found a voice.

Post 2010, public spaces have different narratives of discussions and there is an unusual calm inside the campus. The new Vice Chancellor has stopped giving extensions to retired professors, presuming that their ideologies are Left-oriented. The move is a great loss for the academic world. Their scholarly insights and experiences are irreplaceable in the near future.

Overall, there is lack of difference of opinion in general which used to be the beauty of JNU. The students, especially career-oriented students, have altered their form of interaction too. Unlike in the past, students are always on guard during conversations.

Lately, there has been a change in Husna's behaviour towards Shankar. She has started spending more time with her friend Sleena from Kerala, with whom she is doing a German language course. Husna has stopped spending all her free time with Shankar. She avoids any public show of affection now. Earlier, when they were apart, she used to frequently message or call him. It has not stopped altogether but the intensity and passion are missing. Her fascination for him has lessened. Earlier, she would meet him every evening, either in his house or a cafe. Now, she avoids him.

Shankar, on the other hand, keeps asking her to take a decision about their future. After all, she is back in Delhi after two months. He had given her time to discuss it with her family and make up her mind once and for all. She gives him the same story on repeat mode—that she does not want to part ways with him but at the same time she does not want to displease her parents, who are against their relationship. Husna's ambiguity makes Shankar restless, robbing him of his peace of mind. He is a divorcee but young and handsome enough to marry again. He is an intellectual, a great orator and is loved by everyone in his circle. He has already told his parents about Husna and they accepted her reluctantly but gracefully. Shankar's mother gives gifts to Husna and many a time Husna visits their house. Now Husna's fickle-mindedness bothers Shankar's mother.

Shankar has no one other than Parash to discuss his messy relationship. He is eagerly waiting for his friend to visit JNU. He hopes that Parash's counseling would help him nudge Husna towards a decision.

Next morning, Shankar receives a message from Husna that she wants to meet him in the evening. He is happy and hopeful that their relationship still has a chance. Of late, the feeling of a widening chasm between them has saddened him. He misses the time when there was a natural flow to their interactions. He is haunted by her deep black eyes, curved sharp eyebrows and rosy lips. Her feminine fragrance is always fresh in his mind as if they have just made love. He craves not only her body but her companionship and conversations.

'Husna's growing friendship with Sleena has made her confident and less emotionally dependent on me', Shankar thinks. During breakfast, he sends a message to Husna saying he misses her. She replies with a simple 'Me too'. He promptly calls her to ask, 'What are you doing?'

'I'm having breakfast with Sleena. She stayed with me for the night', she replies.

'Ok, ok, carry on. I called you to inform about Parash's visit next Saturday. I have invited him for dinner with us. Please make sure that you are not otherwise engaged that day', he requests.

After the call, Sleena asks, 'What's new, Husna?'

'I feel broken, as if I fail in everything I do. Everyone is unhappy and dissatisfied with me. I have four fronts to face: my family, the *tanzeem*, Shankar, my conscience. It is like I am under pressure from all four directions. I have no escape. My family wants me to marry and settle with a Kashmiri Muslim and abandon my PhD but I don't want to do that; the *tanzeem* wants me to lure intellectuals like Shankar, spread anti-India venom for our cause but even that mission is incomplete; Shankar wants me to marry him which I can't; and then there is my conscience. I have made the situation worse by getting too deeply attached to Shankar. I feel guilty about deceiving an innocent person like him who is ready to sacrifice everything for me. What should I do and where should I go? My Allah!' Husna cries.

'Husna, listen to me. We did everything to complete our mission. They know it well. Now things have changed. We need to concentrate on our studies. We are always ready for our mission. But we cannot do anything openly and get blacklisted and ruin the image and honour of our family. I am a part of this mission too but I have told them that I will do it in my own way. You have gone too far with Shankar. After all, he is a *kafir*, no matter how good he is. You should save yourself from this emotional drama and blackmail. You cannot marry him. It will not only bring disrepute to your family but it would also be difficult to convince the *tanzeem*', says Sleena.

'I understand all these things and that's why I am in a dilemma. The mission of *jihad* is the ultimate priority, even if it means compromising with my virtue. I wonder how they could exclude my emotions, intellect and my natural instinct to live a good life, treating me like a means to an end. I am bound to lie all the time', says Husna dejectedly.

'We are all in multiple roles', Sleena advises. 'We have no choices, everything is decided by our religion. We simply can't break out of our circle and move to another orbit. Our socialisation and worldview has clipped our wings and we are meant to keep moving in this orbit and not take flight. You cannot be with Shankar because that means moving to the next orbit and taking a new flight. Shankar understands you like no other but you need to gradually distance yourself from him until the passion naturally dies between the two of you. You can focus wholeheartedly on the mission only when you break up with him'.

'Sleena, I am sure about one thing. Whether I go back or stay here, I am not going to marry anyone. This perhaps is the safest way for me. Let everyone judge me and put the blame on me'.

It is 10.10 am and Sleena has to go for classes. Husna has to prepare a paper on Kashmir for the next conference in Chandigarh. Shankar has suggested a title and helped her in framing the research design of her article. He has given her many good books to read on nationalism and ethnicity, including his friend Ashok's novel on Kashmir, *Nativity Reclaimed.* Husna always enjoys Shankar's company and wishes he had been a Kashmiri Muslim.

In the evening, Husna meets Shankar at the canteen near the main administrative building. Shankar starts on a neutral topic, 'The weather is so hot and dry. I feel exhausted all the time'.

'You should come to Kashmir with me. September is full of flowers and autumn lays a golden carpet of apples for lovers and welcomes them with a cool breeze. You would have respite from everything including the mad Sleena who always enquires about you', Husna says teasingly.

Shankar ignores the last and takes her earlier statement seriously. He asks, 'How can I go there with you? Your parents don't like me and I don't know anyone else. What would I do there?'

'Come on, become a Musalman. You will have a job in the university and I shall have you'. Husna jokes as they head towards the campus ring road for a stroll. It is a walk of forty minutes. The road is serene and calm in the evenings, dotted with only a few regular walkers.

Shankar replies, 'Not a bad idea. I don't want to lose you and even my parents won't mind it. You are my life, my jugular vein. Is it necessary to get converted? Is there no other choice? Can't we get married and still follow our respective religious beliefs? How does it matter?' Shankar asks.

'The world would have been so different and beautiful if only everything was so simple', she says bitterly.

Shankar, in a light mood but with serious intent, says, 'How tightly have these boundaries throttled you.' He sighs and recites Eliot:

> Let us go then, you and I,
> When the evening is spread out against the sky
> Like a patient etherised upon a table;
> Let us go, through certain half-deserted streets,
> The muttering retreats
> Of restless nights in one-night cheap hotels
> And sawdust restaurants with oyster-shells:
> Streets that follow like a tedious argument
> Of insidious intent
> To lead you to an overwhelming question...
> Oh, do not ask, 'What is it?'
> Let us go and make our visit

'I don't want to rush you into anything but I'm exhausted. You gave me hope. You were there for me when I was alone. You helped me overcome my nightmares. I had your shoulders to weep on and regained myself. Now I just want you to be mine. But I feel that you have changed', Shankar says.

'I am simply stressed. I have no job, my father has retired and my mother has become too peevish to understand anything. Do you think I'm being spared by my brother and parents for even suggesting the idea of marrying a *kafir*? I have nothing', Husna says bitterly.

'You should try to take a decision. You are not able to concentrate on your studies. If you cannot clear JRF, how would you clear KAS? I have managed this fellowship for you and I will try my best to get you a good job in some college. You should go look for relevant publications and try to finish your thesis', says Shankar, trying to knock some sense into her.

'I am trying my best. You don't know how difficult it has become for me to persuade my parents to allow me to come to Delhi. I told them that you were no longer my supervisor. I lied that some other professor is now guiding me. They think I have ended my relationship with you. I had no other choice than to lie about us. You have to be more understanding.' says Husna. She changes the topic and asks about his new book.

'I am still writing, another fifty pages are left. I am writing about the issue of divide which has been brought to the surface only after the new government came to power in 2014. Modi's intentions are well sold to his subjects but his populism might boomerang'.

'Remember, you promised me you would write a

pro-minority Left-oriented book about how minorities are unsafe and the poor have become vulnerable to Bhakt goons. I'm eagerly waiting for it', says Husna.

'I have given so many presentations on the emergent crisis in the country; the trust deficit in the institutions and the useless rhetoric of surgical strikes and demonetisation. In fact, my colleague Tatra was telling me that I am vigorously toeing a line which harms the country's interests. But I take it as my intellectual duty to see that India's evolutionary march does not come to a halt. My dissent is positive. I believe in an inclusive nationalism that does not crush differences. Be it Nehru, S Radhakrishnan, Abul Kalam Azad, Dr Zakir Husain or Rabindranath Tagore, they all worked for it. That is how India has grown over the centuries. We have undergone different transitions in history while rejecting things which we could not digest and retaining what could supplement our civilisation. I think you are also affected by the false information of your maulvis and muftis. But this is a scientific era which moves on market rationalism. It is finally the nexus of ideas and power that makes this world move', says Shankar.

'Kashmiris want separation from India and India promised a plebiscite in the UN; the Security Council passed the resolution, but we are still subjugated. We do not want to become stone-pelters but how do we protest when no other means work?' asks Husna.

'The UNSC resolution has given two options to Kashmiris: Stay with India or go with Pakistan. There is no third option. What would Kashmir achieve by getting annexed to a state like Pakistan? You have seen life here in Delhi. Don't be like your brethren of the Valley, who have many imaginary tales to narrate. These maulvis treat women as a commodity. They spit venom against Mehbooba Mufti because they are unable to accept her power and position. It is blind patriarchy that prevails in Kashmir. I don't say anything against the Book but in practice you lag miles behind. I have no objection to anything you do but I have a problem with your worldview which does not allow you to look beyond your community and geography. You have hatred for non-Muslims in your head and heart. Please come out from this mindset', says Shankar.

'Why are you saying these things to me? I am what I am and you have no right to humiliate me or demean my religion like this. I can also say that you are prejudiced and narrow-minded. I am a human being and I have emotions. I am not an issue which you can analyse to come up with a solution', explodes Husna.

There is an abrupt silence. The street light illuminates their faces that have opposite expressions; Shankar is trying to force a smile and lighten the mood but Husna has turned hostile and completely ignores Shankar. She walks swiftly towards her hostel. Once they reach the gate, Husna says loudly, 'Don't call me. I shall be busy tomorrow'. Shankar is baffled by the sudden change in Husna's mood. It was becoming more difficult to predict what makes her happy and what makes her sad. A normal conversation ends with a heated argument.

With a heavy heart, Shankar concludes that he is destined to have bad relationship experiences. In order to ease the pain, he calls Parash and asks, 'When are you coming? Have you fixed your schedule'?

'Yes, everything is planned and we are meeting on Saturday evening. We will have a nice time together', replies Parash.

'*Yaar*, I fail to understand Husna's mindset. Are all Kashmiri girls like her? She is nice and pleasant at one moment and starts snapping the next moment. Today again, a normal conversation ended in an argument. She does not argue logically but only cries and remains in victimised mode', says Shankar.

'I think she is passing through a phase where her conflicting roles have deeply affected her. You only told me that she had a very difficult past. Her father did not accept her as his own progeny. Try to understand how this experience must have affected her innocent mind and emotionally damaged her. You need to understand her current situation too. How insecure a Muslim girl coming from a conservative middle class family without any fellowship must be feeling. Your criticism, even with good intentions, provokes her. Therefore, give her time', advises Parash.

'No, I think that she has become whimsical. She once told me that she was expected to sit at home after graduation. Her brother, though younger than her, used to beat her. Her mother would stop talking to her for days together. It made her lonely and she started talking to animals and trees. But look at it from my point of view. I have given her everything she asked for. I gave her love, time, money and academic guidance too. Still, she is not sure about our relationship. My mother is worried and I'm unable to decide anything. Anyway, I hope she listens to you when we meet', says Shankar.

'You should stop worrying about it. Everything will be alright. Have a good sleep. We will talk about it in detail on Saturday', Parash assures Shankar.

Brigadier Kamal is very impressed with Barkat. After his return to Pakistan, he speaks highly of him during the briefing at ISI office in the Ojhri Camp. Barkat is recommended for the honorary rank of Colonel. Brigadier Kamal, in charge of Kashmir operations, himself gives this news to Barkat. In code words, he conveys the information along with conferring the freedom to take decisions regarding different aspects of the operation. Barkat is now accountable to headquarters only. He is supposed to send his report about developments and progress to the HQ in Ojhri when asked for it.

This favourable development is a boon and Barkat wants to exploit the opportunity. In his first decision, he puts the youth wing research programme on abeyance and asks Bilal to go home. The order is approved by HQ.

He instructs changing the name of *Valley* magazine and increasing its circulation in Kashmir. He proposes Bilal as its advisor. Barkat changes his hideout from Bandipore's dense forests to Sumlar village. He has been in Kashmir for over three years, yet he has managed to remain unknown to the public and intelligence agencies. His work now is to monitor the role of the main commanders and analyse the tasks of different organisations. Brig. Kamal had given him a large amount of cash to distribute among the commanders discreetly. Barkat's new hideout is a two-room *kotha* (cottage) in a Gujjar cluster of ten families. They rent it to him because he tells them he is an orphaned child of a Gujjar family from Banihal. In exchange, Barkat gives them homeopathic medicines he had brought from Baramulla.

The *kotha* becomes his safe, inconspicuous abode. A mobile and transistor were given to him when he came to Kashmir and was assigned a specific wavelength for the purpose of communication. He is fond of reading, always keeping some English and Urdu books on hand to read in his free time. He never talks about political issues or militancy with anybody.

Some local boys often help him in his household chores. He pretends to be poor and never refuses offers of free maize flour and rice from the locals. They think he is doing his Master's in English via correspondence and respect him. The local headman is informed that he is an orphan of *jihad* by some Pir in Banihal. The Pir asks the locals to allow him to live in peace.

A week has gone by. One fine morning, Barkat is sitting under a deodar shade in a contemplative mood. He has Jigar's *Atishe Gul* (a collection of Urdu ghazals) with him. '*Jaise har shai mai kisi shai ki kami pata hun mai*' makes him reflect seriously about the dynamics of day and night. Nothing gives him more joy than his long conversations with Razz *Babb*, who has a genuine understanding of the web of interactions. His promotion to the honorary rank of Colonel has brought him no joy. He thinks of the reasons the Pakistan army promoted him and feels self-loathing.

He remembers the difficult years in Syria, fighting the war and counting dead bodies. At that time, he hardly had any understanding of the Arab Spring, but was part of Salafi Jihadist groups including the Al-Nusrat Front. He remembers the pleased faces of commanders in Pakistan when they read the list of Shia Kurds and state forces sent to their graves. It was not a US-Russia war, but a war between Iran and Saudi Arabia. In short, it was a Shia-Sunni divide which had engulfed the Muslim world.

Here, many experiments had failed to bring Kashmir into total *jihad* mode. Despite huge funding, concealed budgets, proper monitoring by ISI and Pakistan army and non-stop political discourse run by public and private media houses, Kashmir could not become homogenised for insurgency against India because of its cultural contradictions, urban-rural divide, linguistic differences, class contradictions as well as the lag between traditional mindset of the community and forced worldview of the ideologues.

On top of that, Pakistan wanted to minimise the influence of Iran-backed *jihad* in Kashmir. Here again, PDP cut short the influx of Iran-influenced fighters. 'How many cuts would Kashmir get, if by any chance India decides to let it go?' he speculates.

He ponders over the latest report by a militant group, which would have one believe that there are unexpected stakeholders in the affairs of the Valley. Iran thinks it is a spiritual land of its Imams and therefore it is a religious duty to free it from Salafi influences, China links it with its big project One Road One Border (OROB). Abrogation of Article 370 would enable India to crush radical Islamic violence. And then, what about the claim of the original natives, the Kashmiri Pandits, who think that they are the real stakeholders? Therefore, the standoff suits all the stakeholders, including India and Pakistan. It is this report that has alarmed ISI enough to marginalise newly established Iranian influences in the Valley; Barkat was chosen for this secret project.

Shia influence is now becoming visible in Kashmir, especially in south Kashmir, which used to be a Sunni stronghold. He has to cut off funding for the Shia madrassas and encourage Sunni madrassas to engage more children. It is an experiment which was implemented in Karachi and yielded results. He thinks about how all the conflicts are for this world only and not for the world after it, and this bothers him. It is a war of domination and power; God is nowhere in the picture. '*Aur bechare mujahideen ko sirf wada-e-hoor*' (and the poor freedom fighters are fixated on the beautiful girls who await them).

He is about to go for lunch when he gets a call that Bilal has been sent home and his cell is dismantled. 'A good piece of news', he thinks. There is an atmosphere of happiness and joy at Bilal's place in Watapora, Bandipore. Rashid has also come from Srinagar and many other friends, old as well as new, are present in Muza's house. Previously, such receptions were given to those who had performed Haj but now, they are given to offspring who return after trips to unknown places to join militancy. Uzma and Razia look very happy and are busy receiving guests, relatives and a few neighbours too. They think that it is a miracle to see Bilal back at home. Muza and Zoya cannot stop stealing glances again and again at Bilal, who has lost a lot of weight and seems more mature due to his experiences of the last one year.

Next day, Bilal takes Rashid to the backyard to talk about Husna in privacy. Bilal says to his uncle, 'Husna should not continue her PhD in JNU if she has not been able to clear JRF. I think that we need passionate and honest qualified persons to run our newly established research centre and Husna can help me in publishing the journal *Morning Light*. I think it would be a waste of time for her to stay in Delhi without any genuine fellowship'.

Rashid is pleased by his suggestion and quickly inquires, 'Do you think she will abandon her incomplete doctorate? She has not been listening to her parents who have been asking her to quit right after she completed her MPhil in March 2017'.

'I think she needs an academic atmosphere: We shall try to give it to her', suggests Bilal.

'This indeed will be good for her parents who want her to settle down here in the Valley,' Rashid says happily, adding that a ray of hope and harmonious consensus are emerging in their conversations after years of discord and brooding.

They both head towards the house and see Hasan. 'What a joyful sight', calls out Rashid. They go inside, chat with others for an hour and then decide to take the blessings of Razz *Babb*. Rashid drives Muza, Hasan and Bilal to Razz *Babb*'s cottage. He is alone, the door of his cottage ajar. They go inside and find Razz *Babb* sitting like a statue with the hookah pipe in his hand.

They greet Razz *Babb* with '*Assalam Aleykum.*' *Babb* opens his eyes and Muza says cheerfully, 'Bilal has come home. Do bless him now'.

Babb speaks softly: '*Rum gayem sheshs begur gava ban muen, saqiya khali gachha piaman muen*' (My mirror is cracked, hence the image has lost its sheen). He then takes a drag from his hookah and addresses Bilal sternly,

'Did you not have food at home?'

'Yes, *Babb*, I had', Bilal replies.

Again *Babb* asks, 'Did you not have clothes to wear?'

'Yes, *Babb*, I had'.

'Did anyone stop you going to the mosque, go anywhere else or indeed allow you to sit at home?'

'No *Babb*, I was free to do whatever I wanted', Bilal replies.

'Then what made you run away? During our time, people left home because they were deprived of the basic requirements of life. You have everything in plenty. It is not wise to leave your home for causes you do not even understand correctly and let your parents live with their agony', *Babb* says bitingly.

'Yes, *Babb*', replies Bilal with his head down.

'There is a collective loss of identity as well as roles. We have money, but not dignity; we have dignity, but not peace; we have peace, but neither dignity nor identity', Razz *Babb* says sadly.

The smoky smell of the hookah is spreading in the dimly lit room and everyone is silent.

Rashid breaks the silence and asks, '*Babb*, Bilal is back just like you said but what would happen to Husna? Will she marry and give peace to her parents? They blame Bilal for her admission in JNU'.

Instead of asking who Husna is, *Babb* replies, 'We

live at one place, but our mind is somewhere else. This is not binary, but a split in everything. We are walking from order to chaos; from life to death and from consciousness to ignorance. In the name of religion and region, we have taken the violet out from the amphoral.[27] Why should anybody kill anybody when death is inevitable?'

Babb's metaphoric talk alarms everyone in the room. Muza asks, '*Babb*, when will this killing stop?'

Babb raises his brows, looks down and says scornfully, 'In 1989, our boys took the gun in their hands. Back then, I had a friend in Citarnarr who was a retired teacher. One day, his ten-year-old grandson came running to us and said that his father had brought a gun. My friend became very angry and said to me, "Razz, the gun that my son has brought is a God of death (Malkun-e-maut) which will bring untimely deaths".

'His words came true. They killed a *Batta* in Habbakadal, Srinagar, because he was supposedly against their movement. Since then, the bullet is alive and engaged in a death dance. It has no fear of power or domination. It does not have any conscience nor does it recognise religion, language or region. It will be in action until it finishes the system which has given it this power.'

27 Tall jug with two handles.

Rashid pleads, '*Babb*, when will we see the new dawn? *Babb*, please bless us and our Kashmir'.

'The problem is not with Kashmir but with its inhabitants. Social metamorphosis will occur in the new generation. They will put an end to this crisis and sow the seeds of a new beginning which our generation refuses to do. Our thoughts and actions are never in alignment. We pretend to be interested in peace but our engagement is somewhere else. It is a plain doctrine of cultural estrangement. Our individual voice can get strengthened only when it becomes collective. Our leaders are looking somewhere else for cultural reference points and are hugely mistaken in presuming it to be a political dispute. It is a problem of centuries-old cultural estrangement, which broke the moral thread and suppressed social capital.'

He then sings Mirza Ghalib's full Persian ghazal:

> '*Beya-o-josh-e-tamanna, deed num binigar, chu asq az sare mijgan chekeeda num binigar...dar intizar hun mada...zbanam b juram maytapedan...biya ba khak ki manu av dedanam binigar... demedano baliyid ghahe shud...cheeda num binigar...*'

Razz *Babb* sings it in a tune more rhythmic and lucid than the one made famous by Fareeda Khanum. Although nobody understands the meaning of the words, they are spellbound by his soulful singing. When he finishes, Razz *Babb* takes out a handful of walnuts and almonds from his *phiran* and asks Bilal to distribute the dry fruits to everyone. Muza fills up the chillum with tobacco and they all take leave from Razz *Babb*, with a feeling of blissfulness.

Shankar comes to the university guest house to pick up Parash at 6 pm. Shankar gets a call from Husna when they reach the administrative building where Husna is supposed to join them, informing him that she would not be able to come due to a language class. It upsets Shankar for a while. He calls her back to express his wish that she talk to Parash. Husna obliges, repeating to Parash that she is in an important class, which would finish late at 8 pm.

Shankar is taken aback by her rudeness and says angrily, 'How can she ignore us? She knew about our plan for more than a week. She even knows that you will go back tomorrow. She should have come to meet you. She said she respects you. Is this the way Kashmiri women show respect?'

'She must be busy with her studies. You are unnecessarily getting angry', Parash tries to mollify him, though he too feels offended by Husna's last-minute cancellation.

Shankar, though upset, does not want to spoil the evening and takes Parash for a walk on JNU's ring road, where he often walks with Husna. Looking at his friend who seems lost in thought, Parash decides to counsel him as best he can. He says, 'Shankar, you need to read between the lines. Her refusal to meet us today says a lot about how she feels now. She is intentionally trying to distance herself from you. Love is definitely fizzling out in your relationship, at least from her side. Her erratic behaviour means she has not been able to decide about you. Only a year ago, I had seen her effervescent with joy in your company. She was so possessive about you and never left your side throughout the conference.'

Shankar says sadly, 'Three months ago, everything was good between us. We used to talk to each other about anything and everything but now it has become difficult to even exchange pleasantries without a row.'

Parash is listening intently. He asks, 'Tell me, how did you meet her?'

'I was giving a lecture in my MPhil class against saffronisation and confessional politics. After it, she came up and said she loved my lectures. We interacted casually over the next few days and then I appointed her a research officer in a major project on Kashmir I had recently taken. We gradually became close. We even went to Kashmir together and I met her family at her house. We attended innumerable conferences and seminars related to Kashmir issues throughout the country. I used to prepare all the presentations and take care of all our expenses. Her family knew about us. I was confident we would live together for the rest of our lives', Shankar says sadly.

'Why did she change her mind then?' Parash asks, confused.

'Her mother warned her against non-Muslim men. Her mother said that my people would burn her alive after some time. Strange lies are fed to her about non-Muslims. She has become very indecisive. Sometimes, she wants to go back to the Valley and prepare for KAS. Then suddenly, she asks me to convert to Islam', says Shankar.

'Did she really ask you to convert?' Parash asks in astonishment.

'Yes, she did ask me in a fit of passion. I really don't mind changing my religion but she never talked about marriage or long-term commitment', Shankar responds. 'Her attitude has changed since Sleena has become her close friend. Sleena is from Kerala. She and her cousins often brainwash Husna against marrying a non-Muslim. They don't mind about our physical intimacy but always insist that Husna should not marry me. They say that marrying a non-Muslim is *haram* in Quran. This is strange. Does religion allow one to become intimate with a non-Muslim?' Shankar asks irritably.

The revelation makes Parash pensive. He understands

that this is no Romeo-Juliet story. He guesses the reason behind the abrupt change in Husna's behaviour towards Shankar. Being a Kashmiri, he knows that the aim of 'love *jihad*' is not to increase the Muslim population, but a doctrine of instrumentality of women's bodies used for an invisible agenda. Parash thinks she is perhaps not wholeheartedly involved in the agenda; otherwise she would have not faltered. She would have not been so indecisive and hysterical at times. Parash thinks that the chip in her heart is more dominant than the chip in her mind.

But he does not give voice to his fears and instead says, 'Shankar, Husna belonged to a conservative Kashmiri Muslim family and lived all her life in a conflict zone. She found herself liberated in JNU with you by her side. She enjoyed her new-found freedom for some time but realises that she cannot become an empowered woman like she wants. She was not able to clear NET, nor did she find a job on her own. She could not even write a scholarly paper for any research journal. All this while, she was involved with a Hindu man and was dependent on him too. The series of disappointments might have led to disillusionment and her fascination for this glamorous life faded away.'

They complete the circle and reach the spot where Shankar's car is parked. They drive to a restaurant for dinner in the nearby area. Once they are seated and the food order placed, they resume their conversation.

'By the way, do you have any idea what you would do if she insists that you convert?' asks Parash.

'I'm unable to think about it. I have no reservations as such because I truly love her. She was a huge support to me when nobody was around and I was extremely lonely. She was like the monsoon, bringing green shoots in my barren garden. We gradually became closer. She knew everything about my past; from my love affair to my failed marriage of a few months. The more time I spent with her, the more I became attached to her. I always remained by her side and supported all her choices', replies Shankar.

Parash abruptly asks, 'Shankar, you once said that she loved your looks and the way you live your life. Why would she want to change your personality? If you get converted, it would change the very things she likes about you. You would lose your individuality as well as identity. You would be branded as Al Hadis, Salafi, Barelvi or Deobandi. You might start keeping a long beard and dress like a typical Muslim. She was critical of the Islamic ideology in our conversation during the Golden Temple visit so I thought she left her religious orthodoxy behind when she came to JNU. I guess I was wrong in my perception. Would she like to go back to that orthodox religious realm? If yes, then why would she take you along? It is a big contradiction and a puzzle to me as well.'

'What should I do now? Should I stop her fellowship? Should I stop talking with her? Tell me what should I do?' Shankar asks Parash helplessly.

'You need to give her time and keep a distance from her. I know that it would not be easy for you to detach yourself but the relationship has significantly lost its warmth. You must not rush her to take a decision but start dropping hints that you would no longer be able to financially support her', Parash suggests.

'Yes, I shall try to follow your advice. I need to stop torturing myself and simply wait until she decides something on her own'.

When Shankar drops him at his guest house, Parash tries to apply balm on his hurt pride by saying, 'I can understand her mental agony. She is a child of that conflict, when her father denied that she was his child. Her grooming is such that her brother, who must have turned a Salafi, beats her for talking to you on the phone. They do not give her money and they want her to get married. I remember you told me she had run away from Kashmir and first joined Jamia Milia Islamia. Her father recommended her rejection to the Head of the Department of Political Science, pleading worsening conditions in Kashmir. So she has had to deal with a lot from her family. Your support put her back on her feet and in turn she nursed your wounds from a broken marriage. Even if this is the end, you were two human beings who helped each other and also had a good relationship.'

At the time of this conversation, Husna is with Sleena. They too are talking about Shankar and Parash. Sleena advises Husna that she should return to religion to restore the faith of her parents that she is not anti-Islam. She should tell her father that it is men who are deceitful, not women. She has to go back to restore the dignity of her mother. She must not be dazzled by this liberated culture, which she thinks would be wiped out soon. She must be true to her roots.

They are discussing this when Husna receives a call from Shankar. He asks sarcastically, 'Is your language class not over yet?'

She replies sweetly, 'Of course. I just hope Parash Sir was not offended by my absence.'

Shankar cannot stop bursting out, 'Why are you behaving like this? You embarrassed me in front of my friend. You are intentionally keeping me at arm's length these days. I find it difficult to convince myself that you are the same Husna who loved me'.

Husna flinches at the truth in his words but says bitterly, 'I am suffering too. My parents are angry with me and you also don't understand me. I did not give in to their demand to marry a Kashmiri Muslim but I need time to settle down in my professional life first. I need to take care of my parents as well. My brother is unemployed, father is retired and mother is unwell. How can I give them another shock? They are not ready to let me stay outside the Valley'.

Her response dashes Shankar's hopes further. Before disconnecting the call, he tells Husna, 'You might not miss me. But you will miss my worrying for you'.

'I already do', is the reply.

A few days earlier, Bilal had invited all those who were tired of violence for a meeting on the pretext of a discussion on 'Kashmir: Way Forward'. The meeting was held in the private house of a contractor who had political affiliations with the Congress party. Shujaat Bukhari's murder had puzzled them. 'Although he disliked India and was against Pakistan, he wanted peace and dignity for Kashmiris. He was contributing peacefully in that direction through his media connections. Still, he was killed along with his guards, poor policemen who were leaving for their homes'.

He kicked off the discussion by informing the gathering that the main political parties would strengthen the Hurriyat by announcing boycott of the local elections. There had been consensus to corner the Indian state to compel it to talk to Pakistan. For the first time, they had sensed the coming together of Muslim countries to bail out Pakistan from its financial crisis and bring India to the table for talks.

Most of the participants at the meeting were middle-aged veterans of the movement. Rafiq, a college lecturer, impatiently asked, 'Why are we really gathered here?' Saif, a *tanzeem* member, quickly replied, 'The leadership wants us to give inputs to the *tanzeem* and Hurriyat for bringing a logical conclusion to the movement for which martyrs have sacrificed their lives'.

Kaleem, a school teacher, exclaimed that the leadership had no agenda. If India and Pakistan do not fight, Kashmiris would keep dying without any reason. He was of the opinion that blood would no longer change the colour or name of the Jhelum: it would remain Vitasta and Jhelum. Bilal intervened, 'We should leave *tanzeem* to their leaders and focus on establishing peace in present circumstances rather than arguing on thorny issues'.

Munawar Sahib, a college principal, was asked to speak. In the 1960s, he was the leader of Al Fatah but later became disillusioned with armed militancy and quit. He spoke, 'We should focus on bringing back to Kashmir our girls and boys who were sent to outside universities for the mission. They neither completed their degrees nor did they change the political landscape of the universities. Therefore, they should concentrate on their professional careers or come back to their homes. We are losing our young children and in return, we bring guilt and moral degradation to our future generation. We have heard enough that "All is fair in war". There has to be a stop to all this'.

Bilal had a list of the names of students who were sent against the will of their parents to campuses outside Kashmir. Husna's name was on top of the list. Saif was not happy with this decision. He spoke, 'The *tanzeem* had instructed us that Pakistan cannot help us unless we bleed India. Therefore, we have to train our boys and girls for more sacrifices and longer *jihad*'.

His blind faith in the *tanzeem* irritated Munawar Sahib, who retorted, 'We went into jihad as per their instructions. They beckoned us to bring guns to Kashmir, due to which we lost our children and widowed our young women but we blamed India and its agencies. How long should we dwell in the euphoria of late 1960s? Pakistan had a chance to conquer Kashmir when multilateral bodies were lending their support. Now, it is impossible to conquer Kashmir when Pakistan is backed only by China, which is known for incarcerating Uighur Muslims and destroying historical mosques. Allah will never be pleased with this contradiction; we rely on those who are determined to finish Muslims in their country. I understand that China is a completely anti-religion country. It does not allow Muslims to observe their faith in true spirit or even allow them to give names they cherish to their children. They have created their own name bank from where one has to pick the name of a baby. Of late, it wants to dismantle the historic mosques.

'Does Hurriyat talk about this vindictiveness against our religion? Does the *tanzeem* speak about it? What type of Islam are we professing? God does not go by half-truths and half-lies. The time has come to unfold the reality and let our children know about it too. *Sajda Khaliq ko be, Ablees say yarana be, Hshar mai kis say ikedat ka sila mangayga*. We are not true Muslims because we are playing political games for others instead of helping our people'.

That Munawar Sahib was stating these facts so bluntly astonished everyone in the room. There was an awkward silence, as if the wind had knocked them into a state of introspection over their fate.

Those involved in militancy, in the past and present, were also anticipating some political changes in Pakistan. With the emergence of Imran Khan's political party Pakistan Tehreek-e-Insaf (PTI) at the helm of affairs, ISI's role had become subdued. Imran wanted to start afresh with a clean slate. Kashmir was on his mind but not with intense urgency. It was clear to Hurriyat that Pakistan was at the threshold of economic bankruptcy. Imran's priorities were driven by the economy rather than politics or *jihad*. The other side of the Valley, called PoK by India and Azad Kashmir by Pakistan, had become numb, voiceless.

Bilal broke the silence. 'We need to hear from the Pirs—both the older Pirs on our side and the younger on the other side—or we will plunge into deep darkness of uncertainties'.

Saif reacted, 'We were rejoicing over the victory of Imran, but the *tanzeem* leadership was sceptical about his stand on Kashmir's *jihad*. There is deep silence in Muzaffarabad. Although the younger Pir never favoured Imran, he came to power. Therefore, we have to pressurise Imran more through the Establishment'.

Kaleem was not impressed by what Saif said. He spoke, 'Pakistan is undoubtedly going through a metamorphosis. We simply need to wait and watch. Imran's interest lies more in the stability of Pakistan than in its volatility. He might roll back the *jihad* project. He is a leader who does not care for old-style policies. He will take all powers from the General in command or Army Chief and will not care for public opinion. He will undertake new experimentation to set the economy right and try to bring back the rule of law. He has his belief in democratic institutions but he is a dictator, a West-oriented Eastern showman. His policies annoy middle-rung army officers and die-hard religious organisations. It is time to put things in their rightful perspective and avoid further embarrassment'.

'That is true; the time for Hurriyat is up. The new leadership has to emerge and it has to be durable otherwise another generation would bear the consequences and perish', lamented Bilal.

Saif said, 'Our agenda is affected by policies across

the border. The bosses there are worried by Imran's reign. His role model is Qaid-e-Azam and he talks about Allama Iqbal. There seem to be definite contradictions in what he professes'.

Bilal requested Munawar Sahib to throw some more light on the political changes in Pakistan. In his typical cranky style, Munawar Sahib said, 'Imran is very popular. He had a populist agenda even before coming to power. Such an agenda is difficult to achieve quickly, therefore, his success would not be measurable in such a short time. He has his social agenda for which he will have to make tough political choices. It would not be surprising if the army rejects him in the long run. His austerity measures, trimming the government's expenditure, won't be liked by many and it would not be surprising if he becomes another John F Kennedy'.

This diatribe made Saif edgy. He proposed that they should consult the *jihad* commanders and *tanzeem* leadership for the line ahead. He was not happy with the emergence of Imran Khan, whose cricketing background made him popular with Indians as well. For Saif, this was a disturbing element because he did not want peace with India. He would imagine, '*Ki bhar udhuey khoon mai nhane kay baad aati hai*'. He thought that Imran would wish for peace with India without the settlement of Kashmir.

Coming back to the concerns he expressed earlier,

Munawar said, 'We should get our girls back from the universities. The rich have houses and businesses all over India and their children study in technical colleges and institutions like normal students while our poor girls are sent to play with fire on the pretext of higher studies. The solidarity of the family and our dignity have gone with the wind. The market and fluidity of globalisation have exposed our women to more vulnerability and they are treated like a commodity. Please call them back before they are consumed by the politics of power. Moreover, the Frontier *tanzeem* thinks that Imran is a Niazi[28] and not a real Pathan and he would never like this type of *jihad*. The changing scenario in Pakistan would also affect us. We have to think of our people'.

Amidst the heated discussion, Bilal gets a call. He abruptly informs the members that an important *tanzeem* leader has summoned him and he had to leave immediately. It was Barkat on the phone. He asked Bilal to meet him in the forest of Ahuthwatu and spend the night there. Bilal informed his brother about spending the night with Barkat and rushed to the site.

28 Although the Pakistan PM's full name is Imran Khan Niazi, the reference here is to defeated General AAK Niazi who led the 1971 war that led to the Pakistan army's defeat and the creation of Bangladesh.

Ahuthwatu is a beautiful dell over Bandipore township. It is an enchanting little valley surrounded by lush mountainous forests, framed by drifting clouds and the foaming Madhumati hurtling downhill. Barkat loved its scenic beauty and wished fervently for its peace and tranquility to sustain, although he had no roots here. The mist and forest fog stirred with the melodic breeze and turned the pages of memory in Barkat's mind. Barkat had asked Bilal to meet him here because he wanted to impress upon him the unique beauty of Kashmir, a paradise worth guarding by those born on its soil.

Once Bilal reached the hideout, both settled for confabulations which extended until midnight. Barkat began by expressing his disillusionment with the policies of *jihad*. He said, 'Bilal, Imran wants to build a new Pakistan. He will put emphasis on development and rebuild the institutions. He has taken the judiciary and military with him. This has implications. It would impact Kashmir structurally'.

Bilal reacted, 'What do you mean? Would he stop supporting our cause? So you think that he can deal with India and convince the world more effectively?'

'Bilal, he is a popular leader and to some extent, he does resort to populism and play with rhetoric, but he is more patriotic than religious at heart. He knows that it will be difficult to snatch Kashmir from India in the present circumstances. Kashmiris would have to go for a total uprising of their own without any damage to Pakistan's faltering economy. Perhaps, he would secretly and vociferously convince Muslim countries, especially Iran and Saudi Arabia, to directly send more financial assistance for the Kashmir cause. This would be a paradigm shift in Pakistan's agenda in Kashmir. Even the deliberations at HQ have led to a consensus that Kashmir's political parties should join hands with local separatists to corner India. They should leave Muslims of India to their own devices.'

Bilal became agitated with the revelation and asked, 'Does it mean Kashmiris should plunge into total war against India without any help from external sources? Would ISI support for Kashmir's *jihad* be cut off?'

'Imran will not support *jihad* directly. ISI HQ gave a different proposal. They predicted political violence in India in different states where they will extend their latent and concerted support. This time, they will rely on communal fringe politics of India; be it the cases of lynching, reservations or change in school syllabus, national names and symbols. Imran is more interested in internationalising Hindu terror through these fissures in Indian politics. Unlike his predecessors, he can easily play the Hindu terror card on the world stage. The middle-rung officers are not at all convinced to leave

Kashmir's *jihad* solely to politics. They want military operations to continue. Therefore, many organisations active in Kashmir and dormant in India will not be in complete accord. There will not be complete control of any *tanzeem*. It will result in more violence in days to come. Unless we act maturely, Kashmir will plunge into deeper darkness'.

Bilal was shaken, realising that in all these great games, his own society had reached that point where morality was disconnected from community feeling. Cultural discourses had been hijacked by religiosity and had become bankrupt. He read out a clipping he had brought along from local newspapers, thinking that Barkat would not have read them in his forest hideouts.

> The recent killings in Kashmir point towards a much dangerous and horrific situation. These killings are very different from the usual deaths and killings in Kashmir because these were not done by forces—neither by suspected militants and neither did they die in clashes or violent protests. These were planned murders and had silly reasons and motivations behind them. I am speaking about the murders in the Valley in very recent times like the most recent Uri gang-rape and murder of a very young girl, where a woman plans this whole crime along with her son and his friends. This is

a crime of different magnitude because a woman who herself is a mother of a girl waits for her son to gang-rape her step sister and mercilessly kills an innocent child and then destroys her body.

In another crime in Baramulla, a boy kills his fiancée brutally, accompanied by a woman with whom he was in relationship. This boy did not leave his fianceé because the marital contract (nikah) was signed, so he would have had to pay compensation for divorce. He preferred brutal murder of a young poor girl. Even more shocking thing is that the woman culprit who was married and had children, one of them handicapped, accepted that the plan was to kill her husband and handicapped child and marry her lover.

Down south, a wife kills her husband in the night along with her lover who was a mosque head (imam). Also in the south, a child is kidnapped from his house and is slaughtered by unknowns, the heart-wrenching thing is that the boy was the youngest child among many sisters. The horrific sight is that the boy's arm was cut with a knife, there were blade marks on his body and acid was used on a four-year-old child.

Barkat was struck dumb. The bright glow of the gas lamp on the side table near Bilal was making it difficult for Barkat, who was sitting on the opposite side, to look at him. He lowered its flame and said. 'Bilal, the other *tanzeems* have asked again for *lataluki* (disengagement) from state jobs. This will be a new phase of violence. The best thing is to get all our girls back to the Valley who have had little role to play in bringing sanity to the men in their families.'

Bilal said, 'We are caged in our own prison. People from across the border want the conflict to continue. It has given birth to escalating violence for which no one is held accountable. The commanders want us to go to Indian universities and spread *jihad* all over the country, especially Punjab and Kerala. We will only lose more boys and girls in this game. Hurriyat should have thoroughly thought about it before executing this plan outside the Valley. It has become a structure to give legitimacy to unaccountable deaths and destruction. The tragedy is that our society has become dehumanised with displacement, death and continuous violence. The leadership should have taken responsibility for the repression, alienation and terror over the decades and tried to break the vicious circle of violence and destruction. That has not happened. Instead, the big umbrella organisation which has been seducing society in the name of *azadi* for the last three decades continues its romantic deception. In return, we have been committing collective suicide. There seems to be no formula for creating a fresh political initiative'.

Barkat could not help revealing his own plans. 'Bilal, I am tired of all this and want to move out from the Valley. The way Muslims are killing Muslims, I find Kashmir might plunge into further violence. Pakistani political leadership would be indecisive and ISI's hidden support would further complicate the matter. You also get all the girls back from the Indian universities and decide to live a better life. Let us leave everything to Allah.'

They both knew there were new alliances forming in the neighbourhood. Imran Khan wanted to bring Saudi Arabia in the fold of Asian investment priorities and closer to China. Imran was willfully trying to sideline the US and bring about a new axis with the Muslim world to distract attention from internal conflicts. There was no knowing in which direction the new winds would blow.

The night had penetrated the darkness of the forest. The roar of the Madhumati along with the murmuring of the dishevelled bushes and trees of the forest, ruffled by strong winds from the west, made for a frightening scenario. Barkat and Bilal decide to retire for the rest of the night.

The next morning, before parting ways, Barkat tells Bilal that it would be their last meeting.

Bilal thanks him for his help in restoring him to his family and explaining the dire situation and says, '*Khuda hafiz, dost*'.

'*Allah Hafiz,* take care', replies Barkat. He stands there looking at the retreating figure of Bilal for a long time.

Barkat stays at his hideout and waits for Badar of Bahawalpur and Asif of Layari Karachi camp.

The meeting was scheduled in order to draw up new strategies for the movement. Barkat wanted to understand their thinking after ten months in Kashmir. It turned out that both Badar and Aisf were mesmerised with the lavish lifestyles of Kashmiris. Their costly mobile phones, luxurious bikes and cars and spending power amazed them. Back home in Pakistan, they had no such luck. Their world in Pakistan was dominated by Islam, Wadehras and Choudharys,[29] army, ISI, landlords and maulvis.

Soon after they arrive, Asif bursts out, 'Faizan of Muridke told me that he had nice time in Sopore along with Wahab and had enjoyed the hospitality of some local girls. They drive around in a big Scorpio and seldom think about fighting. In Pakistan, *mujahideen* do not even have bikes and they are deprived of such merrymaking

29 The leading landlord families of Sindh, Punjab.

with young women. Faizan and Wahab have decided not go back and stay in the Valley'.

Badar's observation is more sarcastic. He says, 'Kashmiris curse everyone. They sing "*Allah huo*" in madrassas and then enjoy life with their families. Whether they live in rural or urban areas, they enjoy excessive religious freedom and affluence. They enjoy more freedom than any of the Muslim countries, including Saudi Arabia'.

He then asks Barkat, 'What would a Kashmiri get if annexed with Pakistan? They have everything already. If it is true that the Indian army was in barracks before 1990, it must have been a heaven in peace and tranquillity. They have everything here: Islam as well as total freedom. No jagirdars, no Bajwas, no maulanas and no ISI. If my parents and my neighbours had these things, they would have never sold us to the madrassa for earning our wages to fight this un-Islamic battle. How can Allah be with us to support this *jihad*? Allah is punishing us'.

Before Barkat could comment, Asif adds, 'The method of recruitment has changed. The new commander Ishtar who gave us a briefing the other day, said that the training camps are now established here only. Batches of twenty are to be chosen for different camps and local commanders would give them three weeks extensive training. Commander Sahib now has put emphasis on local commanders to lead and have targeted attacks as envisaged in the big programme. We are only to supervise it. Youths are given training with guns to fight the local police to get the arms. We shall only provide ammunition to them from different channels. Pakistan cannot afford to be visible now. The new government does not want direct linkage. In fact, had it not been for the army and ISI, Imran Khan would have abandoned us. They do not want to leave any discernible proof of our intervention and are calling back some of the commanders.'

'Are you also returning, Sahib?' Asif asks.

Barkat replies, 'Things are changing rapidly. Since Kashmiris are divided in their outlook, they do not need our support. But I have not yet received any order to return'.

Barkat is restless after the tiring conversation and wants to go to Razz *Babb*'s cottage. Badar and Asif also ask him to take them along. On the way, he is mesmerised by the glow of chinars and wonders if autumn has come early. He did not even notice spring and summer this year.

In Kashmir, autumn is like a second spring, the red leaves of chinar blazing like flowers.

The early winter in Kashmir is very chilly, even without snow. The sun stays hidden in the dense fog. The black clouds, trickling streams and naked trees give the Valley a bleak appearance.

On one such wintry afternoon, Habib Sahib along with his colleagues Iqbal and Sadiq come to Razz *Babb*'s cottage. They are disturbed about developments in the mosques built over the last two decades which have become centres of political discourse of *khatibs*[30] and imams of competing sects. The cottage seems like a haven untouched by these changes. They have come to him for peace of mind and blessings.

They are all retired school teachers. Wali Sahib, once principal of the school and a frequent visitor to Razz *Babb*'s cottage, is already there to welcome them. They start talking about Kashmir's plight, how it is in the grip of contrived narratives and individual campaigns. *Babb* is in high spirits, unusually sanguine, listening to the conversation with interest.

30 Khatib is a person who delivers the sermon, during the Friday prayer

All of a sudden, Razz *Babb* is reminded of the dream that Manzoor Sahib shared with him before his death. 'Two months ago, Manzoor Sahib had come here for a while. He was tense due to a dream he had the previous night which was as vivid in his mind as a lived memory. He told me that he saw Ghulam Qadir in his dream. The fine rich gentleman had died long back in the previous century. He was a noble man of Khuoma and had a house near Jama Masjid at Bandipore.

'In the dream, Gulam Qadir had invited Lal Ded and Nund *Reshi* to his place for lunch. Qadeer Sahib, Usman Sahib of Grul, Ahad Sahib of Sopore, Vedlalji Razz, Neel Koul of Kalusa, Nand *Babb* from Srinagar and Dar Sahib from Ajas were also there to welcome the two. There were other noble-looking persons with turbans whom Manzoor Sahib could not recognise.

'They were seated on the beautiful carpet in the main hall of the two-storey house. Manzoor Sahib said that he was also present in the feast, therefore he had rushed to my place to share the dream with me. The interesting part was the absorbing conversation between the two main guests, Lal Ded and Nund *Reshi*. The other guests were keenly listening to them.

'The conversation was started by Lal Ded who

asked Nund *Reshi*, "Do you know what Kashmir has become after you left? It has turned into a place of wretchedness, frozen in uncertainty. It is now left with dark patches, thin rivulets, naked mountains and empty houses. Due to displacement and misplaced priorities, there is only continuous violence and unrelenting suffering. Bonds have weakened and intellect has dried up. There are only weeping daughters, mourning mothers and helpless parents everywhere in the Valley. I am pained and concerned. Why did all this happen?"

"It was bound to happen. Kashmiris are united by the fold of *Reshi* culture which had space for natural evolvement. That space I left is filled with the ignorance and distant vulnerabilities of our guests from the west. Our guests had different value systems. Their formalism and codifications caged us. Our *Reshi* tradition became subdued and their domination prevailed. One can resolve the religious formalism, but Kashmiris have gone beyond the point of resolve. I failed. I should have not left them room for manoeuvre. They filled up spaces with tales of power and domination. It became a new formalism of codes and verdicts. The schism between the two parallel lines has produced these catastrophes", replied Nund *Reshi*.

"You could not remain what you were supposed to be, a Trita.[31] You were neither Vaishnavite nor Islamist. You were Shaivite, in a non-codified order where names were unsubstantial. You made them ritualistic, searching for dictates and guidance from outside while blurring the inner self from a commingled tradition they have opted for, a Wahabi mode of living, unknown and unheard of till recently. *Mauj* Kashir (Mother Kashmir) is unwell. This does not augur well for its subjects. There is no glow; there is a glare that hurts", said Lal Ded.

"Yes, I know nobody was happy with these developments. The ire of the angels and of Shakti was severe on the night of 1 Aushid, 5093. It stirred the chief. I think the chief had to leave Kashmir on the morning of 2 Aushid, Sunday 5093 (26-Dhu al-Hijjah-1438, 17 September 2017).[32] He left disgusted and troubled. It seems Shakti has been angry with him and he had to go unceremoniously", added Nund *Reshi*.

"What about Shakti worshippers?" asked Lal Ded.

"They are spread all over the world, but only a few in Kashmir", replied Nund *Reshi* sadly.

31 A blend of the tenets of Shaivism, Buddhism and Islam.
32 Dates on the Hindu calendar.

'Then Qadeer Sahib intervened, "What are we in for, *Mauj*?" Lal Ded looked towards Nund *Reshi* and urged, "Tell them. They need some respite. They are tortured and miserable".

'Nund *Reshi*'s white eyebrows lifted and with a tight-lipped smirk he said, "The youth in sects defy culture. Today their religion is flourishing on human weakness.In our time, it would live on human strength. Then they were aware of that joy and now they are aware of its limitation. Sects are alienated and disconnected from the cord. Internal homogeneity will need to be stitched up. The chief has failed and left them divided and displaced. His tenure is over. The misplaced will come back to their original fold, maybe to that core, after a half-century from Aushid 5093. They have to suffer till then. Violence will not leave them and they will be at each other's throats. Tongues might get silenced".'

Usman Sahib did not grasp all these references, but Ved Lal and Razz *Babb* understood the meaning of the dream. Manzoor Sahib could not remember those times. Before his eyes opened, they were singing together *lalwaakh*, like a Darud and Leela.[33]

---

33 Musical style of rendering Lal Ded's native poetry.

Narration of the dream leaves each one in the gathering guessing and working out his own interpretations, some bitter and some questionable, but nothing pleasant. Razz *Babb* is busy with his hookah, listening calmly to what they have to say. In a couple of days, the tale would spread out to homes in the Valley. Late Manzoor Sahib is not an ordinary mortal and Razz *Babb* is a venerable sage. The dream has some serious messages which are not clear immediately.

The topic of conversation changes and they start talking about the changes in Kashmir due to militant leadership and radical youth.

'What cruelty has been unleashed by society that an eight-year-old helpless daughter was kidnapped, raped and killed? Shockingly, this happened three months after this Kathua rape case appeared in the newspapers. Some say that it was her uncle who was involved tacitly, others say that a few Dogra boys wanted to teach the family a lesson. Anyway, we never heard of such a thing in Kashmir before this *Azadi* Movement. *Batta*s' presence was a cushion offering peaceful conflict resolution. They have gone, it looks like they have taken the good times with them', laments Habib Sahib.

Wali Sahib nods, adding, 'We have seen what we had not seen in centuries. We had seen physical hard work, *begaar* (bonded labour) during Dogra monarchy and in the cruel Pathan régime. Never had we killed our own people. We were a protective and caring community. This is now our pathological psychology: killing our own people, raping children and leaving families to the mercy of elderly men. What we despised in other non-Kashmiri communities has become common in us. They say it is a new normal. But we can't say these things before the young men. They hurl insults at us and we weep in privacy. Families are together not because of farming and its requirements, or by shared values and filial warmth, but because youths have nothing better to do than killing their abundant time at home and loitering in the shops and on roads. These children do not help their parents in their agricultural activities any more. We have to be dependent on Biharis and people from UP. What can be expected other than fluidity, uncertainty and mistrust? The children are unemployed and girls remain unmarried. Men and women of our generation are most unfortunate living these divided lives, burdened with the sorrow of loss and failing to do anything to retrieve their lost culture.'

Wali Sahib states, 'The faith healers are mostly from outside the Valley. A few amongst us went for religious education outside the state and have become new Pirs on return. They are not our creation. The case of Aijaz Sheikh is giving shock waves. He abused so many children and got away with it because he was a religious figure. He was first engaged by a madrassa as religious preacher, then an imam in a mosque at Handwara and finally, a school teacher in Sopore—where he was finally caught in the crime. Even the profane has become sacred under the umbrella of religion.

'Concurrently, Sheikh had floated this theory in the market that he has *jinns* at his command who can get rid of anyone's trouble. However, there is a condition. Unlike other faith healer *jinns*, Sheikh's *jinns* would not talk to anyone, not even to Sheikh. This is the stupidity of our people. We are sinful. Hundreds of our children have suffered because of the perverted sexual desires of people like Gulzar Pir and Aijaz Sheikh. Still, women throng to have a glimpse of him in jail.

'I think it is the need of the hour to have a detailed account of the staff and students at madrassas. All masjid committees have to have full particulars of imams. It is a fact that here, in Kashmir, agents of different agencies have led prayers for years together as masjid imams and it is still in vogue. Moreover, we need to develop a consensus among the masses to have a law to ban all kinds of black magic and witchcraft, which no doubt has had severe ramifications on our moral, social, religious, ethical personality and mental makeup. It is not just his sin but we all are sinners helping in creating such a kingdom.'

'The *Babb*s we knew before 1990 had just one long *phiran* and the hookah. They abhorred glamour, avoided even the company of people and were content with little. Here, with the new Pirs, you have jamborees for a select few, increasing number of diehard followers, especially women. Look at their style of travel, lavish way of life, dress and diet which is akin with market branding of a cult culture. Their increased numbers in the towns and villages have changed the social landscape of these places. Gradually, we have become obsessed with them. Our land seems to be a fertile soil for such false notions to grow', he adds.

'Yes, Sahib, we are a nation of obsessions. Life's uncertainties scare us and trained mystics sell us the illusion of being a distinct community. In that segment of time, it only overwhelms us, like a magic wand that controls us', says Habib Sahib.

Babb suddenly puts aside his hookah, lowers his eyes and speaks. 'Between orthodoxy and fluidity is the space of illusion and obsession. We plunge in when our structures are weakened. Even history and memory are disconnected. You cannot hold one and leave the other; rather, history and memory move together in the rhythm of time. It has to be merged in continuity. Parting with the consensus of history and forging a new collective memory has created the present chaos.'

Iqbal Sahib cannot hold himself back and asks, 'Why do we believe in things which are not true? Why do we get obsessed with stories and burn ourselves in the fire of qualms? We are not sure what we really want and desire. Why do all of us say unfair things about Big Pir and maulvis, yet follow their dictates? I fail to understand our stupidity and have no reply to these questions. Why are we so obsessed with the power elite of Pakistan? It haunts me now. Why did we take revenge on our friends and neighbours when Bhutto was assassinated in Pakistan? We tried to finish Jamaatis then and back in 1989, we listened to them. We drove out *Batta*s and tried to annihilate them. This is what we have been doing.'

Wali Sahib reacts, 'We never encourage our own imams in mosques to speak about religion within our universe. We do not believe in intellectual queries and rely on the stories told to us. We know that it is not the truth but we still propagate it because we want uncertainties and victimhood to prevail. We believe what our non-native clerics and less educated Muslims leaders tell us.

'KK Aziz's book *The Pakistani Historian and The Murder of History* tells us "Millions of young minds are being fed on a diet of lies, inaccurate facts, misrepresentations and blatant official propaganda". This is what has been transferred to us too.'

'True,' Iqbal reacts, 'A death is a death. Whether a

policeman dies or a *mujahid*, both are Kashmiris. But the reaction to the funeral of a policeman and a *mujahid* is different. Funerals of 'martyrs' are well announced and arranged at sunrise. Multitudes of youths are brought from neighbouring villages through mosque calls on loudspeakers. *Mujahideen*'s funeral processions get publicity in towns and villages, are branded as martyrdom, religious chanting and then coverage in papers and national electronic media. This is what we are witnessing in Kashmir. On the other hand, a policeman's death is a silent funeral in the darkness of night attended by villagers, relatives and the family members.

'Each family has the same story of their happiness being consumed by militancy. They violently express it in public places but they silently mourn in private spaces. The sobbing is in silence, tears are internal and sorrow is hidden, untold and unsung.

'See what it says in this newspaper: "Such is the political climate of Tral: If you die for a side which is seen as the enemy, then you even don't get a fitting goodbye." That was how the funeral of Lateef Ahmad Gojri went: quiet, unnoticed, and unsung. He was a policeman who died in a shootout with the four guerrilla fighters of Jaish-e-Muhammad in Tral. The poor fellow was given a quiet burial at his village Kangdoora-Kahlil in the darkness of the night with just his relatives and neighbours in attendance.

Some three miles away, the two villages of Handoora and Khangund, in contrast, bore the sacrifice of their two young guerrillas with pride. In fact, no one slept as songs of freedom and resistance on mosque loudspeakers kept the villagers up all night. And as the first rays of the sun touched Tral, tens of thousands of mourners came into the two villages to give the two guerrillas an emotional sendoff. Ishfaq Ahmad Khan and Abid Maqbool Bhat died in the gun fight in the forests of Tral with two of their Pakistani compatriots dying by their side.

'Policeman will be missed more by his family, children and friends and the boy's death might not even get lip service in days to come. We have witnessed it.

'There is another trend emerging of telling the stories of martyrdom with much drama. Now turban-wearing maulvis come to neighbourhoods in towns and the villages. They come with 4-5 persons with an indirect plea for the recruitment of militants. They spin narratives of the wretched condition of Kashmir and in melodious narrative arouse the passions of young boys in the name of our Sheba and Kalifa.[34] Anyone who listens to these maulvis is moved by their speeches. They recite verses that serve their agenda.

'Look at this maulana on Facebook. He sings, weeps

34 Great women champions.

and brings passion and pathos to change the mindset for radicalisation of our youth. He urges even doctors to quit their profession and join militancy. Lyrical songs mythologising death and killing of young boys are given a religious colour. This is in fashion in mosques and selective houses in towns and villages across the Valley. They make the taking up of guns so charming, as in the 1990s, that crossing the border seemed like a passage to heaven.'

Usman Sahib, silent till now, speaks, 'It is a cruel joke on us that we lose children for nothing. Since they use religion, nobody has the courage to defy them. They mix our real tragedies with rewards in the world after this. Despite our education and suffering, we do not doubt them.

'The worry is that young boys from schools, if not doing well in their examinations, would not be left with any other choice of jobs. Militancy thus becomes a form of employment and religion has become political exigency.'

As they are discussing this, the door suddenly opens and a young boy rushes into the room.

'*Babb*, *Assalam Alleykum*'.

Babb has his own way of responding to greetings. He very rarely says '*Walekum Salam*'. Instead, with his eyes closed, he gives a tight-lipped smile. Others in the room are silent and Iqbal Saheb whispers, '*Mehman*' (literally guest, here meaning non-native militant). They convey their salaams to *Babb* and leave the cottage hastily.

Barkat enters Razz *Babb*'s cottage at sunset along with Asif and Badar. It is a murky night with a slight chill in the air, faint sunlight filtering into the dark room, casting multiple shadows. After greetings, Barkat says to Razz *Babb*, '*Babb*, Asif and Badar are in Kashmir for the last one year. The poor fellows are from the villages of Sindh and Punjab. Their families are financially weak and need their help. They desire a good life with their families back home. No such thing is in sight here. They feel that they are fighting an unwinnable and meaningless war. They need your blessings'.

Babb looks at them and says, 'Malkin-maut (death god) is rejoicing. They give you guns to kill your own brethren. It will not stop unless innocent killings of Habbakadal[35] are accounted for and exonerated through confession. Our lived religion was our fragrance, spreading and enlightening the *Reshi* nativity but you made it liquid. Instead of flowing, it has turned torpid and thick with human blood. Our religion was not religiosity; it was a comingled evolved culture of different faiths, where Kahnov, Dastigeer, Sharika *Mauj*, Shankaracharya and Dargah were divine invisible forces who protected us. In any difficult situation, they used to come in the form of bird, animal or sound from the sky to protect us. We

35 Predominantly Pandit neighbourhood in Kashmir.

preserved our culture for centuries and we lived on. You broke this chain. It is better for you to go back. Look what happened in Fatekadal. Human beings cannot be substituted'.

'*Babb*, Indian army has gone berserk, intoxicated with its fire power', says Badar.

Babb immediately recites, *'Dooldapa us sarapa naaz ka shaveh n tha, Hum he kar baithey thhey Ghalib, Paishdasti aiek din* (It is we who started it, otherwise she was nice and naïve). Who killed first? Now the circle has to be completed. The message was vividly clear in 2005 when a mountain was burnt and one lakh people died before our eyes in that manufactured massacre. Ali Sahib gave me the whole account of that autumn morning when God's fury fell on that mountain'.[36]

Badar looks at Asif. Their eyes meet as if they are trying to compress the wisdom of ages in moments. *Babb* takes out something from his pocket and gives it to them to rub on their chests. Barkat signals them to go after taking *Babb*'s blessings, while he stays back.

Outside, the evening light has dimmed. There is no electricity in the cottage. Barkat lights a candle, keeps it on the shelf. He seats himself close to Razz *Babb* and says, '*Babb*, Asif and Badar think that Kashmir has an excess

---

36 In 2005, an earthquake felled a mountain in PoK.

of affluence. Money, sex, food and fruits are available in plenty. This is the only attraction that keeps them in Kashmir. They think that Kashmiris are people of easy virtue. They extract money from any source and say whatever suits their convenience and interest. They eat too much and swear by religion to prove a point in their own interest. Men and women both tell lies and make up stories. It is sad that the destitute, deprived and illiterate are sent as *mujahideen* from Pakistan. They have no compatibility with the locals. They joined militancy due to financial hardship and ignorance about the religious rhetoric of Kashmir, but in Kashmir, they are confused by identity politics, entertainment, vengeance against the rich and competition for material gain. That is why they get caught and killed without any résistance.

'*Babb*, I wish Masterji had told me about this off-putting character of Kashmiris. He taught me for many years, yet he did not say a word against Muslims of Kashmir. He was a living angel, but he should have showed me the other side of the Valley too'.

Razz *Babb* looks at Barkat with his big eyes wide open. There is an intuitive understanding in his looks. He then takes a long drag on his hookah and says, 'You have not met the mothers and sisters who lost their loved ones in this struggle. What have these mothers done to deserve this pain? They believed their men, who brought them this misery. Their miseries and misfortunes are cumulative, resulting from actions and reactions. The stories of their lives are not different from yours.

'Your first guardian gave you a roof and wanted you to go to school; you exchanged it for loitering in the automobile workshop. Thus a priceless gift was shunned. Providence gave you a second guardian who helped you in getting an education with a degree; you exchanged it with struggle and *jihad*. You should have chosen public service which would have given you an opportunity to help people who were orphaned like you, but you chose a path of death and destruction.'

Barkat is miserable. He remembers how happy and carefree he was when as a beggar's child he was part of a small universe and was wrapped up in his small world. That world had boundaries and those margins kept him secure. What went wrong? He remembers how he thought Teacher *Babb* would infuse new confidence in him and he could lead a more dignified life, leaving the stigma of being an orphan behind. Teacher *Babb* taught him with full passion and had cautioned him to stay with him for more years for capacity building and empowerment through a package of languages and knowhow in computers. He remembers that he was impatient to overcome his precarious past quickly. Instead of becoming resilient, he developed a victim syndrome and could not be comfortable in the setting that he was entitled to. He should have stayed with Teacher *Babb* till he could realise his full potential and frame his boundaries. He got lost and could not stand up to the competition he faced in day-to-day life.

With half wings, he wanted to soar. He abandoned his Masterji's universe. He joined—rather was tempted and induced by an underworld organisation—to gain an identity, money and 'honour'. He lived for years as a member of that outfit, a shadowy life with no place in society. Down the years, it only made him a person of darkness. He feels remorse that he did not listen to his Teacher *Babb*. He let his mentor down.

However, it is a bit late for him to realise that shortcuts are not solutions. Teacher *Babb* would often tell him that he had to go through institutional learning to acquire the basic strength to stand out in a crowd.

Now, he does not want to miss the chance to gain from the guidance of Razz *Babb*.

'*Babb*, show me the path of redemption and survival', pleads Barkat.

'Start the process of individualisation from inside and you would find you are not compartmentalised. You will realise that you are the complete universe and each living or non-living being is within you and is your constituent. If you can understand that, the reward will be salvation, service, love and compassion. Let bygones be bygones. Turn the pages of memory, then shut the book. Move beyond the past and begin a new journey of integral humanism', says *Babb*.

'What am I supposed to do? I am under watch and I have to give them convincing answers', Barkat says in agitation.

'Kashmir has become a theatre of the absurd. Do you think you can continue to play a role in it? Things can happen in peace also. It is love and compassion, not hate and violence that make people live together. Bonding in order to create the "other" has cut you adrift; bonding in order to be with the "other" brings stability. Vulnerability is attached to possibility and you have to move towards the new promise without fear. Promise to save the childhood of those who have been abandoned from the moment they were born. They are anchorless. You can help them from anywhere on earth. Choose your place and devote your life to good deeds until the world order changes into something beautiful', *Babb* suggests.

Barkat is convinced he must make a new beginning, and also knows, in a flash, where he must go for his mission. It is midnight when he leaves Razz *Babb*'s cottage with a resolute mind.

Husna has decided that she would go back to Kashmir after finishing her doctorate. Now she has no intention to stay in Delhi and is to take up a job in the Central University of Kashmir, where her father knows the vice chancellor. Since she cleared her NET,[37] she has been looking forward to life in Kashmir as a teaching professional. Her parents and Sleena have convinced her not to marry Shankar. Conflicting emotions are storming her heart. The eventful and adventurous years since 2014 were a phase of experimentation with life, when she lost herself to the outside realm. She thought she could retain the indoctrination she had been subjected to in school in a liberal atmosphere. In tacit and willful multiple roles, she had played way too much with her body in ways that her mind found unacceptable. Her heart was ravaged. She had received love and in exchange had given religiosity and lust. She treated love as a material referent and in return, it broke her from within. She often wept and cried out for no reason when alone and would pull herself back with repentance and a sense of defeat.

37 Fellowship test for becoming a lecturer.

Before her last meeting with Shankar for parting of ways, she talked with her friend Sleena in her hostel room the whole night. It was difficult to make the right decision and therefore she wanted suggestions from Sleena, who was insisting she leave Shankar. She had pleaded, 'It is difficult to escape his gaze. I have been with him to all kinds of places, spent days and nights with him like a couple living together. He helped me academically and introduced me to his parents and friends. It is difficult to forget him'.

'Husna, you must realise he is a divorcee, ten years older to you and a *kafir*. Why do you mix emotions with your agenda? You changed him a lot. He is no longer a rightist Hindu; at least he is vociferous against state policies. Your role is over. As long as you have gained something, you do not need to be with him any longer or else you will be branded as a *kafir* too. He is of no use to us. You need to go back to the Valley. It is not our fault that the mission cannot be completed as per the plan. We played our role. You should not feel guilty about either your years here or the sacred agenda', said Sleena.

'I can crush my emotions but how can I lie about not loving him right on his face? I crossed all the boundaries to win his trust and fulfill the agenda', lamented Husna.

'You were a Muslim in thought and deed. You drank with him for the religious cause. You stayed with him because you had to win an intellectual to oppose state policies. He wrote many articles against the state and he had sympathetic words for you and your people. We did not succeed substantially but we were successful in running the "intolerance" campaign. It was bought by both print and social media. We did our job. Go say "*Tauba*"[38] and become a good Muslim. It is not difficult to make him feel guilty. You can accuse him of deceiving his first wife and flirting with many girls—that he did the same things with you as well. You can even give the excuse of the big age difference and tell him that he only analysed your culture with crude facts and not as a lover who can value it. You can even accuse him of creating a feeling of uncertainty and inferiority in you,' suggested Sleena.

'That is not possible. I need a better excuse. I would rather tell him that I have decided not to displease my parents. I am not even convinced about the safe shores of religiosity, nor do I feel that the learnings gave me solace to live. Something still pinches me from inside', Husna concluded sadly.

In the evening, Husna meets Shankar. It seems like ages since they enjoyed a quiet evening or a passionate night together. Their conversation is stilted and awkward.

Averting her eyes, she starts, 'I have to complete

38 Confession before God not to repeat a misdeed.

my PhD and go back to Kashmir. My father has some connections to get me placed in the university. He was happy when I cleared my NET examination. I think Kashmir has gone to a more radicalised version of Islam. The BJP-PDP alliance has alienated the average Kashmiri more than ever before. We see daily deaths of our boys and people accept it as the new normal. I have to go back as early as possible. My brother is not settled and my parents need me'.

As usual, Shankar reacts, 'I just don't know what you are made of. Kashmiris should understand that their future lies in the process of development with India. Their *Azadi* Movement has no future and it will make them intellectually bankrupt. They are getting money without working for it and the economy is stagnating, with people seeking refuge in religion. It is a new ritualism advocated by a selfish leadership to gain some legitimacy for the tragedies they have unleashed on people'.

'Why do you talk like this? We lose our boys on a daily basis due to the Indian suppression of our movement. Imran Khan is trying hard to unite the Muslim *umma* and also persuading China to force India to negotiate on Kashmir', says Husna heatedly.

'I can't understand why Kashmiris refuse to ditch their illusions about Pakistan. Imran is trying to bail out Pakistan from financial bankruptcy. He cannot give priority to Kashmir. It is left to ISI, which is feeding you lies and denigration. ISI knows Kashmir is out of reach so they use you as the most trusted rebellious lot to bleed India and send your boys to the plains for anti-national terror activities. It has nothing to do with Kashmir', says Shankar.

Husna is taken aback by the accuracy of this statement. She thinks it would be dangerous to continue talking about this. Though nervous, she also wants to know how much Shankar is acquainted with their agenda. She continues, 'I don't know what that Kashmiri *Batta* friend tells you. I am not pleased with his cooked up narratives', says Husna.

'That is real wisdom. They are different from Kashmiri Muslims. They take a progressive line and are liberal and frank. Muslims are in a state of confusion. With each passing day, they are collectively moving towards primordial religious conservatism. It has happened more with the educated middle class. I see some point in Parash's argument that Kashmir may fall into the Chinese lap in the near future. He can see a trajectory from Hindu Kashmir to Muslim Kashmir and from Muslim Kashmir to Chinese Buddhist Kashmir. It is like a moving circle of time and space in social formations of power and domination. This *Azadi* Movement is meaningless. More Muslims live in India than any other country and are any day more safe and modern in comparison to fellow Muslims across the world. Kashmir remains a fractured society and it is far behind in its goal to be a new nation-state with many stakeholders clamouring for their claim. Kashmir has nothing to gain from being annexed by Pakistan, nor can Pakistan take it. UNSC resolutions have been long nullified by international developments, change in social geography and annexation of part of Kashmir by China', retorts Shankar.

Husna counters emphatically, 'We want an independent Islamic state and we have a common agenda supported by a united leadership. Pakistan will support us and our movement is getting stronger day by day. You'll see, India will succumb to our pressure'.

Shankar is amazed by Husna's statement. She has never spoken like this in his company before. Not long ago, she had aired unfavourable opinions about her religion, society and leadership. She had said that the separatist leadership is a myopic, illiterate lot and Islam is a patriarchal, rigid, pre-modern religion unable to compete with science. He silently digests the flip in her thought process but strongly rebuts her contention.

'You are mistaken. I think you have stopped reading. Imran's emergence is not an abrupt development meant to provide direction to the Islamic movement, as you and your people think. It is the army's ploy to save Pakistan from the embarrassment of bankruptcy and isolation. His pleas for financial aid should be read correctly. How can Pakistan be a chooser? Pakistan has been a client state; it has to be, unless it makes structural transformation at notional and ground level, which is a distant reality. It is hard for Pakistan to sustain itself with its religious contradictions at macro level and cultural fragmentation at micro level as well as huge regional and economic disparities. No country can sustain itself with such social disharmony and degenerate politics.'

He explains to her that as Prime Minister, Khan was vociferous when he returned from Saudi Arabia with an aid package and blamed Iran for the Middle East turmoil. China too gave aid with conditions. He had to come back with a heavy heart and had to convince the military high command. He promised security for China's projects, especially One Road One Belt, making Pakistan a client state with a compromised sovereignty.

'Look at the contradiction: A communist China, dead set against Islam, destroyer of mosques on its soil, brainwasher of newborn Muslim children against Islam, claims to be a saviour of Pakistan, a country that conditions its children for indoctrination in its mushrooming religious schools. On one hand, the Pakistani state takes help from a *kafir* communist dragon, on the other hand its masses are devoted to mullahs.

'The continued Saudi support is in return for the services rendered for the promotion of an orthodox religious project. It is *diyat* (compensation) for the thousands of Pakistanis killed in sectarian violence, and China's package helps pay off national debt. This is how Pakistan plays the role of a client state.

'It has played this historical role right from its inception since 1947—first for the US and now for China. The future of Kashmir movement is nothing but jostling of Hurriyat between Muzaffarabad and Srinagar. Hurriyat wants Pakistan to veer into Saudi Arabian orbit to help it out economically and religiously, while China is expressly opposed to this diplomatic push to isolate Iran,' interjects Shankar.

This gloomy picture depicted by Shankar makes Husna a little nervous but she has a mission to accomplish: breaking up with Shankar. She instead says, 'We can be friends but it is not possible to carry on our relationship. I think that I have been too liberal, forgetting my home, my *deen* (religion) and my people. I need to settle down'.

'I wonder what makes you think like this after living in JNU for the last four years. I am okay with whatever you have decided. But you should not text me anymore or expect me to be around whenever you want. Please give me the books and the credit card I gave you', Shankar says unemotionally.

'Ok, I'll do that', replies Husna, abruptly getting up to leave.

Their intimate relationship comes to a close on a bad note. Shankar is back in his room, lying face down. All the beautiful moments with Husna pass before his mind's eye like a reel. He feels half dead but her sudden change of behaviour stirs his curiosity and he starts asking himself. 'Was it a case of love *jihad*, deliberate and willfully masterminded by someone?' He quickly dismisses the thought. 'No, no, she is not like that', he assures himself. 'She has emotions. She even had nightmares many times, I had to calm her down. No one can be so manipulative. Maybe it is Kashmir's brewing crisis which robbed her of her peace of mind and made her whimsical and unpredictable. I wonder why she became serious about our relationship in the first place if she knew her parents would never allow her to marry a Hindu. Is she really so innocent? Parash told me she comes from the Valley's conservative, conflict-ridden society. The university life of JNU was a joyful phase of her life. For her, it was a new beginning with limitless space and liberty in a time-bound capsule. She found it exciting as long as the freshness lasted. Once it became fusty, the allure was lost and she is back in the bosom of the culture she grew up in. I thought I could draw Kafkaesque feelings out of her. Now, I wonder whether all the facts she shared about herself were lies or the truth'.

For Shankar, a golden phase of his life has ended. Husna, on the other hand, feels relieved. She thinks that the biggest conundrum of her life has come to a close. She would now be a born again Muslim, Inshallah.

Barkat's second-in-command Ishtiyaq, a regular major of the Pakistan army, issues two orders from Manshera camp. One, some informers, including a few women identified as moles, should be killed. Two, the appointment of Pakistani militants as commanders must be stopped and home-grown *mujahideen* promoted, mostly from rural areas. It is a reversal of the 1990s policy, when thousands of militants from Pakistan were pushed into the Valley and urban areas were targeted for *jihad*.

In his elaborate report, Ishtiyaq gives reasons for dismantling the women's cells and requests reformulation of the role of women. Ishitiyaq is a diehard militant. He tends to ridicule Kashmiri militants for being so conscious of their looks, seeking girlfriends, and coveting mobiles and costly western clothes. He sends a hard copy of the report to HQ at Mimshara, 'Our boys wear *salwar kameez*, spend nights in dense woods, eat ordinary maize breads, nuts and eggs, hardly ever have soup and *goshtaba*, while these home-grown clumsy lads stay in bustling settlements, enjoy home food and flirt with the local girls. This kind of recklessness, these cultural differences have made us vulnerable. The recent killing of two of our *mujahideen,* Talha and Mehmood Bhai at Aglar Kandi, shows how easily they target us now. We will continue losing our boys because of these local lads who are so casual and gauche in their interactions with the local girls and women that they forget their duty and even spill secrets in recklessness. Therefore, we are conducting operations only in small groups. Kindly give new orders and directions to these boys. The strike calls are no more relevant. They are useless commanders who have no control on these hedonistic teenagers. I dislike working with them. I request new orders to be given as soon as possible'.

Ishtiyaq has also discovered that the number of new local recruitments is declining and local leaders are changing *tanzeem*s as if they are job-hopping, for similar reasons: promotion and profit. He discusses it with Barkat. Barkat knows that Ishtiyaq is new to the Valley and finds his hatred for local *mujahideen* alarming. Unlike the other Pakistani army commanders, Barkat has no passion left to engage Kashmiris for reconditioning their minds to hurt India by any means. He feels revulsed by this bloody, directionless movement. He has seen the confidential report which illustrates the details of why war did not break out in 2002. He chose not to share the findings of this report with Ishtiyaq which in essence said: 'India had shown restraint in 2002 against Pakistan because its IT industry scrambled to relay the fears of its international customers and the importance of stability in India to the government. India had by then become an important player in the global supply chain of services and knowledge industry and was warned by the likes of General Electric that one slip-up and the outsourcing clients would leave, perhaps forever.' Barkat knows that India can easily play games with Pakistan if it wants. There is no comparison despite China's pledge to give active support. This realisation had dawned on elite Pakistan army circles, but it has yet to dawn on the likes of ISI. There is a running animosity between different *tanzeems* and militant outfits. The commanders are losing their hold.

Barkat has been avoiding Ishtiyaq lately. He seems indifferent and distracted even in the meetings he attends. Ishtiyaq has noted the change in him and secretly appointed a local lad to shadow Barkat. Ishtiyaq does not doubt his integrity but his evident indifference to *jihad* is worrying. Ishtiyaq is keen to find out if Barkat is facing an emotional predicament.

Two months later, Ishtiyaq goes to Barkat's hideout to discuss the issue of the frequent killing of boys by the Indian Army and about inter-*tanzeem* feuds. It is a frosty morning in the dense forests of Sumler where two commanders meet for a private, professional conversation. Ishtiyaq is eager to change the line of action against the Indian army and says, 'The Indian army finds targets easily and the young boys get killed without any substantial gain to the movement. The locals only know how to be noisy but secretly they give information about the targets to the enemy. We are trapped in a strange vicious circle'.

'You are right. Kashmiris are a strange lot. They have more identity crisis than any other community. The new generation has become even more unpredictable and fluid. The elite are cosmopolitan, power yielding, linguistically sensitive and phonetically conscious. The sentiment varies between township and township. There is a salaried middle class in Bandipore-Safapur line which is more interested in education and it is difficult to involve them directly in *jihad.* Sopore and Baramulla districts have an affluent population that is culturally distinct and phonetically discernable and therefore, distanced by the urban elite. They protect their identity through Jamaat-e-Islami's agenda of socialisation. The south is traditionally rich but linguistically different and less acknowledged. *Jihad* can easily fill up the void, they feel. They are late in collective consciousness. Though the south has small towns, they are qualitatively different. People have set their sights on education and salaried jobs, yet there is engagement with *jihad* for consensus on a mystified past in which Pakistan is glorified. There are more linguistic divides and regional variations among the communities of Kashmir than class divisions', replies Barkat.

'Does it mean that they have no religious obligations or love for Muslim oneness?' Ishtiyaq asks angrily.

'Ishtiyaq, Kashmiris are not a homogeneous, stable community. They have inferiority complexes and play the victim card while at the same time pretending to be superior and argumentative. It is their leadership which has infused in them the shades of inferiority and wounded mindsets with multiple standards. They are noisy about Islam and participate in boisterous protests about *azadi*, but their actions are in self-interest and material welfare. Their sick mindset is devoid of trust and needs a cure,' exclaims Barkat.

'Is this why you have become indifferent towards this *jihad* over the last few months? The high command says that we should draw our line of action ourselves so that Kashmir remains on the boil and *jihad* becomes locally evident. They are unable to give us a new strategy at the moment', says Ishtiyaq.

'It is difficult to bring Kashmiri elite to the point of one consensus about what actually they want, individually or collectively. In fact, those who matter never had any choice but to be visibly anti-India. Once I was shown

'Lost Conversations', a seventy-page document, by my senior officer in Rawalpindi. It was a typed copy. I am not sure about its fate now. It was the recorded conversation of Kashmiri mainstream political leaders at some place in Delhi. The political leaders except the old Pir were never sure what they actually wanted. They feel Pakistan is too primordial for them. They are not with India but would not like to go with Pakistan either. They praise China, so long as it is anti India. Privately they praise India for its liberalism, disorder and for free mobility and business. They denounce America, but would like their children to settle in the western countries. It contains amazing confessions and makes apparent, the explicit disillusionment of Sheikh Abdullah and other successive leaders of Kashmir. I don't remember the exact words, but I do remember that it presented a narrative of Kashmir and the reasons why Sheikh Abdullah had a change of heart in 1938 and 1975', says Barkat.

'Can you throw some light on it? I want to know about this', requests Ishtiyaq.

'Abdullah had a special fondness for Nehru. If it had not been for his relationship with Nehru, he would either have been killed by a conspiracy of his own men or directly by monarchy in the period 1932-46. It was Nehru who introduced him to the Quit Kashmir Movement along with the national movement of India. The sense of defeat and deprivation has remained a perennial factor with Kashmir. Nehru felt deprived and Sheikh Abdullah felt defeated, feelings which they managed to pass on to their co-religionists. In order to overcome this historical aberration, they joined hands in 1938.

'Abdullah knew his subjects were poverty-ridden, illiterate and submissive because of centuries of subjugation and yet survived through social-cultural mimicry. They managed to co-exist with subaltern locals as well as with non-native elites. Sheikh Sahib's decision to change the name of Muslim Conference to National Conference was deliberate. For transforming Kashmir into a modern civilised society, he needed the social agency of an educated middle class, which then was none other than the Pandits of Kashmir. In their absence, Kashmir would have been in the slumber of Swat Valley, singing "*Allah Hu, Allah hu*" and fighting for elite power; a *jihad* without any reason or knowledge—as they do now. They were teachers, doctors and administrators until they were replaced by the process of democratisation and affirmative action for the majority population in the late 1960s.

'In post-independence India, Abdullah brought about land reforms and deprived Pandits of their land more than proportionally. In 1947, they had 33 per cent of land of the Valley. After he became a prisoner of Cold

War polemics and an agent of a client state, nobody could stop Kashmir from developing as part of India. There were detailed figures of material assets of Kashmir in 1947 and then in 1975, as also of Azad Kashmir and Swat Valley. There is no comparison. We are in a dismal stage in Pakistan. Syed Mir Qasim elaborated how even in the absence of Sheikh Sahib, Kashmir progressed through state-sponsored programmes and local developmental schemes. It ushered in a new revolution in the lives of the people through the apple industry, handicrafts, forests, mushrooming of schools and well-spread health facilities. Kashmir being a predominantly Muslim state, the government had formulated policies which allowed admission in professional colleges and appointments in the public sector on the basis of population and not through merit lists. This process gradually displaced traditional Pandit elite from all public spheres.

'By the mid-1970s, Kashmir was structurally transformed in the way Abdullah wanted: a burgeoning rich class along with well-spread educated middle class. Muslims became visible in the public realm. On the other side, the traditional elite and middle-class population of Pandits was migrating from the Valley. Kashmir now had more professional colleges, cheap education, increased number of mosques in each locality and well-spread chain of state-run schools than any other state. It only needed an industrial base and big hospitals to make it a leading state, for which Abdullah came out of political hibernation. He wanted to prove that they were miles ahead of the people of Azad Kashmir and other parts which got annexed with Pakistan in October 1947. They had only ridicule for Pakistan and looked down at it in disgust'.

Barkat adds, 'We knew their double standards. We never trusted them but seduced them through religion so that they plunge back into the situation they had started from in the 1930s. Let them become akin to the Swat Valley and Azad Kashmir. The process of shaming is happening from both sides, though they are feigning a movement of grace and salvation'.

'How do you know these things?' asks Ishtiyaq in astonishment.

'I have been involved in this movement for the last thirteen years and was supposed to read reports and analyse developments. I got to know about the secret 'Conversations' when I was promoted to officer rank and was privy to secret documents', replies Barkat.

'This will be a huge disappointment for the average *mujahideen* if they come to know about it', says Ishtiyaq.

'We are not like Kashmiri *mujahideen* who can't keep any secret. No one needs to know about it. Gradually, we shall hand over the movement to them. Let them decide. Till then, be careful with the mission and do whatever the command says', cautions Barkat.

Ishtiyaq does not say anything about tailing him out of fear. His respect for Barkat is growing now that he has got a glimpse of his intellect and circumspection. Barkat is always calm and serene, as if living a normal life. It is difficult to get any information from him about his personal life. He concludes that Barkat is a diehard commander rich in experience and shrewd in his judgments. He has learnt things in this meeting which were beyond his comprehension as a soldier. When he leaves, he feels a bit out of his depth.

Snowfall in the forest makes it look purer than the sky, which is covered with untidy layers of thick clouds. It looks as if the sky has absorbed the serenity coming from the earth in the form of a white glaze. Barkat looks out at the dense forest from his hideout.

Snowflakes are falling on the wide branches noiselessly and there are no footprints or trails in sight. The only sound is the gushing of streams and chirping of tiny birds. Barkat thinks it is time for a rebirth. Early in the morning, he reviews his years as a militant, lonely and secluded for most of his adult life. In a flash, he knows what he must do to get out of this rut: get a personal life. He decides to ask Tahira for her hand in marriage. The very thought is like an elixir.

On wintry evenings, Kashmir goes to slumber much

earlier than usual, especially in remote villages and far off towns. Once he thinks it is safe, he goes to meet Tahira and brings her to Athuwatu jungles where he has a safe hideout in the higher ridges of Bandipore, which he still uses in emergencies.

'Tahira, I like this place very much. It is divine. They say Madhumati, lost in the plains of India, came here to meet her lover, Koka Pandit. This rivulet is named after her. It is a place of romantic worshippers', Barkat whispers, gazing into her eyes.

'Well, the entire Kashmir is like that. If you go away from towns and cities to places with few inhabitants, you shall find nature in romance with the earth. Especially in meadows and the pilgrimages of hills and mountains, the earth is alive with wild flowers, chirping birds, blue sky, wispy clouds, bushy terrains and flowing brooks, about bountiful tales of men and women now—missing and unmentioned in history', she says, adding softly, 'Pakistan sold us dreams through Hurriyat which brought drugs, death and destruction'.

'Yes, my second *Babb*'s family was from Bandipore and often described the beauty of the place nostalgically. I find the essence of the old Bandipore of *Babb*'s stories in the freshness of the Athuwatu forest. I want you to know that my second *Babb* was the one who helped me become a better person. He took an orphan like me under his wing and helped me fulfil my dream to study. I still remember the first time I went to his place to study, *Babb* brought out his *Nichpatre* (sort of religious calendar) to find day, date and time to start my teaching. Kashmiris use *Nichpatre* before starting any auspicious work.[39] I was touched by his sincerity towards teaching', Barkat remembers fondly.

'It is strange that Kashmiri *Battas* live in Pakistan too. How many *Battas* were there at your place in Pakistan?' Tahira asks in surprise.

Barkat realises his mistake and changes the topic, 'Come, let us talk about something more important. I want to spirit you away to a far-off place, away from Kashmir'.

'Ohh, my *Mauje*, where? Pakistan? You want to slay me or sell me? I shall not go', she mocks in a wry tone.

'No, I want you to be my wife. We shall go home', says Barkat earnestly.

'Moen too had promised the same thing and look how it turned out. Do not deceive me with these tales now. I shall perish if I have to go through the same agony again. I have no hope of a happy and normal life', says Tahira sadly.

Barkat holds her hands and says earnestly, 'I would never leave you. We will go to a place where we can live

39 Panchang, an assemblage of astrological details and date.

peacefully like a normal family with our own children'.

'I prefer to die here only. Do not give wings to my long forgotten dreams. It is my destiny not to experience a good life. I am happy here with your closeness. This is enough', replies Tahira.

'Why are you bothered about this place where you have lost everything and each passing day is bitter suffering for you? I want to take you to a different place where you can forget about the bitter times and live happily,' says Barkat.

'From where will we get the money to live a good, happy life in a different place? Unless you are truthful to me, how can I be convinced?' asked Tahira.

'I was not like this before. I am a driver by profession and that driver has become owner of ten vehicles over the years. The vehicles still run at my place and I have daily income that has piled up into millions over the years', replies Barkat.

'I don't understand. You told me that you have no relatives, you are alone and you left home thirteen years ago. How can you still manage to run your business?' she asks.

'This is the reward I will get for giving so many years to the mission. I can quit any time and I would face no problems in starting a fresh life in India, Pakistan or Bangladesh. I have earned this from my masters of *jihad*', says Barkat.

Tahira is not convinced. 'They will follow you there', she says, full of dread.

'No, I am past that age limit. I have survived without any treachery to my employer. I am left free with these advantages after turning forty', Barkat replies.

'Is it possible in this digital world, with so much of surveillance? You will be caught by police even if your *tanzeem* allows you to quit', says a worried Tahira.

'That will not happen. Believe me. I have remained invisible and unknown. Still, I shall first go alone and settle everything to be on the safe side. I shall change my name and transfer the money to a new account opened with the new name. I am thinking of leaving tomorrow. Please keep this a secret. But do pay a visit to Razz *Babb* whenever you get time and take his blessings', says Barkat.

'How does it work? I mean, how did you manage to run your business all this time?' asks Tahira.

'I cannot answer these questions as I do not know myself how it is being done. Every month, a certain amount is transferred into my account like a salary. I was never interested in knowing the mechanism of the long chain through which it functions. There are people to do it but I don't know them. Politicians, bureaucrats do it on the appeal of cult gurus, *qazis*, maulvis and astrologers. They work not only as facilitators but as collaborators with or without non-state actors in getting impossible jobs done. They get huge commissions for it. Their power helps in sustaining this unproductive industry of *jihad* through non-state actors. There is hardly anything spiritual in their dirty world', says Barkat in disgust.

'Then why do you ask me to take blessings from Razz *Babb*?' asks Tahira.

'Oh, take your words back! Even to say something like that about Razz *Babb* is sinful. He is cast in a different mould. Genuinely spiritual, he stays hidden from the masses. He is a human being who thinks beyond materialist attractions. He is a spiritual wanderer, unlike the new exhibitionist Pirs who make it to the news and are visible. There is a thin line between real Pirs like Razz *Babb* and the fake Pirs. You must understand this when you meet him. You need to differentiate between a thug and a truthful person. There is a strange assortment of holy, calm, unworldly pious men and women who are around to make this world safer for common people. They try hard to stay invisible. Razz *Babb* is one of them. They are a rare breed, difficult to find in the modern world. They have been replaced by a new class of gurus and maulanas who sing bhajans, *nats* and narrate *nawahs* in family gatherings, temples and mosques.[40] They are alike in all the religions. They polarise communities in

40 Praise of the Prophet and religious mourning.

the name of their religion and divide them to create chaos and anarchy, all the while claiming to be inviolable and expecting only other-worldly rewards. They have control over politicians and powerful people. They have connections with everyone who holds positions in the power structure. They trick people with the power of their narratives. They claim to be godly and can easily lure women and befool men with their so-called mystical knowledge. They have the power to undermine reason. They remain obsessed with their feigned identity and display it with rhetorical flourishes to hypnotise the masses. This is how they manipulate people for their vested interests', says Barkat.

'Each one has a role here, either construed or constructed. We have been caught in our sins. It is difficult to come out of this whirlpool', says Tahira.

'That's why I insist must you come with me and live in a place which is far away from this chaos. The times ahead are very uncertain. Al Hadis and Barelvis are dominating the other streaks of the faith. They are rich in resources and influence. There are new *khatib*s whose sermons are different from before. They preach anti-culture and rootless traditions of the faith. It is conflicting but still gaining recognition due to the uncertainties of the time. The narrative of return to God is full of vengeance in all the religions. You will not be left free here because they have identified you as soldier on a keyboard. Therefore, it is better to leave this place and live in a different, unknown locality', suggests Barkat.

'I will come with you', exclaims Tahira, finally saying the words Barkat wants to hear. 'I shall send back my nephew to his mother and then leave silently with you', .

Barkat's joy knows no bounds. 'I will return as soon as I settle everything. We will unite within three months, perhaps, when the spring brings the first flowers in the gardens', Barkat says excitedly.

Once upon a time, he had left his home in the spring and never went back. 'Take me to a place where nothing is concealed and men do not kill men in the name of faith,' Tahira reciprocates happily. 'I want to live where dark clouds do not come from the western mountains to kill us with slashing lighting and turn our blue clean rivulets into red, muddy, foul-smelling waters. I dream of living in a place where relationships are built on mutual appreciation and respect. I no longer crave for lustful coupling but for soulful closeness in the path of life we tread together. I am ready to leave this Valley and go to a place where "love has no age, no limit and no death". Take me there, my dear.'

The hard fatigue of years of militancy, exasperation with days and nights of hypocritical discourse and frozen estrangement with place and people vanishes in the spiral of love and oneness. Barkat feels for the first time a yearning for togetherness. He feels optimistic about his future with Tahira.

A line by the poet Jigar he had heard from Teacher *Babb*'s son in Varanasi reverberated in his ears again after long years and he recites happily, '*Taghaful, Tajahul, Tabassum, Takallum, Yeha tuk tou ayae vough aate aate...'* (first ignoring me willfully, then arguments, when still I followed, then smiles and finally conversations and interactions. This way she came to me slowly and slowly step by step.)

'I desire to go to Mukdam Sahib with you before you leave and tie a handkerchief for your return', says Tahira.

Next day, they go together to Mukdam Sahib and then up the threshold of Hari Parbat. While coming down from the Parbat, they notice three teenage boys watching them from the slope near the last stair. They do not bother them but it puts Barkat on edge. The couple takes a taxi and gets down near Said Kadal. Barkat's suspicion of being tailed turns out to be correct. He tells Tahira that they are under surveillance and warns her to stay alert. It is then time for a hasty goodbye and a promise that they would meet soon. Tahira takes a local bus towards the Dargah and Barkat too disappears.

A week has gone by without any word from Barkat to his second-in-command Ishtiyaq. According to the instruction, Barkat was supposed to go to Bahawalpur via

Nepal. The change in strategy is due to failed targets and deaths of *mujahideen* without any significant dividends. Barkat has told Ishtiyaq that he would be returning to Pakistan, but instead of taking the border route, he takes a train from Jalandhar to Mughalsarai. He carries a new identity card bearing the name of Madhav Kishor Mishra. He has already thrown his mobile into the Ravi river near Madhavpur, a town in Indian Punjab.

Meanwhile, in Kashmir, with the arrest of two women militants, Shazia and Jan, the police claim it has cracked down on the network of the underground women's wing and militant hideouts. This makes the *tanzeem* worried about the safety of its commanders. There is no news about Barkat, a top-ranked commander in the army files of Pakistan. They need to know his whereabouts. His sudden disappearanc makes commanders suspicious that there is a mole in their organisation. Tahira too is under scrutiny.

Early on Sunday, she goes to seek the blessings of Razz *Babb*. She knows that *Babb* does not look at women, nor do women ever dare go to his cottage. She rests near the cottage for a while, till she sees Wali Sahib walking up. After greeting him, she requests Wali Sahib to take her along. He asks her to wait outside and goes to get Razz *Babb*'s permission.

'*Babb*, a woman named Tahira wishes to seek your blessings. Shall I bring her in?' he asks.

'No, no, time has come. I shall go to see her', says *Babb* and hurriedly stands up, which is unusual for him. He puts the monkey cap on his head and moves out. Tahira runs towards him and bends down to touch his feet. Before she can do so, there is a rain of bullets from behind a big tree.

Both *Babb* and Tahira are lying dead in the open field under the cloudy sky of a chilly Sunday morning. A pool of blood spreads on the green grass.

The headline in the morning papers the next day screams: 'Razz *Babb* is dead. A uniformed unidentified person killed him and a lady named Tahira in front of his cottage. The killer was seen running towards the army camp'.

Ishtiyaq's men have accomplished their mission.

Madhav Kishor Mishra settles near Smane Ghat in Varanasi in a two-room house. Abu Tasleem, his identity for years, is gone, buried in the files of unknown deaths in Kashmir. The file in the archive of time that had opened with the first tribal raid in Kashmir remains unwrapped, though fresh names and pages keep getting added.

Mishraji is a typical Banarasi philanthropist who goes unnoticed and serves abandoned children in an orphanage. Nobody knows anything about his past, nor does anybody care to dig it up. People know him as an eccentric middle-aged humanitarian. He is normally a quiet person but becomes animated when attending formal debates and discussions.

Though willfully disconnected from his past, he often thinks of his three *Babb*s who wrote the story of his life and his times buried in his heart. He laughs like a madman and then weeps bitterly when he reads the news about the tragic murder of Tahira and Razz *Babb*. He knows that it had to happen for *Babb* had hinted to him about it. It was long back decided with the killing of

Sabzar, a typical case of factional rivalry and animosity. Yet Barkat has no wish to go back to revenge the death of his dear ones.

Time passes by; his blood-soaked money finds meaning in MKM Mission House. He expands the organisation and shifts to a two-storey building which has five rooms in addition to a hall and a library. It becomes a study centre with a difference, where university students voluntarily spend their free time teaching kids without any fee. The organisation takes care of abandoned children, whose number increases to 110 in five years. Funds come from charities as well as the students who come to teach here. MKM Mission House soon gets social acceptance and he attains the status of Swamiji. The saint gives discourses on the floating population, stray animals moving freely in the city, congested roads and lanes with encroachments, yet eulogises Varanasi as a place connecting the threads of sustainability, a source of enlightenment, where death does not scare and life does not excite. It is peaceful. In its mechanical and organic disorder, the city's life preserves its age-old harmony in the meeting of traditions and faiths.

The choice of place for rebirth of Madhav Kishore Mishra is not coincidental. He knows well that Gautam Buddha chose this place for his declaration of avatar and sermons. The Bhakti Movement originated here with Kabir and Raidas. This is where Mahatma Gandhi gave his first lecture against colonial rule and the maharajas who supported the Raj in 1916, launching the freedom movement. Madan Mohan Malviya established a pioneering institution—Banaras Hindu University—here and even Narendra Modi chose this constituency to elect him to Parliament and become Prime Minister of the country. Mirza Ghalib paid tribute to Varanasi with his famous poem '*Chirag-e-dair*' and Jawaharlal Nehru often visited the city and BHU to renew his pledge and vision. Multitudes have heard reverberating echoes of saints and Sufis, musings of artists in sitars, *shehnai* and *tabla* over the centuries. The sacred city transcends time and space.

The notion of timelessness is not stagnation but a pattern of wandering round a core that has not disintegrated. One needs to cultivate it and enjoy the bliss of the crescent Ganga that takes a turn in Varanasi as if going back to its source. This place has a solution for human suffering.

Barkat is satisfied with the functioning of his organisation. He has made it a rule that a minimum of ten boys abandoned by their parents are picked up every year from faraway places. He makes it a core centre with linkages to Pilgrimage House and Gyan Prava, the enlightenment centres, besides bringing alive humanistic debates and the cultural flavour of Varanasi.

Years go by and the organisation becomes a centre for exchange of academic ideas with discourses on intolerance, rupture of modernity, weakening of states. However, lived religion and interfaith accommodation are teetering due to the process of democratisation. Trust deficit in degenerate politics does not allow humanistic discourse to take over, which is a cause of worry and deep concern for Barkat. He wishes to contribute towards empowerment of humanistic discourse. It has to be a change of subjectivity where power would be synonymous with altruism for public good rather than a vehicle of self-interest.

Can the Enlightenment ethos be revisited, he wonders. He had heard from Teacher *Babb* that Kashmiri traditions were geared for universal peace until these were subdued by non-native insurrections. He has seen its reflection in Razz *Babb*. He thinks that each place evolves according to its own traditions of common culture and shared existence over the years. However, he thinks that sustained traditions emerge from culture at the time of crisis through actors. These actors change the structures and interpret the structural core of love, peace and collective accommodation and should find space and experimentation for alternative modernity.

This interesting academic reformation centre fascinates many teachers and students from the university. Sundays become eventful, absorbing days at this institution. Parash too comes at least twice a month. He gets a sense of peace listening to the ideas that were dear to his father. MKM knows Parash is his Teacher *Babb*'s son. The long duration of discontinuity in their acquaintance is like layers of dust which have made them unfamiliar now. The precious memory is saved in a box which Barkat does not wish to open, preferring to remain unknown.

He has invited Parash to one of the seminars on 'Alternate Modernity' and after a handful of academic interactions, he requests him to be one of the trustees of the Board of MKM Trust. Although Parash does not know much about the organisation, he admires Mishraji as a person and accepts the membership. He gives presentations which provoke discussion and reflective endorsements. He knows that present-day scholarship is not capable of adapting those methodologies. Colonial subjugation and modernity have made Indian scholarship genuflect before the image of modernity by either glorifying the past or negating it. Mythologising history is not elucidation. The problems are grave and the solution is to find an alternative world order which could make morality intrinsic to materialism. Buddha renounced materialism and Marx clinched it. Both knew its power to dehumanise the order. Islamic teaching (*tabliqh*) uses past glory for symbolising the hegemonic expansion of a codified faith. Cult gurus are no less proficient in mythologising history. The only difference is the varying degrees of violence they both provoke in society. If materiality is everything in this world, its distribution has to be without boundaries because boundaries limit unfolding of the self or the group.

Barkat is puzzled about the amazing overarching of the narrations of his three *Babb*s. The illiterate one who saved his life told him that he should not try to make his living by dishonest means. Teacher *Babb*, who gave him education and opened the windows of his mind to see the world, explained that material without morality is fluidity. And Razz *Babb* said that the inner journey was better than wandering in unknown places.

Barkat is convinced his life has come full circle. December is gone. The New Year has brought chill as well as the optimism of spring. Justice Javid Iqbal, Allama Iqbal's erudite son dies at the age of ninety-four but leaves behind a new discovery of Iqbalism[41] through his talk shows, writings and YouTube videos. It is a rebuttal of the mullahs' interpretations of Iqbal. Barkat finds Justice Javid's interpretation close to what his Teacher *Babb* would say about Iqbal. Poor Big Pir proved to be

41 Poetry and philosophy of the poet.

not so conversant with Allama Iqbal's poetry. Therefore Kashmiris do not endorse it much.

After becoming a member of the trust, Parash frequently visits the new MKM centre on weekends. During a morning session, Parash finds a copy of *Kulyate Razz* in his library. He is surprised and asks, 'Where did you find this book? Do you know who he was? Do you read Urdu? This is my father's poetry.'

Barkat replies, 'It is very dear to me. I like his poetry. I know Urdu a little and do not understand Kashmiri but his Urdu poetry is rich and even has the reflections of Iqbal. Parash, I want you to help me to understand his Kashmiri poetry. Just like Javid Iqbal, who explored his father's poetry, with the same passion I want to explore his poetry. It is a treat to learn how Iqbal explains his thoughts in "Reconstruction". I think the human project is about new ideas and research for the betterment of humankind. It cannot be a closed realm of codifications. Codification is incomplete and limiting', says Barkat to the son of his mentor.

'Yes, Mishraji, Iqbal was a rebel against the conservatism of Islam. I was mesmerised by his conversation with God, where he asks a question about the future of the *umma* and God does not say anything in reply. It has a huge message of collective existence and the purpose of historical existence in the service of humanity.

My father would also explain and interpret many shades of Iqbal's poetry. It was basically the poetry of exploration where he was socially caged for being the product of his times but yearning to go beyond religion's finalities', says Parash.

'What else did your father tell you, Parash?' asked Barkat.

'In his last years, he was in pain. He became lonely after the departure of my mother; he was also attached to a private student, who left him without prior notice, without any information. He felt he had failed his orphan student, who disappeared before his education was complete. We could not do much about tracing the boy. What is strange is that when I went to Kashmir after my father's death in 2011, my childhood friend Najeeb also told me that a *mujahideen* commander, a non-Kashmiri, would come to my father's abandoned house regularly; sit there for hours as if in meditative mode. It could be Barkat, who had turned a militant'.

Barkat's heart is beating rapidly but long years of training have ingrained in him the ability to keep his cool. 'Maybe you should have explored this clue.'

Parash dismisses the thought that Barkat could have been that *mujahideen* commander. 'There were not many chances to lead him astray at that stage for he had picked up degrees, learnt languages and was on a linear track after years of loneliness and underprivileged childhood'.

Barkat tries to defend himself. 'You become vulnerable when familiarity brings in your mind a stream of twisted comparisons. Comparisons are derivations that generate repulsion. Maybe your father brought Barkat in the range of competition, where he became frustrated standing in the queue to find a place in society.'

'I think he knew well that he had a long way to go on that path of linearity, for he was late to the race of life. I understand *Babb* did not want him to be conscious of the fact that he was socially at a disadvantage. Barkat himself discovered it and wanted to correct his past, not by taking a break from it but linking it with a world of its own. Perhaps he joined a *tabliqhi* group. That would have been very tragic for my father to hear.'

'Yes, you do not live for money alone,' responds Barkat. 'You toil to erase the stigma and cling onto hope of a better future. Death then is a future that seems seductive and healing in the helplessness of this life'.

Parash looks at his watch. 'I must go home to prepare for the next week's interactive session. My friend Shankar is visiting. I shall bring him to the centre'.

'Banaras is mystical', Shankar says to Parash during their early morning visit to Samne Ghat. 'It indeed is. In case of Varanasi, it is mystical in exteriority. No doubt it is the exteriority, its ornamentation and decoration that attracts the outsider. History here is ornamented and the present is congested with streams of pilgrims, students and professionals pouring into the city. Different steams blend in one, which is the Banarasi way of life. Look at the turn of the Ganges from this Ram Nagar Bridge. Is it not an amazing sight? The Ganges is kissing only the curved border of Varanasi with her thin lips. I wish it could have kissed the full circle', says Parash.

'It has remained like my half-curve relationship with Husna. I had wished to come here with Husna and spend some time exploring the civilisational depths of the East with her', Shankar says sadly.

'Have you two not broken up already?' asks Parash.

'We did. But ten days ago she sent a text saying she is unhappy and in a suicidal mood. Out of concern, I suggested she consult a psychiatrist and do what her parents want. I fear that she would turn to be another Anna Karenina. Her conflict is the conundrums of Kashmir. She continues texting me even after I asked her not to contact me at all. It seems as if she wants me but not enough to go against the wishes of her family. It is a strange case where a willful rebel has turned into a remorseful victim. She argues that I have no cultural warmth to give her. Tell me Parash, what is all this?'

'It is a paradox of being. A reversal of role of God and Society creating confusion and existential crisis for a person', replies Parash.

'What do you mean? Explain!' pleads Shankar.

'This material world needs a moral core. Therefore human agencies created God and religion to bring order in the universe. Morality was replaced by God to justify instrumentality of self-interest rather than collective welfare. God remained personified for the other world after death. It should have been here to strengthen the moral core rather than justifying the break of moral core'.

'Shankar, we have almost reached MKM centre. Mishraji is a saintly philanthropist. I have developed a liking for him. He is a great listener and offers solutions for any problem you put before him. You can discuss anything with him without hesitation. Your formal presentation is tomorrow. Today, we can talk about your personal life', says Parash.

'My riddle is Husna's change of mind; I would feel great relief if I could solve it. Husna had become a part of me. Her decision to break up with me has made me lonely and introverted. It was her love which made me sympathetic towards Kashmiri Muslims. I even reached a point where I thought that their hate for non-Muslims is justified', says Shankar.

'Love is a bridge between the self and the other and glues it into one core', responds his friends.

They reach Mishraji's centre and go in to meet him. Shankar finds it cosy, a place where he can speak out without restraint. Effervescence of the narrative is ready to flow.

Shankar starts, 'My purpose to come to Varanasi was not only to get mature reactions and observations on my presentation but indeed I am interested to discover our source of sustenance. Mishraji, I am told you can solve many puzzles. News of your aura has brought me here'.

Barkat says humbly, 'I am illiterate and naive and this is not my permanent home. I am here as long as God wishes. These children and books are my pilgrims and educated people like you are my teachers. Look at the Ganga. It's our mirror. The image in the mirror tells me my tale, in bits and pieces. You have to find your source of sustenance in the journeying of this river. Stay here for some years.'

Shankar hastily answers, 'I must work hard for some years in academics. I could not get settled in life. My first marriage failed and a girl called Husna came into my life and gave me emotional anchorage. I became obsessed with her and invested time and emotions in her. My break-up with her has ripped apart my heart', says Shankar in a dejected voice.

Barkat becomes curious when he hears Husna's name and he eagerly responds, 'My life has been in breaks and patches too. I was able to gather myself in this seclusion. I know it happens in life. But let me tell you that many of us don't live our lives properly. In the material world, we have lost the art of conversation. Migration and displacement make us multi-cultural but the extension of social geography shrivels us to seek refuge in the monoculture. In a closed social geography where culture complements religion, our lifespans are not fragmented. They are stratified. We invented youth as a separate category. In our tradition, the teenage years were partly spent in childhood and partly in the adult world. Half would be absorbed in Brahmacharya (celibacy) and the other half in Grahast (domestic life). Crusades of *jihad* and modernity have put youth in a category which sounds special, yet nobody understands them and they perish in games of order making. Grahast, the stage of life for marriage and progeny, was in continuity with childhood, with no gap between celibacy and maturity.

'Husna must have been lured by openness of JNU and the glamorous life you gave to her but soon, she went back to her cultural moorings where you are the "other". You need to come to your senses, otherwise you will remain discontented for the rest of your life, without a feeling of peace and closure', cautions Barkat.

'What should I do? I find these Kashmiri girls swing between two extremes. She adored me and despised her home when we became friends. She often said that she had found life and light in me. She appreciated my parents and said that her parents were not only a mismatch but unworthy human beings. But now, she says she wants to take care of her parents and regrets wasting her precious time with me. I don't say that she was a fake, but I do find her unpredictable', says Shankar.

Barkat reacts, 'Why should you worry if you have been a giver? The giver is always a gainer. How long would she be stuck in youthful obsessions? Let her go. She has left you in this misery. '*Huye hasher mein hum jiske liye rusva, jawani ki do-chaar nadaniyan thhi*' (For what we defamed on the Day of Judgement were a few frailties of our youth).[42] If there is an age gap beyond ten years, dissonance is but natural'.

42 Famous verse of Allama Iqbal.

'She broke up with me but still texts me, insisting we remain friends for life despite our history of a failed relationship', Shankar says agitatedly.

'I think you need to understand her better. In your company, she found bodily warmth and economic security as well, but what she missed was cultural tenderness. This dichotomy made her bond with you weak and uncertain. You should be good to her but avoid any kind of intimacy. Prayers are heeded when heart and body are connected. Here they are spilt', states Parash.

'Should I tell her straightway that she shouldn't meet me any more? I too feel sometimes that my pleas are ignored. My prayers to God lack concentration,' says Shankar.

'Yes, you should avoid meeting her, but don't be arrogant. Sensitivity with arrogance is inferiority and shallowness, while sensitivity with modesty is bonding and healing', replies Parash.

He continues, 'Yes, modesty is sensitivity and goodness while arrogance is shallowness and mediocrity. I feel that Husna is restless, nervous. Many career women like her have become unkind to their bodies as they bargain with it for a price. They do not understand that bodies are as pure as the soul and the notion that the body is profane and the soul is pure is foolish. Some career women engage their bodies for material success. They think they can manage men, but patriarchy is so frozen in conflict-ridden societies that in the guise of virtue, discourses are created to eliminate the dissent. Perhaps, she understands that it would be difficult to survive if she breaks out of patriarchal boundaries'.

Barkat goes into the kitchen to prepare tea for them. Meanwhile, Shankar shares something very dear to his heart with Parash. 'I don't know why I am still so immersed in her. The intimacy I shared with her was not just physical. I felt as if she was the answer to all my prayers and the purpose of my existence. All of a sudden, the aromatic fragrance of our relationship has changed into a foul stench. I agree that intimacy is divine when the heart is in it. Then, it is love or else it is trade'.

Over tea, the topic of conversation changes. Barkat says, 'It is communication and language that moulds the interaction. I have not been lucky like you to talk about women and have agreeable conversations with them. My contact and interactions have mostly been with men. I have no experience of gendered language. If my mother had been around during my childhood, things would have been different. I am colour blind about this world. Most boys who do not have normal socialisation with families and institutions are awkward with women.

'Instead, uncommon saints have played important roles in my life. Their teachings were simple but assertive, and they were not persons of temporal power. Power, in any case, is prone to be abused and exploited for vested interest. One has to handle it with care and compassion'.

The sun was high up in the sky. The news of the surgical strike at Balakot had spread like wildfire. Shankar had had a premonition that before elections, a tragedy like Pulwama would bring India and Pakistan head to head. 'There is a paradigm shift in Indian aggression. India could venture deep into the Pakistan's territory. Pakistanis hoped there would be a role reversal in public discourse brought about by its leadership. Imran talks peace, Modi talks war. I think Imran got a God-given opportunity to listen to international opinion to act against banned organisations in Pakistan. He can win on two fronts: save his country from war against India and compel India to engage on Kashmir and finish terror structures in Pakistan as well. If there is no war, it would mean more pressure on India to be proactive in Kashmir, to engage its stakeholders', Barkat tells them.

Shankar reacts, 'I too think the West has only one wish: that Pakistan do more on terror and engagement of India with Kashmir is replicated. I think this would bring army and civil authorities on one page, for Pakistan is in troubled times. If there is no war, I think it would be Imran's undoing and Modi's political closure. Modi's aggression is his political advantage and Imran's softness is for his country's benefit'.

After a couple of nights in Varanasi, Shankar goes back with a puzzled mind, still teeming with questions about his relationship with Husna. Personal experiences, he reflects, influence political discourse.

Summer is gone and rains have come to swell the otherwise limpid streams that flow into the Ganga, making it overflow its banks. MKM Mission House is about to be flooded but Parash continues to visit. On a sultry Sunday afternoon, Parash receives a call from Mishraji to meet him. He goes after the evening *aarti*. The night has put on its curtain of darkness for the stars that were bathing in the brimming Ganga. Its roar on its zigzag course makes it sound like a force of nature to be feared.

'Parash, this is the most crucial night of my life. It looks like this centre might even get submerged for some weeks, the way Ganga is rising'.

'It happens after rains, then we forget about it. I think you should shift to some other place till then", Parash tries to soothe him.

But Bårkat has a larger plan in mind. 'I think I should move out of this place for good. I have decided to hand over its functioning to you. I want to be relieved of my responsibilities.'

'Why, what happened ? Parash asks with concern.

'I have lived here for more than forty years and I am

no longer interested in running this centre, which I think should be handed over to a professionally committed person. You are the most qualified person to make it a sustainable institute', Barket says persuasively. Parash does not say anything, for he has the responsibilities of an ailing mother-in-law, growing daughter and struggling wife. He feels overburdened, the advancing years also slowing him down. He responds that he will take time to give his reply, maybe after the rains.

After the professor leaves, Barkat is in a contemplative mood. For the first time, he feels his aloneness is a blessing. He thinks about how his adventurous experimentation with life had made him understand his *raison d'etre*. He had created a choice for himself, when he found that he was lost in the din at different stages of his life; now he is convinced he has nothing new to experience.

At every crossroads, he has had to erase the past to make a new beginning. He lacks the patience to endure a condition for too long, wants to overcome his limitations and faces identity crisis. He tries again and again to be part of a collective that would give him attainable tasks but instead of getting satisfaction, he gets disillusioned and feels lost. When Razz *Babb* showed him the way to regain himself, he thought he had come full circle and finished his wanderings.

He has no regrets about his next step, for he feels he

has no choice. He created his own world, experimented with it and failed to find any solace. His sweetest memories are the hours he spent with his three *Babb*s. He thinks that those are the connecting knots to the alternative paths he could have charted based on their advice. Tahira made him realise how incomplete he had been and how much agony, pain and suffering both the worlds have construed for power and domination. The first one groomed him till he entered his teens and gave him his name and sustenance. The second one opened the window of knowledge and tried to give him a sense of direction but he found social boundaries difficult to cross instantly.

When the third one showed him the mirror, he realised that he had lost his face.

Barkat wishes he had followed any one of them in full. He failed to stay steady on his course and broke his own spirit. He remained deprived of social capital, purpose and path. He felt caged and wanted to break all boundaries. It was a path of self-destruction, the life of a nomad for elimination and not for assemblage. He should have opted for this-worldly goals with its construed social disparities balanced by legitimate evolved institutions.

Looking back, Barkat realises he had been bequeathed good worldviews but had chosen the worst path. He had chosen to drown in mystified illusions and untrue seductions. He realises that he should have been with his Teacher *Babb* for more years, not turned his back to him with incomplete knowledge and half degrees.

The sudden, abrupt decision to abrogate Article 370 with one stroke on 5 August 2019 took everyone by surprise. It shocked Pakistan, for it implied that its game was over in Kashmir. Kashmiri Muslims went into shock, unable to come to terms with what had happened. Imran Khan's new avatar unfolded a messiah of the Muslim *umma*. To distract from the challenges of domestic opposition and external compulsions to rely on China, he came out stridently against Modi and started a hate campaign from the UN General Assembly. For the first time, Pakistan state and non-state agents, media and think-tanks went berserk, urging the government to punish India, baying for its blood. War clouds gathered but international pressure defused the tension. Restrictions in Kashmir saved the Valley from the mayhem that Pakistan wanted to unleash.

Shankar was upset, Parash watchful about the developments. On phone, they would talk daily to share the news and vent their apprehensions about instability in the region.

'Parash, once the restrictions are over, do you think there will be an eruption?' asks Shankar.

'Two months have gone by, there is a sense of realisation that Kashmiris might get reconciled to staying within India, especially after the loss of special status. However, Pakistan will never allow that Kashmir shake off its dystopia. It will do everything; use all its capacity and agencies to bleed India on caste and community lines. The game will now be played by revealing secrets and sharpening animosities.'

'What about Kashmiri Pandits?'

'They are non-players in the game but sanguine that the developments which started in 1931 have come a full circle. It will take a decade from now, when a century has passed, to reveal its brunt. Pakistani threats can be countered only if peace and development in the country and normalcy in the Valley remain fail-safe'.

'I have yet to find out Husna's reaction. I think she might become harder in her approach. I feel that in their heart of hearts, Hurriyat or mainstream, literate or illiterate, they had been given this feeling that there was a possibility of Greater Kashmir on the lines of Musharraf's package. What they have got is a dismembered union territory. Separatism and conventional politics have all been made irrelevant in one stroke'.

'True, the uncharacteristic assertion, charisma and

popularity of Modi and Imran in their countries and their image in the world have given them an advantage to take bold decisions, which other leaders did not have the courage to take. But both of them are caged in their structures. The structures are dictating to them, jolting them when they get a little independent. Therefore, they will only outsmart each other rather than engage in cooperation. I would have desired Imran to accept the change, for he knows that neither wars nor negotiations can decide any formula on Kashmir. India can no longer delink it, Pakistan could not annex it. India had to integrate it, which in the longer run is good for Pakistan as well, if it decides to settle for peace. No further changes of boundaries can happen now.'

'This abrogation does not augur well if Pakistan is not prepared to accept it. It will not allow Kashmiri youth to think about their future'.

'Shankar, the problem with the younger generation is that they don't have a sense of history. What they learn from the media and the digital world is final for them but actually they are half-truths and lies. Families and parents hardly have any impact on them. They blame the older generation for the baggage of historical liabilities forced on them. There is a generation gap. By blaming their parents, they get the justification to break out of their embrace. It is a trust deficit. Values change with changing times but they don't realise this.'

Parash continues, 'Shankar, Mishraji has decided to hand his centre over to us. He is unusually generous. If you are convinced that we can carry on his mission, then I shall accept it or else it would be difficult for me to shoulder the responsibilities of this institute'.

'Yes, it is a good idea,' Parash responds immediately, seeing light at the end of the dark tunnel of his personal miasma. 'You will remain engaged with it after your superannuation. I shall try to create resources for it and we will be able to make it a viable self-sustained institution'.

Two months after this conversation, Parash went to MKM Mission House to convey his decision. Barkat was glad to hear from Parash that he, in partnership with Shankar and others, would carry his mission forward. Parash presumed that MKM would be around to help and guide them.

Late October, before sunset, the light breeze on the banks of the Ganga makes it a delightful place for animated conversations. Barkat feels more relaxed than he had ever been in his life. Finding him in a serene mood, Parash seeks some blessings for Shankar as he would be starting his life afresh after being jilted in love again.

'Shankar wants to remarry and leave behind his sad past. He needs your blessings'.

'My good wishes are with him. I think that he should marry an enlightened, thinking person in public life or someone involved in intellectual pursuits. One should either stay alone or forge a relationship with an understanding partner. Spouses transform your worldview: if you change your life partner, your worldview changes abruptly. You could turn fundamentalist, conservative or you may go radical-progressive, such is the impact'.

'True, we have observed it in the case of Imran Khan. When he was married to Jemima, non-orthodox in her outlook, Jewish traditions were ushered in. He became truly professional, built a world class hospital in Pakistan and was critical of his own creed. His second marriage, although it did not last long, had its impact and made him a follower of enlightened moderate Islam, for his second wife was a progressive modern Pakistani woman. Now his third wife, an extremely religious woman, who not only rejects modernity but any other cult of Islam other than the codified one, has made Imran a ritualistic Muslim in the public realm.

'As he contradicts his own previous understanding of religion, they call him a leader of U-turns. No wonder he has turned messiah of Muslims and openly preaches like a cleric in public forums about the religion.

'His strength is drawn from his ambition to become a world leader like Zulfiqar Ali Bhutto. However, unlike Bhutto, his manifested grounding is in his faith. Modi, Trump and Imran represent the same tribe—not trusting other politicians but speaking directly to their constituencies. Assertion with majoritarianism, blaming predecessors, mixing up the past, they draw legitimacy for their dictatorial tendencies.

'I think that these are structural constraints that do not allow linearity but make us move again and again in circles. It might not be a repeating of history but changing history in different forms from the same spring.

'In Pakistan, the army might not go against civil democratic system, but will not allow a civilian to dictate anything that goes against the interest of its establishment. The army in Pakistan sets the script. It might not jump in directly but always has alternatives to give jolts to the ruling party through structural dynamics. Imran no longer remains its favourite. You will have circles of power dynamics in Pakistan. It has taken them a long time and a large toll, but Kashmiris now understand this. The present leadership might cure Kashmir of its age-old ailments. I think the vicious circle is coming to a close, a virtuous cycle will begin. It happens in individuals and it happens with the collective.'

Parash interjects, 'You seem to know many things—religion, dharma and politics—like present-day cult gurus, all in one. But unlike them, you prefer solitude, not the multitude'.

'Parash, solitude or multitude are the inner and the

outer conditionality of the self. The human quest to date has been to prevent divisions but trying to bring order in time and space has brought out its dualism. If you replace power and domination with love and parity, the split of self can be prevented. The human quest is order-making by splitting the self through material conditionality, which invents the other. It seems a path through stage-wise linearity, which in fact is overlapping of circles.

'This is a strange paradox that we call development.

'I found rich answers in simple conversations, contented life in routine conduct, divinity in the multitude and restlessness in solitude. If you explore these narratives of day-to-day life at the common collective meetings, I think you will find your father. You will have to read biographies of ordinary people. I think you will find answers'.

'What do you mean, Shankar?'

'I mean, it is either complete integration or absolute separation. The ailment is in mixing them up. Blend it for new formations. We live in blurred boundaries, while our *Babb* lived in blended traditions.'

Parash replies, 'Our discussions always seem incomplete. I will come to Delhi next month on a Sunday afternoon for more conversations. Give me leave until then. I shall be out of station for a month'.

Barkat sturdily moved out towards the enduring and

serene Ganga. He looked into its depths. The water has become clear over the years. The November moon is in the sky. Barkat has come to the conclusion that his work on earth is done. His shadowy life in the war zone, in hideouts for years has taught him that he lived a life of engagement without attachment. His three *Babb*s lived their lives with sincere engagement to which attachment was intrinsic; freedom and security were grantee and granted. They were different from common people. They were simple in their routine but dogged in their pursuits, which essentially were divine and spiritual. He, on the other hand, broke his attachment with engagement, playing the role not of giver but consumer. He has come to realise that love with compassion is the human project, while domination and power play does not lead to consolidation. He looks at the moon and then washes his face in the Ganga. He realises that 'There are two kinds of light: the glow that illumines and the glare that obscures'.

He goes to bed late and rises early in the morning to leave. The early morning haze covers him and the breeze sighs a farewell.

December has come with its pale shadowy sunshine. Ganga has receded into a rivulet, a serpent curving around Varanasi's banks. On the afternoon of the fifteenth, Parash walks along the Ganga towards the centre, where the caretaker Gautam is sipping a cup of tea.

'Gautam, where is Mishraji?'

'Sir, Baba has gone to the Himalayas. He will not return. He left a letter and some keys for you. I went to your house but it was locked. He told me that he has posted some papers to you.'

Parash had received a copy of the will making him the legal heir of the centre. Gautam brought the sealed envelope and handed it over along with the keys.

Parash opens the letter. It reads:

'Teacher Babb would often mention that he could not get his two boxes, which were in the small library cum worship room (*Haankuth* he would call it) of his home in Kashmir. He would call it his real spiritual cultural capital that he had inherited from his elders. I failed to find the boxes. But, I found some books and a few belongings scattered in the room. I assembled them and kept them safely under lock and key. Most of it is a strange mixture of Sanskrit texts, such as *Panchastavi*, the *Spandau* by Vasugupta-Natha, a commentary on three transcendental states of *Anavopaya*, *Saktopaya*, and *Sambhavopaya*, a jumble of three hundred pages in Sanskrit, the works of Abhinavagupta including *Tantraloka*, *Paratrimsika Vivarn* and *Kavyalamkara*. The descriptions on Ananadvardhan's *Dhanyaloka* and Bharata's *Natyashastra*. Lal Ded's *Vaakh* in Sharda script, Kalhana's *Rajataragni*, *Nilmata Purana*, Janraja's history, pocket book of *Bhagavad Gita* and Gayatri mantras, *Sandiya* and *Ritiratma Kavyasa*. There are some books on *tazkiras* and *tarikhs* in Persian chronicles too, like *Taufatulahbab* and *Baharistani Shahi*, and some hand-written poetry, mainly in Persian and Sanskrit, the diary filled with *Vaakh* of Lal Ded and lyrics of Habba Khatoon. Besides, there was a cloth bag containing mirror, *Nichpatre*, *sandiya*, *qazul* and *chandan* (piece of sandal wood), headgear (*taranga*), phiran and old *zatuks* (horoscopes old and new). Perhaps this is your nativity that becomes the basis for the episteme of universality. I wish that I could have found those two boxes, which are lost now.

'Do not search for me. Find me in these biographics of unsung people and poetry of saints. Its language is in the multitudes of people mingling on the banks of brooks, toiling to satisfy their hunger and dreaming to save their honour. You will find in those narratives your father, a trustee, my adoring Teacher *Babb* smiling with my two other *Babb*s. You will find us all.'